The Road to LaReta

The Road to LaReta

A Novel

BONNIE BATEMAN KING

Based on a True Story

The Road to LaReta
By Bonnie Bateman King

PUBLISHED BY
King-Haverly Publications
802 15th Ave SW
Puyallup, WA 98371

This book is a work of fiction based on a true story. Characters,
incidents, and dialogue are drawn from the author's imagination.
Bateman and Boe family names are authentic.

If not available at your local bookstore, this book may be ordered
through King-Haverly Publications or its online distributors. To
order the book directly, visit:

www.BonnieKingAuthor.com or
www.facebook.com/bonniekingauthor

Please review the book on Amazon Books

Library of Congress Control Number: 2016914922
ISBN: 978-0-9979391-0-1(Paperback)

Images: Family albums. Map and telegram: designed

For LaReta Lois Bateman Harrington Curtis
They loved you. We all do.

To forget one's ancestors is to be a brook without a source, a
tree without a root.

Chinese proverb

CONTENTS

The Road to LaReta

PART ONE
Cat Skinner

Dorothy Adeline Boe

1

The Road

March 8, 1939

Webb hunched his muscled shoulders toward the steering wheel. His deep-set blue eyes scanned the road ahead through fading light. There was little traffic, but Webb knew snow-filled ruts were waiting to blow a tire on his 1930 Chevy.

Wind brushed across berms of snow on either side of the road, creating a translucent scrim of white through which Webb drove as he headed westward. He felt for the whiskey bottle beside him on the seat, found it, took a swig and exhaled slowly with appreciation. *Jim Beam, Kentucky Straight Bourbon Whiskey, 90 proof, my ol' friend,* he thought.

Ahead of him, the winter sun disappeared behind snow-covered mountains, softening the sharp point of trees.

It was almost 5 pm before Webb left Ogallala, Nebraska, heading west for Cheyenne, Wyoming. It would take another three hours on Highway 30 before he turned north onto 87. Exhaust clouds roiled behind the sedan, thoughts churned in his head and his brow furrowed into a scowl. He looked ahead, but what he saw was not the road. Webb saw her face, her sad face. He shook his head in disbelief. *Dorothy's too young to be dead. She was only 26, for God's sake!*

The speedometer indicated the automobile could reach a top speed of 65 miles per hour, but that was just a hope and a prayer for the old Chevy. Webb hit the faulty gage on the dashboard a couple times. *Is the damn thing stuck at 45 miles an hour or is this as fast as she's gonna go?*

He grabbed the whiskey bottle again and took another drink. *I don't know if I can make it in time. At least it's not snowin' like it was four days ago.*

Webb, not a regular church-going man whispered, "Thank you, God, for small favors—any favor." His thoughts shifted to the destination.

I gotta make it to North Dakota to pay my respects. It's the least I can do. And then there's LaReta…

The sedan's heater was acting up and Webb was cold to the bone. Patches of ice glistened in the headlamps. As wind whipped skiffs of snow across the road, thousands of sparkling jewels danced in view. Her image floated among the crystals.

Dammit! Why didn't I take the time? She asked me more than once to come see them. But how could I? I moved from job to job, lucky to have one. Other times when I could have gone, I just didn't. Now, here I am racin' to get to her on time.

The sky slowly darkened and the lights from his car lit the road a few yards ahead. That's the way things had gone. He was only able to see what the next minute would bring, maybe the next day or month—if he was lucky. He ran his fingers through his hair with anger and frustration tightening every muscle in his body. *Maybe if we'd been together, it wouldn't of happened.* He took another drink. *This is the worst payback a man can get for his mistakes. I ain't worth a tinker's dam.*

Webb crossed the state line into Wyoming where the roads, although paved, saw no repair during winter—only snow plows here and there. Right now the roads were passable, but he worried that might change.

Ogallala, Nebraska, had been Webb's job site until that afternoon. Now it was Wednesday evening and there were still 500 miles to drive through Wyoming and into Montana to his folk's home in Billings, leaving a lot of time to think. He would pick up one of his sisters and drive east another 350 miles to Dunn Center, North Dakota. Dorothy's funeral was scheduled for Friday, March 10th at 1 pm.

LaReta probably doesn't even know me. I haven't seen her or Dorothy for ten months. How the hell am I gonna take care of a three-year-old?

Guilt, regret and uncertainty were a load 27 year-old Webster Warren Bateman wasn't used to. He was known as the guy who could hold his liquor, put on a poker face, shoot pool with the best of them and tell stories until his audience, drunk or sober, was in stiches. Webb liked being the center of attention. The ladies liked him too, long before Dorothy.

Webb was handsome. His six-foot, 190-pound frame had been conditioned by years of labor and construction work. Thick, light-brown hair crowned a high forehead. Prominent cheekbones and a dimpled smile added to his good looks. His facial features were boyish and soft, even though he wasn't. Born on a farm near Milroy, Minnesota in May of 1911, Webb had worked hard, played hard and figured out a long time ago who would decide his future. No one would tell him what to do. But now…a dank wool smell permeated the jalopy. He felt across the horsehair-padded seat to his right and found a damp spot close to the door. The car's heater made the odor worse. *Must be a leak around the window. I'll fix it in Cheyenne. Everything else is fallin' apart. Why should this bucket of bolts be any different?*

Webb's beefy, weather-worn left hand gripped the three-spoke steering wheel. He stepped on the clutch and jerked the stick shift from third to second gear to get more power out of the old rust bucket. The hard-driven 1930 Chevy was all he could afford in the fall of 1938. He needed cheap transportation to get him to the jobsite in Nebraska. This beater wasn't his style, but it wasn't important now. He just wanted to get to the next wide spot in the road, Cheyenne. *Control the rig, stay in charge. Just tackle the next grade and keep going.*

He liked to be in charge and in control. His usual job was operating heavy equipment. Webb also liked being the boss. He knew how to lead and get things done. If he had any doubts about his ability, he'd bluff until he figured it out.

Webb was a Cat Skinner. That's what they called heavy equipment operators and he liked the moniker because it recognized his skill, but he joked with friends about "skinner." It referred to a man who drove a mule team. Skinning a mule just meant you were smarter than the mule. "A questionable gauge of intelligence," Webb would say with a belly laugh and a drink in his hand.

Controllin' equipment is a hellova lot easier than women or marriage or bein' a father. The road will get me to North Dakota, but this is a trip I never expected to make. When we first met, it was fun and easy. The future looked good for me. I had a job with promise and a pretty girl on my arm.

Webb's thoughts slipped back to a better time—for both of them.

Dunn Center 1934

"He's coming up the road. I can see his car." Dorothy couldn't contain her excitement as she peered out her parents' front window. It was a Sunday afternoon and only Dorothy and two of her younger sisters were home. The rest of the family had gone to visit neighbors.

Naomi and Melva, hurried to the window anxious to meet the man their sister couldn't stop talking about.

It had been only two weeks since Dorothy and Webb last saw each other, but for Dorothy it seemed much longer. Webb warned her there would be times when he'd be gone for long stretches on construction jobs. She'd heard the warning, but now she knew how time apart made her feel. When they weren't together, she was anxious, restless and couldn't wait to see Webb again, even though the relationship was still new.

Summer had flown by since meeting Webb. Randeen Hoovestol, Dorothy's brother-in-law, introduced them in late spring. He was married to Dorothy's older sister, Myra, and was also a cousin of Webb's. Randeen and Webb had known each other since they were kids. The two couples went to Saturday night dances together. Every time

Dorothy was with Webb, her heart raced and she felt giddy with excitement. Myra whispered in her ear, "It's just temporary insanity." Dorothy giggled in response.

While she was happy, she was also uneasy, even intimidated. Webb was the kind of guy girls noticed at dances. He was handsome, outgoing and funny and Dorothy wasn't sure if Webb really cared for her. She hoped so, but thought she might be just a convenience for him, someone to take to dances when he was in town. One thing she was sure of; she was attracted to Webb Bateman.

Dorothy was slender with fine features, intelligent, but shy at times. Suitors in Dunn Center were few and far between and those who had shown interest in her weren't of interest to Dorothy. Then she met Webb Bateman. At 22, Dorothy's marriage prospects might not get any better. At least that was what she'd been told.

Dorothy turned to her sisters for their opinion. "Well, do I look okay?" She glanced in a living room mirror, touched her finger waved hair, fiddled with the strand of beads around her neck, and straightened her skirt.

Her sisters saw a well-coiffed, dark-haired, young woman with a big grin, eager to open the door and greet Webb. "You look swell!" Naomi, a couple years younger than Dorothy, was excited for her sister.

"You better watch out, Sis, he might try to kiss you," seventeen-year-old Melva teased. Dorothy waved her off and hurried to the front door just as Webb parked the car.

"Hi girls!" Webb doffed his hat when he entered and nodded at Naomi and Melva, sending them into a fit of giggles. Dorothy blushed at her sisters' reaction.

"Never mind them, Webb. I'll go get the picnic basket from the kitchen."

"Need any help?"

Naomi and Melva grinned at each other, impressed by Webb offering to help.

Dorothy came back into the room and handed the basket to Webb. "Sure, you can help eat all these leftovers from last night's supper. And there's some of the apple pie I baked yesterday." Dorothy hoped the old adage was true: 'The way to a man's heart is through his stomach.'

Webb popped the fedora on his head, tipped it to a rakish angle, and opened the door for Dorothy. "Bye, girls." That sent Naomi and Melva into another round of giggles. They rushed to the window to watch the couple disappear down the country road. Naomi exclaimed, "He's cute!" The girls laughed again.

It was a warm, hazy afternoon. The summer landscape colors were muted in shades of gold and brown. Webb and Dorothy chatted amiably as the car bumped down a back road, followed by a cloud of dust. Dorothy appeared calm and collected, but she was nervous. The two of them hadn't spent much time alone.

Because of the drought, one of many dry creek beds meandered beside the road. A cow chewing her cud turned to look as they passed by. They could smell the warm earth through the open car windows and see what little wheat there was in nearby fields, struggling skyward.

A stand of shade trees by a small lake made the ideal spot for a picnic. Up the hill from the lake was the cemetery. Webb offered Dorothy a hand getting out of the car, carried the basket and helped spread the blanket in tall grass. Webb joked, "Nice location for a cemetery. Too bad the residents can't enjoy the view." Dorothy smiled, not sure of a response.

They made small talk and laughed through lunch. Once the last of the pie was finished, Dorothy started putting plates and utensils back in the picnic basket. "Hang on. I'll help," Webb offered.

They cleared off the blanket and Webb sprawled the length of it, propped himself up on one arm and said, "Tell me more about yourself, Dorothy Adeline Boe." Dorothy blushed. She was pleased he remembered her given name.

Sunlight splashed off shafts of grass and a light breeze picked up and wafted through the trees. From where Dorothy was sitting, the setting was idyllic. Webb's dimpled smile and his muscular physique made her breathing shallow; her body tingled. It was something she hadn't experienced with a man before.

"I know you have a fine family. *Lots* of brothers and sisters." Webb grinned. Dorothy was still nervous and appreciated his effort to make conversation.

"Thanks for asking, Webb." Dorothy's voice was soft. She was glad to be able to talk about something she knew well. "It's still a marvel to me, but my mother gave birth to twelve children, including two sets of twins, in a little sod house on the prairie not far from here.

"Their nearest neighbor was 23 miles away. Without a doctor close by, only eight of us kids lived to adulthood. I have an older sister and brother, Myra—who you know—and Laurel, and five younger ones: Naomi, Miland, Melva,

Aaron and Vernetta."

Dorothy's nerves weren't helped with Webb looking at her intently, but he seemed genuine in his interest. She was drawn to him and couldn't help leaning toward him when he spoke.

"You told me a while back you went all through school in the same grades with Naomi, but didn't you say she's younger?" Webb asked.

Dorothy smiled broadly. "I started grade school and was there long enough to learn to read, but I came down with St. Vitus Dance and had to stay home. It was a strange illness that made me jerk and I couldn't control it. The doctor said it was because I had rheumatic fever caused by a strep throat when I was little."

"I'm really sorry to hear that," Webb sympathized.

Dorothy sat up straighter and touched her heart. "Oh, I'm okay now. About a year and a half later when Naomi started school, I was well enough to go back and from that point on we were in every grade together. We even graduated at the same time."

Webb slowly sat up and clasped his arms around one knee. "You did a lot better with education than me. I didn't even finish high school. He pulled cigarettes from his breast pocket and tapped the pack against an index finger until one slipped out. He lit it and slowly inhaled. "Mine was in the school of hard knocks," he said looking out at the lake. A hazy cloud circled above his head as he exhaled, careful not to blow smoke in Dorothy's direction. He looked back at Dorothy. "It's great you've made somethin' of yourself. I bet your folks are proud."

Unlike most men Dorothy met, Webb didn't seem blinded in awe of her as a school teacher. It made it even harder for her to breathe. She couldn't help but think of the possibilities for the two of them.

"Thanks, Webb." Dorothy blushed again, but her smile was broad. In an effort to compose herself, she continued her story. "My folks encouraged me to get my teaching certificate. After high school, I went for six weeks training at the North Dakota State Normal School in Ellendale. I had my own school by the time I was nineteen and made 80 dollars a month," There was pride in her voice.

"Whoa, that's about the same money I'm makin' now." Webb said with surprise. Maybe I'm in the wrong business." He laughed.

Dorothy caught her breath. "Oh, well—it didn't last long. Times were hard, so they cut my salary to 60 dollars a month in '32. I looked for something else." Dorothy hoped she hadn't put Webb off because she made the same money he did at one time, but continued with her story anyway. While she was enamored with Webb, maybe it was good to test his mettle to make sure he was who she thought he was.

"My uncles own shoe stores in Washington and Oregon, so they offered to send me to Knapp's Modern Business College in Tacoma. I did that in '33 and did real well. I was even initiated into Alpha Iota, the business sorority."

Webb nodded and smiled. Dorothy didn't think he knew what a business sorority was, but he looked impressed anyway.

Dorothy glanced toward the lake. "I would have stayed and gone to work there, but Mother and Dad needed me back here. Things are so bad because of the drought and the Depression, some families are eating their own horses.

She paused at the thought of desperation that could lead folks to such drastic measures. "I hope to get a teaching job again to bring in some income for the family, but nothing has come up yet. Right now I'm just another mouth to feed and they can't afford it." Dorothy sighed and continued, "Myra and Laurel make sure the folks get some money now and then, but it's tight."

"My God, I knew farmers had it rough, but I didn't know it had come to eatin' their own horses," Webb responded, surprised. "But my Ma and Dad did move to Billings, just this spring. They couldn't make it in the hotel and restaurant business in North Dakota either. A lot of businesses have closed their doors. This Depression makes it tough all around." Webb sat with his arms wrapped around his knees, shoulders hunched forward, and a frown clouded his face.

Dorothy nodded her head in sympathy and agreement. "The soil won't produce, Webb. Mother and Dad are talking about a move to Oregon. One of my uncles, Will Harbke, owns the "Hill Billy Ranch" in Scappose. He's offered to let my folks live there and run the ranch until they find a place of their own. Mother and Dad homesteaded their property over thirty years ago. If they do lose the farm, I'm afraid it will kill my dad." Dorothy looked down, tears welling in her eyes. Webb reached for her hand and they sat quietly.

Wanting to lighten the mood and find out more about the man who seemed to have hold of her heart strings, Dorothy said. "Tell me more about yourself."

Webb smiled. "I'll tell you what little there is." He settled himself again on one elbow, his long legs extended off the end of the blanket. Dorothy sat on one hip and smoothed her skirt down over her knees.

"I'm just a Cat Skinner, Dorothy, but I've done pretty well for myself since I started work for Win Coman's road construction company. I have to move around a lot, but so far all the work has been in North Dakota."

The tip of Webb's cigarette glowed as he inhaled again. Dorothy leaned forward, interested in every word.

Webb exhaled and continued. "Win hired me when I was eighteen years old. He's a good man. Believed in me." Webb laughed. "One of the few people who did." Webb looked away in thought and then back at Dorothy. "I'd driven truck before, but Win taught me how to operate all the heavy equipment: graders, crushers, blades and shovels. I'm a time-keeper now. I track all the workers' hours, so I got a little raise. If I stick with 'em, I could move up to foreman and maybe even superintendent in the next year or so. And I don't think that's too bad for only bein' 23."

"I think that's great, Webb!"

Webb paused, smiled, and squeezed Dorothy's hand. "Hey, what do you think about bein' my girl?" Dorothy sat up straight. His question came out of the blue, but it was exactly what she'd hoped for. She shivered with excitement.

"Yes, of course!"

Melva was right. Webb did try to kiss Dorothy. And he succeeded, more than once.

The Road

Five years had passed since the picnic with Dorothy. Now Webb was in Cheyenne and Ogallala three hours behind him. He gassed up and took the passenger door panel off to get a better look at the window crank. It was rusty and needed a strong hand to roll up the glass, but he managed to fix the leak, at least temporarily. *I wish all my problems could be fixed this easy.*

His thoughts drifted back to the car he bought in 1937. Work was steady back then. The 1935 Pontiac had called his name the first time he dickered on the price. It still cost him nearly 600 dollars, but he believed he'd given the dealer a run for his money. He never paid the first price asked on any vehicle—no fun in that. It was about the wheelin' and dealin'.

The Pontiac was streamlined and modern. She had horizontal "speed lines" that extended the length of the car, large rounded fenders and suicide doors with hinges for both front and back doors located at the rear of the door. 'Suicide' came from the fact that oncoming traffic could rip those doors right off, if they happened to be open when a speeding automobile drove too close. He also bragged to friends about the split windshield with a metal piece down the center of the front window that created a V effect. To his way of thinking, this car was a real beauty.

He'd sent Dorothy a photo of himself smiling and leaning up against the driver's door, fedora in one hand and the other hand on his hip. He chuckled remembering her written response to the photo. *"The picture is good of you but rather flattering don't you think?"*

He imagined that Dorothy grinned when she underlined the word 'flattering' in her letter. She had a way of jabbing him about being cocky. Webb thought about the dealer repossessing that same car when he was out of work early in 1938. *Damn, nothin' good seems to last for long.*

Cheyenne disappeared in the rear view mirror. Night opened its curtain for Webb to slip through and he headed north on Highway 87 to Casper, four hours away. His plan was to make it to Casper a little after midnight before he pulled over to catch up on sleep, if he could sleep at all.

He had on the same work clothes and well-worn boots he pulled on that morning, before he left Ogallala. His few belongings were tossed in the back seat, including a shoebox he carried with him from job site to job site. He had filled a couple gas cans, picked up two extra tires for the car's wire spoke wheels, a pint of Jim Beam, and collected on old poker debts. He hadn't planned to leave the job for another few days, but that was before the damned telegram arrived.

Webster Warren Bateman

2

The Damned Telegram
Ogallala, Nebraska 1939

Since the previous fall, Webb had worked for Morrison Knudsen Construction Company as an equipment operator, a Cat Skinner—a blade man to be exact. The construction site was Kingsley Dam, the second largest earth-filled dam in the world, nine miles north of Ogallala. It was called an engineering marvel. The work began the year before Webb arrived and his job, along with other equipment operators, was to move the 25 million cubic yards of earth and other material it would take to build the dam.

Webb thought maybe his luck had turned. He'd either been out of work or changing jobs a lot in the previous years. Building this dam was part of President Roosevelt's New Deal. It provided work for thousands of guys like Webb. It was a good job and gave him "three hots and a cot" in a town called Kingsleyville built near the project site. Workers and their families had their own small houses and the company even built a school for the kids.

Single men stayed in bunk houses. Although Webb wasn't single, that's where he stayed. Dorothy was two states away.

During the 1930's, Ogallala's population had doubled to 3000 because of work on the dam. Where there were men earning money, there were others to help them spend it.

Some provided services: doing laundry, selling sundries, and offering better meals than they got from the M-K mess hall. There were women, too, almost all practicing the same profession.

A stretch of four blocks in downtown Ogallala called to Webb, lured him with excitement, challenges, risk, even danger. There were card rooms and bars, pool halls and brothels, a run-down hotel and dance emporium.

The hotel reminded him of the one his mother ran in Almont, North Dakota, but without women waving and calling from the upstairs windows.

During the day, the dusty streets of Ogallala were sleepy; there was little traffic. But at night, especially Friday and Saturday night, after men lined up at the M-K payroll office, the streets came alive. The "working women" leaned over second story window sills, to reveal their enticements and offer a good time—for a price—to googly-eyed working stiffs. Music poured out of the bars and dance halls. Men crowded into restaurants for cheap steaks and watered-down beer. Card sharks shuffled and pulled hard-earned dough out of victims who sat across from them at poker tables.

After a belly-filling meal, Webb would head first for a pool hall and whiskey. He'd find time later for the card sharks. He liked poker. With any money left, he'd pay for another pint and maybe visit the upstairs "yoohoo girls."

It was Wednesday morning. Webb stretched and yawned. His mattress was thin; he could feel the slats beneath. As many hours as they worked, the thickness of the padding under him didn't matter. He could sleep on the floor, if necessary, and welcome shut eye, any way he could get it.

"Hey, Webb, there's a telegram for you in the office," one of Webb's roommates mumbled as he came in the door after finishing a night shift. He headed for his own bunk, plopped down and took off his boots. The sound of work boots hitting the floor finally got Webb's attention. He had to get up to work the day shift anyway. Webb sat up, scratched his head and swung his legs over the side of his bunk.

"What? Whad ya' say?"

"You got a telegram in the office."

"What the hell?" Webb had never gotten a telegram on the job before. Letters, sure, but not a telegram. He pulled his pants over long-handled underwear, jerked on his boots, work shirt, jacket and hat. "Thanks. I'll catch you later." Webb pulled the flaps down over his ears to keep out the cold. He headed for the office.

An icy wind hit Webb in the face, but helped wake him up. His boots crunched through the frozen snow on a well-worn path past other wooden bunk houses toward the M-K company office. He wondered if something happened to his mother or dad, but if that was the case, he would have gotten a call, not a telegram. Why a damn telegram?

"It was delivered by Western Union earlier this morning, Webb. Must be pretty important for *you* to get a telegram." The guy behind the counter folded his arms across his chest and struck a pose as though he expected an explanation.

"Right, Swede. Probably President Roosevelt himself asking for my help," Webb quipped.

Webb turned his back to the counter and to the clerk, tore open the envelope and read the telegram. It was from Dorothy's father who, although he couldn't afford it, had to pay for every word. It was painful in its brevity: "Dorothy Boe Bateman died in hospital March 7. Funeral Friday March 10 at 1 pm at Dunn Center Lutheran

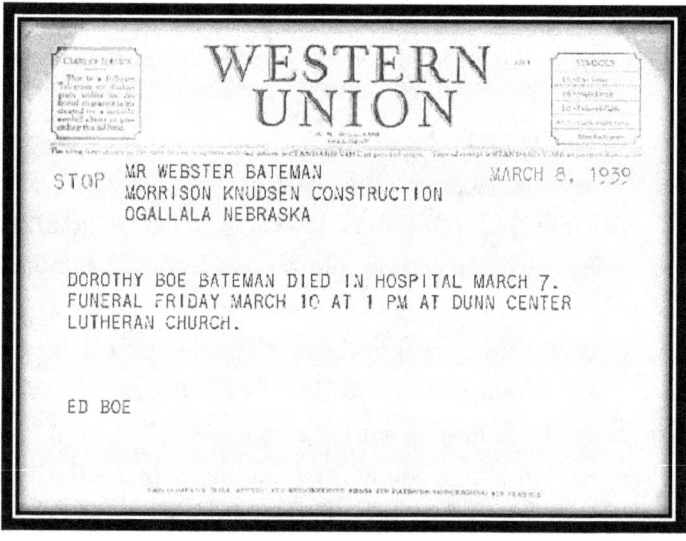

WESTERN UNION

STOP MR WEBSTER BATEMAN   MARCH 8, 1939
      MORRISON KNUDSEN CONSTRUCTION
      OGALLALA NEBRASKA

      DOROTHY BOE BATEMAN DIED IN HOSPITAL MARCH 7.
      FUNERAL FRIDAY MARCH 10 AT 1 PM AT DUNN CENTER
      LUTHERAN CHURCH.

      ED BOE

Church." It was simply signed, "Ed Boe."

Stunned, the letter slipped through his fingers to the floor. He picked it up and hastily stepped outside onto the wooden porch. He needed to read it three more times before the significance sunk in.

Webb grabbed the pack of Chesterfields from his

breast pocket, tapped one out and stuck it between clenched lips. His hands shook as he struck a match and lit the cigarette. He took a long drag. The exhaled smoke mingled with his frosty breath. It was cold, but Webb's numbness wasn't because of the weather. He needed to get control. *I don't believe it. I don't believe it. It can't be. She just wrote me last week to say she was better. I even wrote her back.*

Webb thought about how brief his letter was and wished he'd said more.

Dear Dorothy,

I am terribly sorry to hear of the tough luck you had. I hope that this letter finds you back in good health. I wish that I could help.

The job here will only last about 10 days longer and I haven't even saved car fare to Billings. There is another job about 100 miles from here. I may try to get down there and get a job.

The weather here this winter has been fairly agreeable. Last nite we had to work in a small snow storm tho!

I haven't heard from home for a long time. It's my own fault 'cause I don't write to them.

Dorothy, please excuse me. I just can't think of anything to say except I do hope you are okay. Will send this to Dix [Dickinson Hospital]. *But hope it catches you at Gladstone.*

Please write and let me know how you are. Love to LaReta. Love, Webb

He wondered if Dorothy had seen his letter before she died. He stuffed the telegram in his pocket, straightened himself, flicked the cigarette into the snow and strode back into the office. "Family emergency, Swede. I have to leave today," he said, trying to steady his voice. His usual, calm, easy-going demeanor was gone.

"Get my final pay cut." Webb pushed the words past the choke hold on his throat. "My wife died yesterday."

The Road

As he drove on toward Casper, tears welled in Webb's eyes. Jim Beam unraveled his emotions. He thought about the telegram, the funeral and the phone call to his mother.

"Webb, I am so sorry!" Dena was shocked. "What happened to her? What's going to happen to little LaReta?"

"I'll tell you what I know when I see you. Got a letter from Dorothy she wrote from the hospital." Webb's voice was hoarse from guilt and fear of the future. The words Dorothy wrote from her hospital bed hit him again. "You didn't know how close you came to having a daughter all of your own."

"I need one of my sisters to go with me to the funeral—Vivian or Blanche? I haven't seen LaReta since last year. She may not even know me." What he didn't say was more telling. *They may blame me, even hate me. And what do I do about LaReta?* Webb didn't want to face Dorothy's relatives alone.

"I'll talk to the girls, Webb, but things have changed since you were here. Vivian is working and met a salesman. They plan to get married this summer and move to Portland, Oregon. Blanche works as a bookkeeper for a Chinese herb doctor. Neither one of them may be able to go."

"Just find out, Mom." Webb was impatient. "I already called the Bailey's in Gladstone where Dorothy and LaReta boarded. They said they would get word to Laura and Ed Boe—you know, Dorothy's folks. I told them I'd be at the funeral in Dunn Center on Friday. I have to pay my respects."

Webb cleared his throat. "And I'll need to borrow some money."

There was a pause. "Webb...we're short ourselves. Don't get me wrong. You've helped us out when we needed it, but there's some problems at your dad's pool hall and your brothers have their own troubles. Ray's got his small radio repair shop and he's making records for musicians just to make ends meet. Walt drives truck, but has a wife to support. You know it's hand to mouth for all of us. I can't promise anything, but get here safe and we'll work something out."

Webb made one more phone call to Billings, but only had time to explain the bare facts to Julia before they lost the connection and the line went dead. He hoped he'd have time to see her so he could explain more in person. Maybe she would help him figure out what to do about LaReta.

Webb grabbed the whiskey bottle again, unscrewed the cap, and hoisted the bottle to his lips. He lost sight of the road, but the quick backward tip of his head ensured a familiar spicy warmth from lips to belly. He recapped the booze, swiped the back of his hand across his tear-filled eyes, and pressed harder on the gas pedal.

Webb reflected on his undisciplined spending. *Hell, I can't keep two nickels to rub together.* Guilt brought to mind that he hadn't sent money on a regular basis to Dorothy and LaReta; ten or fifteen dollars once in a while with months in between. Although it was expected, he didn't send his parents money on a regular basis either. Webb's earnings were decent—eighty-five dollars a month, but he couldn't save a dime. When he had time off, he headed to town with the other guys to let off steam. It didn't help that Ogallala was full of temptations. Liquor helped Webb forget his responsibilities and rationalize his choices. It dulled, but didn't completely destroy his conscience.

The road meandered north passed Chugwater, Wheatland and Douglas, Wyoming. The sky was black around an orb of the moon.

It was just before midnight. Webb had been lulled by the monotony of the road when his travel-induced stupor was suddenly interrupted by a loud bang. The steering wheel vibrated in his hands and he struggled to keep the car on the road as it veered toward the ditch. Webb hung on, forced the clutch to the floor and stomped on the brake pedal. A blowout. Just what he needed in the middle of nowhere with the temperature below freezing.

He turned off the motor, set the brake, grabbed his oil lantern, some tools and a tire from the back seat, then swung himself out the door and onto the deserted road. He slipped on his gloves and in the biting cold, wrestled the flat tire off and fit another on the wire spoke wheel. The oil lamp gave just enough dim light to get the job done. Rubbing his gloves together and jumping up and down to thaw his icy bones, he heard something off the side of the road. Startled, Webb stood still. The snow-covered frozen grass crackled with heavy footsteps. Two big brown eyes came closer.

"Well, I'll be damned," Webb laughed out loud. A cow ambled onto the road, attracted by the light. "Didn't think I'd have any company tonight."

He lit a cigarette and took a couple of puffs before climbing back in the Chevy and starting the motor. The lonesome cow ambled on, but it had already stirred memories of Webb's Granddad Bateman. *George Washington Bateman. Hell, as a kid, all I saw was an ol' man with a cow who was an easy mark for a prank.*

Webb pondered his life then and now. *Guess I've been told by a number of women in my life that men never grow up, but how is it that wantin' to have fun can cause so much trouble?*

Tomine Teodine (Dena)   James Robert Bateman
Ramsland

Granddad Bateman and the Stoneboat

31

3

Dena, Jim and Granddad's Cow

Almont, North Dakota 1921

On a late August afternoon, ten-year-old, Webb, and his buddy, Alvin, kicked rocks and planned mischief in front of Webb's mother's hotel and cafe. Alvin put his hand up to whisper in Webb's ear, afraid someone might hear the plan to spook Granddad Bateman's cow. "I got the hokey-pokey liniment from my dad's shed, Webb. We'll make that cow dance, by gosh."

"That should get those water cans to the hotel real fast," Webb giggled at the thought of the cow kicking up her heels. "Hey Alvin, you think Ol' Bossy will run so fast she'll get that sled off the ground? Maybe it'll fly like one of them airplanes." Webb wrapped his arms across his stomach and doubled over in laughter. He'd seen airplanes, but only in pictures.

The street was a wide dirt road, hardened by automobiles and livestock. Flat-faced buildings, no more than two stories, sat across from one another looking like a showdown when viewed from one end of the street to the other. Plank sidewalks attempted to keep pedestrians out of the dust of summer and the snow of winter. Scalloped canvas awnings flapped in the breeze over store fronts. There was the smell of dust and horse manure. When the occasional Model T chugged by, gasoline fumes added to Almont's aroma.

Within a stone's throw from the hotel, Webb and Alvin could see folks going about their business at the bank, merchandise store, meat market, drug store and confectionary. They pressed their noses against the candy store window almost daily, in hopes their put-on hangdog looks would gain enough sympathy to generate a tasty hand out or two. It usually did.

Another young guy stood in front of the Almont Arena newspaper office barking about the day's news and offering fresh press to anyone with five cents in their pocket or purse. Webb and Alvin imitated his stance, one foot and arm extended, head swung back to bellow out attention-getting headlines. Theirs was more bellow than recognizable news.

Across from the hotel, two men relaxed in straight backed chairs tipped against the clapboard siding of Jim Bateman's pool hall entrance. Hands clasped across their bellies, cigars dangling from lips still moving in conversation, they also kept track of Almont, for lack of anything better to do. Or so it seemed. Jim asked them to keep a look out for the sheriff while he did some "business" out the back of the building. He paid them for their surveillance in booze.

Jim's pool hall was an illegal tavern called a "blind pig." The strange handle came from establishments in other states that circumvented the law by charging customers to see an attraction, a pig or other animal, and then serving a "complimentary" alcoholic beverage. In North Dakota, alcoholic beverages were against the law, period. No such thing as a blind pig allowed, but those who frequented the Bateman Pool Hall gave it the nickname anyway.

North Dakota had entered the union as a "dry state" in 1889, but prohibition, which began in 1920, made alcohol even more tempting. The law banned the production, sale, and movement of alcohol in and out of every state. Alcohol was allowed for certain religious purposes, but Jim's pool hall clientele claiming they wanted to become spirit-filled, didn't qualify.

Minot, North Dakota, just 136 miles north of Almont became a supply hub for Al Capone's liquor smuggling operations. "Little Chicago" it was called. The smugglers used a network of underground tunnels to conceal and move illicit cargo entering from Canada. Some of that cargo found its way to Jim's pool hall in Almont, along with home brew brought in by local "Moonshiners."

Almont was a busy, growing town with a relaxed and congenial air, but with secrets and illicit activities. After the site was laid out in 1906, businesses flocked to town because of the railroad and promises of prosperity on the prairie. The first grain elevator was used by farmers as far away as South Dakota, who brought grain to Almont for shipping. The grain was shipped east in the same railroad cars that off loaded machinery, livestock and furniture. The Northern Pacific Railroad put in a stockyard in 1916 which created additional sales opportunities for ranchers in the area. All east and west traffic across country went through Almont on a "highway" called the Red Trail bringing tourist trade with it. Almont was ready for a decent hotel and restaurant and that's what Webb's mother, Dena, decided she would provide.

Dena Ramsland was no stranger to hard work and the challenge of survival on the prairie. Her parents had emigrated from Norway, to the Dakota Territory in 1881 to obtain free land, given away by the Federal Government.

North Dakota promised farming opportunities in "a land of majestic crystal lakes." The ads in foreign newspapers read, "Land fair enough to tempt the angels in their flight to pause and wonder whether a new and better Eden had not been formed." Dena's parents, like so many others who emigrated, dreamed of having a farm in this land of promise. They homesteaded in Sims.

Dena was born in Sims in January 1885. Her oldest brother had been born in Norway, but three younger siblings were born in Sims. The family later relocated to a homestead southwest of Almont, an area better suited to ranching, with trees and a good supply of water from artesian wells. It was referred to as "The Big Woods" and later the "Ramsland Hills." Their home, built of rock and logs, boasted a cellar containing a spring.

Dena's father died suddenly at age thirty-seven in 1889 when she was four years old. Within a year, her mother remarried and the couple had six more children, four of whom lived to adulthood.

Until she was eleven years old, Dena spoke only Norwegian. As the oldest daughter in the family, it was decided she would live with another family about twenty miles away. She helped with the children and went to a local school where she learned English, but her education was cut short. The family thought education less important than helping with household chores.

She returned home a few years later, but earned her own way, working as a housekeeper and later at the State Hospital in Jamestown.

Dena, at the urging of her parents, homesteaded land adjacent to the family farm and with help, built a small stone and sod house. In order to homestead, she had to live on the 160 acres and work the land.

Dena's future husband, James ("Jim") Robert Bateman was born on a farm in spring Valley, Minnesota, in 1883. He was the youngest of four sons born to George Washington and Sarah Bateman. After eight years of schooling, Jim declared he'd had enough and quit. There was always work for him on the farm and he could learn what he needed to know on his own without further "schoolin'."

Dena and Jim met when he came to Almont in 1907 to visit an old friend. When he first saw Dena, he knew she was the girl he would marry and they wed in June 1907. Dena was 22 and Jim 24. The couple lived in Dena's stone and sod house on the prairie and their first child, Evelyn ("Toots") was born there in July 1908.

Jim and Dena wanted to move to Almont to start a business, so they sold Dena's homestead to her mother and stepfather and started their first restaurant in Almont. After Dena gave birth to Ray in 1909, Jim's mother became ill so the family moved to Milroy, Minnesota to assist with her care and the farm. Minnesota was where Webb, Walt, Vivian and Blanche were born between 1911 and 1918.

Jim operated livery stables and gas stations in four different Minnesota towns, teaching his children nomadic ways at an early age. Ten years after Jim's mother passed away, the family moved back to Almont. By the 1920's, there were three hotels in town with one abandoned by former operators. That was the one 37 year-old Dena decided to rent. She saw the hotel and café business as reliable income for her, Jim and their six children. It also provided a roof over their heads and when Dena made up her mind about something, that's the way it was. She called it the Merchant Hotel.

Thirty-nine- year-old Jim ran the livery stable and pool hall across the street. Webb's granddad, George Washington Bateman, moved with the family to Almont. He set up his own small hauling business, using a cow.

The Cow and the Stoneboat

"You lift her tail, Alvin, and I'll put the grease under there and then we run like hell!" Webb grinned ear to ear at his friend. He was antsy to do the deed and skedaddle out of there. Granddad Bateman was out of sight, around the corner of the three story school building filling the last of the five-gallon cream cans with water.

Water from the town pump and trough next to the hotel was no good to drink. It wasn't even much good for washing, because it was full of alkali and dirt. Horses and cows would stand at the trough "takin' in water at one end and lettin' it out the other." Webb laughed at his description of the sight. He knew or should have that their "piss and crap" returned to the well through rotten wooden curbing.

Private wells in the city weren't much better, but water from a well near the school about a mile out of town was clearer and softer. No one owned trucks to do hauling, but Granddad Bateman and Miles Purfeerst ran dray businesses—heavy hauling. Mr. Purfeerst used a horse drawn wagon to haul freight, mail, cream cans and other commodities to and from the railroad depot.

Granddad Bateman's dray business was more modest with a sled pulled by a cow. Most townsfolk called it makeshift, but the old gent felt useful.

He put a horse collar upside down on one of two cows owned by a banker in town. The cows were tended by Ray and Webb and the Bateman family got to keep half the milk. Granddad Bateman used the cow to pull the stoneboat, a flat bottomed sled used to haul stones, bales of hay, or in this case, cream cans full of water from the school's well.

A strong harness contraption was fashioned to hook the wooden sled to the cow, using homes and tugs. On a daily basis, Granddad Bateman filled two ten-gallon cream cans and a five gallon with fresh water, then coaxed the cow to pull the sled to town. It took several trips a day. He brought water for the hotel and served other families in town, particularly on Monday morning when the ladies wanted to use the "good" water to wash clothes. The importance of Granddad's business was lost on Webb.

Alvin complained, "She's really a switcher, Webb. Hard to hang on to her tail and hold it up at the same time. You got the easy part."

Webb was used to Alvin's complaints because he could talk him into just about anything. He shouted back at Alvin, "Just grab with both hands, fool! We don't got much time. The old man's coming back any minute."

Alvin held on tight and lifted the heavy tail high enough for Webb to smear hokey-pokey, a burning liniment, under the tail. They both took off running around the other side of the school house. So did the cow. She took off like a cyclone, kicking and bellowing and scattering cream cans and parts of the stoneboat all the way to the barn. The clatter could be heard for a mile.

Webb and Alvin took back streets to town. They hooted, laughed and imitated the cow kicking up her back legs. It brought stares from housewives sweeping their front porches and questions from kids playing in the street.

At one point, it dawned on Webb he'd have to face his mother and when he did, she would have heard the tale from Granddad Bateman.

He took his time getting home.

"Webb! What do you know about the cow and the stoneboat?" Dena, hands on her hips, bent over toward Webb to look him in the eye. He knew Granddad Bateman had already told her what happened. He could feel his mother's breath.

"*Someone's* got us back on water from the town pump. Was that you? And the stoneboat's a goner." Dena's exasperation spouted from every pore.

Webb twisted in his spot and looked at the floor. "What happened, Ma? I was in the pool hall with dad most of the day helping him sweep up. Maybe Ray or Walt know something."

Webb's attempt to plead innocent wasn't selling with his mother. "I know where Ray was and Walt's only eight, not even tall enough to reach that cow's tail! I'll be talkin' to your dad about this."

That was a relief. Webb knew he could count on his dad not to remember whether he was there or not. While Webb was in the pool hall, Jim imbibed in "soft drinks," as advertised on his front window. Jim's definition of a soft drink was hard liquor and he had plenty of access. He'd been known to go on binges for days. Dena was left to do the disciplining. With six kids and a hotel to run with ten boarders, there was little time to keep an eye on Webb or his two brothers.

"In the meantime, you and your brothers will be haulin' water in here from the trough. We'll have to boil it or put bricks in the big crock to do some filterin'. Can't drink or use it the way it is. And I'll have to figure out a way to pay Mr. Purfeerst to haul us some good water from the well at the school."

Dena attempted to make the consequences of "someone's" actions very clear to Webb. He kept his head down, stuck both hands in his pockets and kicked at the wood floor, feeling sheepish about what he and Alvin had done, but not willing to admit to it. He'd made more work for the whole family, especially his mother and older sister, Toots.

The Road

With nothing but time on the road to think about the past, memories of those early days were keeping him company. Trouble. Webb knew how to get into it from a very early age.

Webb drove past darkened windows in Glenwater, Wyoming. Not many people awake at 11:00 pm.

Early to bed and early to rise… Not sure it ever made me healthy, wealthy or wise.

Glenwater, a small burg—barely a dot on the map, slipped past. It would be another hour to Casper before he pulled over to catch some rest.

Small town. That's who I was. Not a lot of people ever thought I would amount to much. It seemed I was always in trouble for one thing or another.

There was a hotel on the outskirts of Glenwater with a No Vacancy sign in the window. Webb's thoughts faded again to the Merchant Hotel.

I guess there was one person who saw something good in me. Wonder where she is now?

Almont's Main Street

4

Elsa

Almont, North Dakota 1922

Previous owners of Dena's hotel went broke, left a dirty mess and rooms full of bed bugs. Fouteen-year-old Toots was old enough to roll up her sleeves alongside her mother. Vivian was seven and Blanche four—too young to help very much with the huge job of making the hotel habitable again.

The first back-breaking task for Dena and Toots was heating huge containers of water. They added lye to break down the minerals and carried sloshing buckets to every room in the hotel. The narrow back stairs were uneven and the railing unsteady, but these undaunted females managed to carry and dump the contents in every room where they scrubbed each crack and cranny on their hands and knees. Mattresses were scalded and left to dry in the heat of upstairs bedrooms.

"Do we haftoo, Ma?" thirteen-year-old Ray, eleven-year-old Webb, and nine-year-old Walt chorused their complaints when told to help.

Webb pleaded, "I think Dad needs us at the pool hall." The whining didn't work. The boys washed dishes and brought in wood for the big black cast iron range in the kitchen. If they wanted to eat, they helped. It was a threat that motivated.

In the fall, there was more for them to do. Ray and Webb, with Walt helping as much as he could, brought in coal for the furnace that heated the hotel. It was in the basement, down rickety wooden steps. The old metal mammoth used lignite coal from mines near Almont, coal that produced a lot of ashes and left heavy clinkers, minerals that melted and fused together. The boys had to haul the ashes and clinkers back up the stairs to dispose of them out back of the hotel. There were days they could have been mistaken for chimney sweeps.

The old barn of a hotel required a lot of coal to keep it warm, so the first winter, Dena offered her handsome, younger half-brother, Thorvald Larson, free board and room if he would haul coal to the hotel. He farmed about eight miles from town. Dena also convinced Jim to let Thorvald have livery space for his two teams of horses. Thorvald referred to his larger team as the "heavy team." It was for hauling coal. His second team, the light team, was to go "girlin'." Dena had a strict rule about no girls in the men's rooms at the Merchant Hotel, but her rule took a beating when Thorvald moved in.

When school started in the fall of 1922, the Bateman clan, including Toots, headed for the three-story school house a mile from the hotel. With more work than Dena could manage by herself, she hired a woman from town to help with chores.

"I'll be home right after school to help, Mamma," Toots assured Dena as she gathered her school books. "I got some beds made and took a few of the slop-jars to the outhouse. Elsa said she would get the rest."

The screen door banged after Toots scooted the boys out the door. Toots made sure her small flock headed in the right direction. As the oldest, mothering the boys came naturally and Dena expected her to fill the role. She had a business to run and for now, Dena had Elsa to help manage the endless day-to-day chores.

Thirty-five-year-old Elsa lived a short distance from the hotel. She was married, but had no children. The one child she carried for seven months had died at birth and left her barren. Her husband worked now and then, but spent most of his time in the Bateman Pool Hall where he imbibed in "soft drinks." In spite of having a husband she couldn't depend on, Elsa's income kept them going and she kept her outlook positive. Hard work at the hotel kept her mind off her troubles. She once told Webb, "Being happy doesn't mean everything is hunky dory. It means you have to look past the bad to find the good."

With the beds made, Elsa hefted one of the heavier slop-jars, a large metal container with a handle and lid. Some of the more "citified" folks called them chamber pots, but whether jars or pots, they were the indoor outhouse, since the hotel had no plumbing. There was one in the corner of every bedroom. Large enough to squat on, they had to be handled with care, particularly down the steep, uneven, narrow back stairs.

Dena, Toots and Elsa took on this unpleasant, smelly task. If left to the boys, one of them was sure to trip on a floor board.

Elsa stepped carefully down the back stairs. One hand grasped the handrail and the other clutched a heavy, sloshing slop-jar. This was the task Elsa disliked the most, but she was getting paid three dollars a day for all her duties. "A good wage for a woman," Elsa bragged to a friend. Most days, she made it outdoors without a spill.

As winter set in, Ray and Webb brought in coal, wood and water before school each morning.

Coal was for the furnace; wood and water for the kitchen stove. Dena stoked the fire and added fuel through a door in the front of the cast iron range. Every day the large, black contraption roared with heat to boil water to drink and wash clothes and to prepare meals for up to twenty folks at a time.

The kitchen was the warmest room in the hotel when the range was heating. There was rarely a day it wasn't hot to the touch. Dena wiped her brow with the back of her wrist and tucked a stray strand of hair into the knot perched at the nape of her neck. Perspiration trickled down her back.

Dena was solidly built and always wore sensible shoes and an ankle length dress covered by an apron. A furrowed brow telegraphed her serious approach to life. There was little time for anything but meeting the back-breaking demands of the hotel.

The boarders in the hotel, besides Thorvald, were men who worked in Almont businesses or at the stock yards on the outskirts of town. The thirty dollars a month rent for a room included two meals, breakfast and supper, and once-a-week laundry.

Every day there were jobs to be done. Monday was laundry day for the boarders; Tuesday ironing day. Wednesday the family laundry was done along with mending or sewing. Thursday rooms were dusted and floors scrubbed. Meal preparation and some cleaning had to be done every day, but more meals were prepared and baking done on Friday and Saturday to feed farmers who were in town to clean up and have fun or for tourists traveling the Red Trail through Almont.

Elsa finished emptying slop-jars, checked to make sure there was kerosene in all the lamps—there was no electricity in Almont—and came to help with laundry. The two women scrubbed clothing on rigid wash boards in tubs of soapy water. Elsa brought a lighter mood to the work when she joked about the condition of some of the men's long-handled underwear.

"Thorvald hasn't had these washed for at least a year!" Elsa's front side bounced up and down keeping time with her hearty laugh.

"Yah, doesn't matter to me, if they want to pay full price and wait to give us their long johns till they're so stiff they stand up on their own," Dena chuckled. "Less work for us."

With weather too cool to use the outdoor clothesline, Elsa fed each item through the rollers of the manual wringer on the enclosed back porch after she'd rinsed them in another tub of clean water. She cranked the L-shaped wooden handle and garments spilled one at a time into a pile of heavy dampness in a basket on the floor. "Uff da," Elsa exclaimed as she hoisted it by both handles, holding it close to her ample midriff. She stepped carefully down the basement stairs. The winter clothesline close to the furnace soon sagged with Monday's laundry.

"I need some more potatoes for soup, Elsa," Dena hollered down the basement steps. "They're in the bin in the corner."

Dena was known for her good cooking and with so much of it to do, she and Elsa shopped almost daily. There was no way to store perishables. They could use an ice box in winter—an outdoor shed full of ice blocks, but spring, summer and fall meant daily trips to the market down the street. The adage "A Woman's Work is Never Done," described the Merchant Hotel to a T.

Elsa took a liking to Webb and along with Toots, attempted to do some mothering; Elsa because she didn't have a son and Toots because she was born with a soft heart. Dena was busy with boarders and guests and Jim spent his days at the pool hall. Ray was a bookworm and a tinkerer. His interests kept him busy and out of trouble. Walt spent most of his time on the farm with his grandparents. The younger girls, Vivian and Blanche, helped when they could, but spent most of their time playing by themselves or with friends.

Webb raised himself and his interests usually led to trouble.

"Ma, I really want to go to that show that's playing down the street," Webb begged Dena as she prepared supper in the kitchen with Elsa. "It's *Dr. Jekyll and Mr. Hyde*! You know the one where he goes kinda crazy? I've heard it's really swell. Can I go, Ma?"

Dena stopped stirring a pot of soup and looked at him. "Webb, if I had money to spend on movies, it wouldn't be to send you to something like that. Where do you get such ideas anyway?"

"But Ma... Other kids from school get to go to that movie. How come I can't go?"

"I said 'no,' Webb. That's it. Now skedaddle outta here."

Webb was crushed. He'd heard so much about the movie from other kids at school. In the afternoon a couple days later, with the dining room cleared of guests and the women in the kitchen cleaning up, Webb spied something shiny on the dining room buffet as he passed by. He went over to investigate.

Fifteen cents! Just the price of the movie. Someone must have left it here. No one's lookin'. Bet no one will even know it's gone. He pocketed the change and sauntered over to the pool hall.

That evening after supper, Elsa called Webb out to the kitchen when no one else was around. He liked her. She spent time talking to him and paid attention to what he said. Her hearty laugh drew him in. It was round and full, like she was. Normally her face carried a broad, kind smile, but not tonight. There was a different look.

"Webb, I did so want you to see that movie." Elsa's words were soft. She had tears in her eyes. "I saved fifteen cents for you to go, but I must have mislaid it. I can't find it. It's tough, honey, and I'm so sorry."

Guilt stabbed his heart. He felt ashamed, but couldn't admit what he'd done. With head down and tightness in his chest, he climbed the stairs to bed, her words still echoing in his ears, but perhaps there was a way to make things right again.

Early the next morning before Elsa arrived, and when Dena was out of the kitchen, Webb put the fifteen cents in a kitchen cupboard. He was too ashamed to go to the show now. He'd made Elsa cry.

When the evening meal-time bustle subsided, Elsa called Webb back into the kitchen. "Honey, I found the money in the cupboard, but I know that's not where I put it. Do you know how it got there?"

A long pause. "Well, may…maybe I do," Webb stammered. He looked at the floor and then out the door. There was another long pause. Then with a rush of words, Webb found himself confessing. "I just saw it there and thought someone musta forgot it and I really wanted to go to the show and no one was around and I didn't know who it belonged to and I thought they probly wouldn't miss it anyway and then you said it was yours and I felt bad so I put it in the cupboard." There—it was out and now he could breathe.

Elsa tried hard not to smile. "I know Webb, but when you find somethin', make sure it's yours." She put her hand on his shoulder. 'Cuz if you don't, it's called stealin' and I know you're not a thief." Elsa made sure Webb was looking her in the eye.

"You have to think before you do things that might hurt somebody else."

Webb had tears in his eyes. "I'm sorry. I won't ever do bad things *ever* again." In the moment, Webb meant what he said.

"I know, Webb. You're a good boy at heart."

The Road

The tension of night driving with only his thoughts to keep him company took their toll. Casper was in view and the city lights grew brighter as he drove.

That's what I wanted—a brighter future, more than I had as a kid. Just wanted to prove myself. Webb lifted the whiskey bottle to his lips and tipped it up. The bottle hid the light. *But seems provin' myself also meant hurtin' people in spite of what I swore to Elsa. Dorothy was one of 'em.*

Webb shook his head, trying to quiet the regret which kept creeping up on him. He took another swig.

"Dammit!" His open palm pummeled the steering wheel. He was fighting his own demons, but in a moment of clarity, stopped to wonder at Dorothy's perseverance. *I don't know what kept her lovin' me.* Webb shook his head again. *I gave her plenty of reasons not to!*

He grew maudlin, tears welling once more. *Hell, what do I know about marriage? What I saw growin' up… Ma tryin' to make a livin' for all of us and Dad in the pool hall…*

I saw a lot when I should have had good examples, but prohibition was in full swing. The pool hall was where guys did their drinking on the sly; me, too. I learned more than most boys ever needed to know. Was laid-out drunk, chewed tobacco, smoked cigars and had a profane vocabulary that would put a mule-skinner to shame, all by the time I was thirteen. And then there was the bettin'…

L to R: George Ims (friend), Jim Bateman,
Tenius Ramsland (brother-in-law),
Ole Ramsland (brother-in-law)

 # 5

Frank Duggan

Almont, North Dakota 1923

The wind blew dust in the door of Jim Bateman's Pool Hall. It was fall and another raucous Saturday night at the local watering hole. Twelve-and-a-half-year-old Webb had finished his chores at the hotel in the afternoon and was ready to shoot pool and have a few with friends and strangers. He wasn't particular. The pool hall, quiet during the week, always bustled with locals and visitors on the weekend. This was Webb's favorite place to spend time, a haven filled with smoke and the smell of liquor.

"There's money on this one," his dad whispered to Webb before he grabbed his cue stick, gave it some chalk and headed to the far end of the pool table. He'd won the coin toss and opted to break. The balls had already been racked. All eyes were on him. He could feel the tension. This wasn't just a friendly game.

Betting on pool players was nothing new, but it became apparent to Jim that Webb was becoming a real pool shark and he wanted to take advantage of his son's skill with a stick. For his age, Webb was a damned good player. He'd learned to control his nerves when all eyes were on him and it came time to make a difficult shot. He won more games than he lost and Jim pocketed the winnings. Jim would slap Webb on the back and congratulate him for his wins, occasionally handing over a few coins. Webb fancied himself his dad's favorite son.

The pool hall was big enough for a couple pool tables, a card table off to one side, and a bar where "soft drinks" were served. A door behind the bar led to a storeroom where Jim's other business was conducted.

Bootleggers and moonshiners brought in their wares, got paid and headed out as quick as they had come. Some circled around to the front door, acting like one of the crowd—just there for a good time.

A barber at a hotel down the street from Jim's establishment added two pool tables and a card table. Since Saturday was the busiest day of the week, and at times, the only day farmers would take off work to come to town, Jim knew their first stop would be the barber shop to get cleaned up. He added a barber chair in the front of the pool hall to bring in additional business, hired a barber and added to his profits.

Farm hands picked a number which gave the time for their haircut, shave, or both. Some appointments were as late as midnight. The posted price for both a shave and a haircut was six bits [75 cents].

While men waited for their appointment, they shot a little pool or played cards: whist, pinochle, penny ante and poker. Money traded hands quickly. Those who lost all their money at the games of chance, ended up without the shave and haircut.

Webb grew accustomed to men in work clothes and a few "city slickers" waiting their turn for the barber chair, who bellied up to the bar, shuffled cards at the table, or sat in straight-backs around the room. They talked, laughed, and did a lot of back-slappin' and one-upping each other with tall tales. There was a cigar, chaw or pipe in almost every mouth; a blue haze filled the room.

This was a place where Webb felt at home, but he knew how quickly this congenial scene could turn ugly. Booze spurred fisticuffs—bare knuckle fights that took their toll on the combatants. The fracases needed little, if any, provocation. Webb was not one to start a fight, but he wouldn't back away from a brawl either.

As the sun sunk in the west, low kerosene lighting cast long, secretive shadows which hid some faces from view. According to Webb, those were the unpredictable ones you had to watch out for. "If a guy won't talk to ya', he's probably got something to hide," he figured. The brightest lights in the room came from lamps over the two pool tables where wicks were turned up as high as they would go.

The hubbub quieted down as Webb stepped up to the table and laid his cigar on the edge. He knew he'd have time to pick it up, do some swaggering and flick ashes on the wood floor between shots.

He'd also take time to glance at his dad to make sure he was still smiling.

All eyes were on Webb. Most of the men in the room had money on him or his opponent, Frank Duggan. Frank was new in town. He'd strode into the pool hall with a half dozen guys from his road gang hired to do maintenance on the Red Trail, the main road that brought more tourists to town every week. Frank walked with his shoulders thrown back, chest and chin thrust forward, a posture which said, 'Hit me if you dare." He cocked his head to one side and with a smirk, bragged about his pool playing expertise. His force of character or lack of it got his friends and some tourists to bet on him. Those who knew Webb stuck with their "sure thing," the local kid.

Webb leaned his tall, square-shouldered frame parallel to the table to make the break. He drew back the cue with his right hand, steadied the tip and created the slide with his left. The cue ball cracked into the triangle of balls.

It was a legal break. He pocketed both a solid and stripe. Webb called solids and continued to shoot. The next shot required the cue ball to bank before it hit another solid. Frank told Webb to call the shot—tell him what pocket the object ball would drop into. Webb did and missed—on purpose. It gave Frank reason to believe this match would be a shoo-in, that play with this kid would be a waste of time. On the other hand, he could teach the kid a thing or two. And there was money on the line.

Frank pocketed a stripe, but before he set up for the next shot, he placed his chalk cube on the rail. It looked like he marked the table for his next shot.

"Hey, Frank," Webb called with a laugh in his voice, "not trying to mark your next shot are you?"

"You callin' me a cheater, kid?" Frank retorted.

"Hell no. Just payin' attention." Webb smiled again and took a puff of his cigar. Guffaws erupted around the room at young Webb's bravado. Frank curled his lip, spit on the floor and moved the chalk cube. The game continued.

The two players pocketed solids, stripes and the eight ball. Frank won the first game. Webb the second. Bets were placed faster and the stakes were up. Jim kept tally behind the bar and Ray helped out. Two out of three games would determine the winner.

During the second game, Webb pointed out that Frank had illegally jumped a ball by digging under the cue ball. Frank was indignant. "What the hell are you talkin' about, kid? That was an accident, not a foul. What are you belly achin' about?"

Play continued into the third game. Bottles of booze were brandished. Bystanders became more vocal about their favored players. "What's that kid tryin' to do? Give Frank a bad name? We otta take him out behind the place and show him who's boss," a guy with a face like a wanted poster slurred.

"You and who else, stranger," came an angry response from Tobias, a local farmer whose bulk filled the doorway.

"Hey fellas," Webb broke in. "We got a game to play here. Right, Frank?"

"Yeah, let's finish this. Your pool playin's not worth a plug nickel anyway. Not sure why I agreed to such a cockeyed match."

Webb's dander was up with that insult, but he controlled his anger. He'd get even.

Toward the end of the third game, Webb was ahead in pocketed balls with one stripe and the eight ball to go. It was Frank's turn. He had a couple solids in the way of the eight ball. A shot he'd used before would drop all three and, if executed fast enough, could not be detected. He would follow through with the stick and at the same time hit one of the balls with the cue stick. It was illegal, but would get him what he wanted, the winnings.

He made the shot; the balls dropped and Frank claimed victory. Webb and a couple other guys in the room saw what he'd done. All hell broke loose.

Tobias grabbed Frank by the back of the neck and tossed him backward. "You lousy polecat cheatin' sonofabitch." Some of the tourists bolted out the door as Frank bounced off a wall and headed back toward Tobias with fists raised and fire in his eyes.

Frank's friends, itching for a fight, were all in. One of them, head down to plow into Webb's bread basket, found himself on the floor instead, when Webb sidestepped and the guy bounced off the end of the pool table.

Almont men and the road gang went at it, arms flailing, words flying. Everyone was into the fracas now with one exception. Jim grabbed loose change and booze bottles off the bar and hurried into the back room. He figured the law would be on the scene in short order and he'd better "tidy up," just in case. He'd seen his place erupt before.

Ray rolled up his sleeves and rushed from behind the bar to help Webb. Muscles on fire, Webb wanted to tear into Frank himself. Ray grabbed his arm. He'd watched the strangers from the back. "Webb," he shouted, "that guy might be packin'."

Not one to take advice in the midst of a fight, Webb flew at one of Frank's sidekicks, pounding his fists into his face and gut. Ray took on another one with equal zeal, but less success.

Webb was making mincemeat out of someone's face when Frank briefly caught Tobias in a headlock and yelled, "Get em!" to a sidekick.

With a banshee scream, Tobias crumpled to the floor. He writhed in pain and blood gushed from his back. A long-bladed knife glinted in the hand of the man who stood over him. The room stood still at the sound and sight. In a flash the culprits raced out the door, crammed themselves into their jalopies and sped out of town. Men from the bar gave chase with the sheriff not far behind. As Jim predicted, the sheriff had been called because of the ruckus in Bateman's pool hall.

Someone went to fetch the town doctor, but by the time he arrived, it was too late. The farm hand who'd come to town for a few "soft drinks" and a game of cards, was dead.

The Road

Webb needed to get some sleep. He wanted to stop thinking about death and his role in it.

Did I cause that? What if I hadn't shot pool with Frank that night wanting to impress my dad. Would Tobias still be alive? What if…What if I'd done things differently, would Dorothy still be alive?

The gas station in Casper was closed when he rolled in, but the Chevy's lights caught a sign in the window. A pretty girl held a bottle of soda. Alina. Webb thought she looked just like Alina. She had the same pretty face and innocent smile. He hadn't thought about her for years. *Why now?*

Maybe I just need a break and some shuteye.

He'd sleep in the car in Casper for a few hours and then keep going. He had to get to Billings as early as possible. There were things to explain to the family and another 350 mile drive to North Dakota.

Webb grabbed a blanket from the back seat along with a clothes-filled satchel to use as a pillow. He was careful not to disturb the shoebox in the corner.

Stretched out across the front seat, coat and blanket pulled tight around him for warmth, and even with his eyes shut, he could still see the picture of the girl who looked like Alina.

L to R: Ray, Blanche, Evelyn (Toots),
Webb, Vivian, and Walt
Mid 1920's

6

Alina

Almont, North Dakota 1923

By Christmas, the Merchant Hotel was the most popular hotel in town. The food was good, beds decent and the family well liked.

To celebrate Christmas, Dena, with Elsa's help, threw a two-day party, inviting all of Dena's siblings, their hired help, the hotel boarders, and friends. It was a large crowd who came for the food and fun. A fiddler, piano player and accordionist provided music adding to the merriment.

The accordionist, twenty-year-old Lawrence Welk, was a local boy who brought his accordion to play on other occasions at the hotel too. He had an eye for Toots. When he later became a well-known celebrity, the family told the story over and over, much to Toots' embarrassment.

In keeping with Norwegian tradition, Dena served large helpings of lutefisk. Preparation of the fish took two weeks. The dried white fish was first soaked in water, then a solution of water and lye and finally in water again.

It was a painstaking process, but the fish was finally baked and served with lefse—a soft Norwegian flat bread, bacon, green peas, potatoes, gravy, and geitost—a Norwegian sweet cheese. Guests brought even more food and, of course, Jim provided the "soft drinks." This was the biggest party the hotel had ever seen.

Dena's relatives filled the small hotel: three brothers, one sister, three half-sisters and one half-brother, all who lived a buggy or Model T ride away from Almont. They brought their families and friends. Most were Norwegian, but the territory had also enticed Germans and Russians.

Webb had grown from his mother and Elsa's good cooking. He was as tall as fourteen-year-old Ray and had almost caught up to his dad's six-foot height. Ray would slick his hair back and make an effort to look dapper. Webb on the other hand, looked like an unmade bed more often than not, but girls still turned their heads and smiled when he walked by. Perhaps his unkempt look was part of the attraction.

The night of the Christmas shindig, merriment was fueled by Jim's supply of booze. While the adults made merry, another one of Webb's uncles arrived with his family and a pretty young girl Webb didn't know. He figured she was probably the fifteen-year-old Russian girl he'd heard about who worked on his uncle's farm.

Not one to hesitate when it came to a pretty girl and knowing if he didn't approach her, Ray would, he made his move.

"Hi, my name is Webb. What's yours?" He offered her a 'soft drink.'

"I'm Alina." She said with a strange accent. She dipped her chin, looked up at Webb and seemed to blush. Or maybe it was just warm in the room. Webb couldn't tell for sure, but he liked what he saw.

"Ya' want some food? There's plenty, and then maybe we could dance?" He wasn't going to waste any time laying out the plan. Alina smiled, batted her eyelashes at him and said, "Yah, sure." That sounded more Norwegian to Webb than Russian, but he figured she was learning her English from Norwegian's who learned their English from other immigrants, so what could you expect.

Webb led Alina through the food line at the buffet table. She hesitated about the lutefisk, but he assured her it wasn't half bad, but the lefse was probably better. He watched her dainty fingers put butter on the lefse and roll it up. He liked it that way, too, and they eyed each other as they nibbled away at the food in their fingers. Webb wolfed down heartier servings, while Alina took her time. Impatient to get his arm around her waist, Webb started tapping his foot to the music as a hint for her to join him on the dance floor.

A few more "soft drinks" served with hand clapping, thigh slapping dance tunes had the two of them giggling their way through made-up dance steps. The slower tunes found them oblivious to the rest of the room as they swayed cheek to cheek. The rest of the guests paid no mind. They were working on their own oblivion.

Webb knew about Dena's rule of no women in the men's rooms. He also knew it had been ignored by many and as far as he knew, no one was ever caught. Besides, was the room he shared with Ray considered a "man's room?" On this occasion, he thought not.

A little before midnight, they found their way up the steep back stairs to the second floor. Strains of *Condu*

Glemme Gamle Norge—Can You Forget Old Norway?—floated up the stairs with them. The boys' bedroom was at the front of the hotel.

The room had a couple single beds, a small wardrobe, and a table with a kerosene lamp, which they lit. Webb closed the door, grabbed a key that hung on a hook close by, stuck it in the lock and made sure he heard the tumbler click into place.

"Just makin' sure we aren't bothered by some drunk." Webb said excitedly. He'd never invited a girl to his room before. He hooked his thumbs over the top of his belt, not sure what to do next.

"I can teach you game," Alina teased in broken English. She smiled. The small gap between her front teeth made her seem even more playful. Her honey blonde hair was pulled back with a scarf tied around her head, Indian style. There was no reason for her to follow fashion and wear a cropped hair do like some of the women in town. There were a couple of women with those hairstyles downstairs. Even Toots wore her hair shorter these days.

It was also obvious Alina didn't wear the breast flattening, hide-every-curve kind of corset he'd seen his mother cinched into a time or two, although he found his mother's Sear's catalogue—the women's underwear section—riveting.

As a hired farm girl, a corset wouldn't have been practical for Alina, Webb thought, and she couldn't afford it anyway. He was happy about that. He had ogled what he could see of her curves all evening, but he only imagined he would see more.

Alina sat on the edge of the bed. Her hazel eyes glistened as she inched up the hem of her long-sleeved, drop-waist wool dress and revealed shapely legs in dark stockings. Earlier as Webb and Alina stumbled up the steep back stairs, he watched her hips sway from side to side and noticed what seemed to be about a hundred buttons down her back. He was up for the challenge—in more ways than one.

"What kinda game are you talkin' about?" Webb asked. Somehow he knew it wasn't going to be 'Kick the Can.'

"You take off…" She paused to think of the word. "Clothes. Not all. One first. Then I do."

Webb hesitated a moment. Under his shirt and pants, he had on long-handled underwear with a long row of buttons down the front and a flap in back, the same kind he'd worn every winter as long as he could remember. The difference was that now they were his own. He'd outgrown Ray's hand-me-downs and, thank God, his mother didn't make him wear his dad's left-overs.

Webb unbuttoned his shirt, pulled it out of his tight belted pants, took it off and flung it on the floor. He'd figure out what to do with his underwear when he had to.

"Well, I did mine. Now you do yours." Webb was panting. The anticipation of what might be happening already had a strange effect on him.

Alina kicked off her shoes and pulled her hem a little higher. Webb's eyes got bigger, his breath more rapid.

"You done this before?" Webb asked to fill the awkward silence.

"Maybe. You?" Alina smiled.

"Oh hell. I've been with a girl with no clothes on," Webb blurted out. His approach was anything but romantic, but Saturday night baths with younger siblings made the statement somewhat true.

Alina laughed. "You like that?" she taunted.

"Oh, yeah."

"Then come here," she patted the bed, "and let me help you."

The game progressed more quickly. Webb's boots, belt and pants were soon in a heap on the floor. His long johns were in full view in the dim kerosene light. Webb spied Alina's bloomers as she slipped off her knee high stockings. She inched her hem even higher. It was cold in the room, but neither one of them noticed.

"Webb, like to kiss?"

"Oh, yeah. I kissed a lotta girls." 'Spin the Bottle' after school came to mind as Webb proclaimed his prowess.

He grabbed Alina's face in both hands and planted one on her puckered lips, forgetting to tip his head to one side to avoid a nose collision.

"Ouch, Webb!"

"Sorry, Alina. Didn't mean to do that. I'll be more careful. Just got excited, I guess."

At least that was true.

Webb's meaty paws fumbled with Alina's passel of dress buttons. She helped him with his. With bloomers and buttons out of the way, and in spite of his awkwardness, Webb's introduction to the wonders and excitement of the game—proceeded.

 **7**

The Road

March 9, 1939

It was 4:00 am, Thursday morning, only one day after finding out about Dorothy's death and the day before her funeral. It seemed longer—as if time was expanding and contracting depending on Webb's thoughts, and yet, there were still miles to cover before the funeral in Dunn Center, North Dakota.

Webb found himself still shaking his head in disbelief. *How could she be dead? So young. It's not fair. What the hell am I gonna do?* There were many more questions than answers.

The road turned north, away from the Medicine Bow Range, heading through the Thunder Basin Grassland. Webb saw the glint of eyes, deer he thought, as his headlamps scanned the road ahead. It was cold, but not much snow on the road. He'd changed one tire so far and the Chevy was guzzling gas and needed a refill for the tank and the gas cans in Casper. Sheridan would be the next chance to fill them again before heading north to Billings.

Jim Beam kept him company. He'd picked up another bottle in Casper along with a sandwich. Now he took a swig. It was still dark and there were no other vehicles on the road.

Webb had caught some shuteye in Casper, but not much—four hours at most. He had to keep going; it would take another six hours from Casper to Billings. *Hope to God, I can make it by noon.*

Holding the steering wheel and bottle in his left hand, he screwed the whiskey cap back on, put it on the seat beside him and grabbed the sandwich to quiet the rumbling in his stomach. He took a bite and glanced up at flickering stars and a three quarter moon sliding from behind a cloud cover. It lit grassland and prairie, the same land laid bare by dust storms just a couple years before.

Maybe there's another job in Nebraska in the next couple months; who knows. No goddam guarantee in this life! It's the 30's. Everybody says the last few years have been dirty, the "dirty thirties." Hell that's why we're building dams—just to hold dirt in place and irrigate so somethin' can grow again.

In the past decade, there had been nine years of drought and dust storms that scoured the Great Plains from Canada south to Texas. It caused folks who earned a living off the land to move west, including Webb's family in 1934 and Dorothy's in 1938.

Webb remembered April of 1935, the month before he and Dorothy were married at the Lutheran Church in Dunn Center. Twenty of the worst dust storms in U.S. history turned day into night. People couldn't see five feet in front of themselves at times. *Maybe that was a sign of things to come for us.* Webb drove on.

I did the best I could, I guess. At least I married Dorothy when she found out she was in a family way. Ray didn't do that when he got another girl pregnant, just the year before. But then he'd already been married, had a baby and was divorced. And Blanche didn't marry—had her baby boy in Fargo at the Crittenton Home for Unwed Mothers when she was seventeen. Big year '35, for Batemans and babies. Walt got married in '36 'cuz Juliet said she was havin' his kid. He denied it, but married her anyway. Too bad the baby died. They divorced the same year.

Almost forgot—Toots had her baby girl in '35 too, but she'd been married for six years. No scandal there.

He finished the sandwich and tossed the paper wrapper on the floor.

The view of the moonlit, snow-covered landscape caused time to stop and shift into reverse once again. *I thought gettin' married was the decent thing to do.* Webb smiled at the memory. *Dorothy loved to dance.*

Dunn Center 1935

She was excited. Webb would be in town for the dance, from Friday until Sunday. She missed him more and more when he was gone. At Dorothy's insistence, Webb stayed at Laura and Ed Boe's farm home near Dunn Center. Dorothy's parents were welcoming, but somewhat skeptical about him being the best choice for her. He moved around so much, and after several months, Webb still hadn't asked Ed Boe for his daughter's hand in marriage.

Dorothy looked forward to this January weekend and their plans to attend the President's Ball at the local grange in Dunn Center. The ball had nothing to do with an inauguration. President Franklin D. Roosevelt celebrated his birthday by encouraging cities all over the country to help in the fight to cure infantile paralysis. His birthday celebration became a day to raise money for polio research and treatment. Roosevelt had contracted the disease in 1921 at age 39 and was paralyzed from the waist down.

Even though there was an admission fee to the dance, Webb smiled and laughed as he paid when he and Dorothy entered the hall. It was for a good cause and he liked Roosevelt. Here was a President who was finally helping the country get back on its feet.

The gathering was well attended. Prohibition had ended in 1933 and it was legal to drink in the open. Most of the younger folks, including Webb and Dorothy, brought their own beverages, which they shared on the sidelines of the dance floor. Webb carried a flask in his jacket pocket on this occasion as he did on most occasions.

They danced non-stop from the time they arrived: the foxtrot, waltz, swing and jitterbug, and finally took a break to go outside and cool off. They shared the whiskey flask again. Webb lit a cigarette.

"Webb, have you heard about the dance marathons in some of the big cities?" Dorothy asked catching her breath. "I bet we could win, if we entered." They were outlasting most couples on this dance floor—with ease.

Dorothy had read about these events, popular for a decade, but in the 30's they were a way for couples to win hundreds of dollars. These events proved how desperate people were to make money during the Depression years. Marathoners danced, walked, shuffled, sprinted, and sometimes cracked under the pressure and exhaustion of round-the-clock motion. They had to keep moving at least

45 minutes of every hour. Some contests lasted days, others even months. A 25-cent admission price entitled audience members to watch as long as they pleased.

"I bet we could," Webb agreed. He exhaled smoke and frosty breath into the night air. The moon glistened off the snow and Webb wrapped his arm around Dorothy to keep her warm. From inside the hall, strains of Webb's favorite waltz tune could be heard. He pulled Dorothy even closer and sang softly in in her ear:

> I'd like to make your golden dreams come true, dear,
> If I only had my way.
> A paradise this world would seem to you, dear,
> If only I had my way.
>
> If I had my way, dear, forever there'd be
> A garden of roses for you and for me,
> A thousand and one things, dear, I would do,
> Just for you, just for you, just for you.
>
> If I had my way, we would never grow old,
> And sunshine I'd bring every day,
> You would reign all alone, like a queen on a throne,
> If I had my way.

Beaming, Dorothy snuggled in to Webb's arms. He whispered, "Let's get our coats and move the ol' buggy down the road a piece. Someplace more private." Webb waited for a response with a big grin on his face, but he was sure of the answer.

Dorothy hesitated. There were times with Webb when she found it hard to breathe. It wasn't from too much dancing. She felt jittery just being with him, but couldn't get enough of those feelings. Wondering if he could feel her heart pounding when he held her close as they waltzed, she would move her hand to the back of his neck and pull herself even closer. She wanted him to know he excited her. He always smelled so good and his broad thick hands were gentle when he held her.

She nodded. "Sure!" Webb smiled and took one last drag. A two-finger flick arced the remains of the cigarette into the snow.

Sitting close in the front seat, they drove a couple miles down a two-rut, snow-covered road. Webb parked the car off the road and suggested they get into the back seat to keep warm without the interference of the stick shift.

Dorothy hopped out and grabbed a handful of icy snow, perfect for packing as a frozen weapon. She took aim, but Webb got her first and sent showers of ice down the back of her neck. She squealed with delight and attempted to hit her mark. Webb grabbed her and tipsy as they were, they both tumbled into a snow bank, crazy with laughter. They hugged, then struggled to get up and took turns brushing one another off before they bounded into the back seat of the car to get warm. Moonlight danced off the crystals of snow.

Dorothy giggled when Webb kissed her neck as they cuddled together. He took a drink from his flask and handed it to her. She took a sip. He kissed her cheek.

Dorothy was smitten, but she also knew where backseat cuddling could lead. She was a school teacher. She could be jeopardizing a job. Her parents needed her help with income. She loved Webb, but what if he wasn't ready to settle down? What if he didn't love her? He hadn't said it yet. Her thoughts were fuzzy. Logic was losing to libido and booze.

"Webb, do you think we should get married?" Dorothy blurted.

He pulled back for a moment and then nuzzled her neck again and whispered, "Nah, not right now. I need to get a better position so we'll have more money." He caressed her arms and then her legs. More kisses and whiskey were exchanged.

So we'll have more money. He said 'we.' He must mean the two of us. Dorothy tried to analyze what she was hearing. Webb took her coat off.

"I'll keep you warm. I promise." Webb's smile deepened his dimples. In the moonlight, she could see the devilish look in his eye.

"Webb, you *do* love me, don't you?"

"Of course I do." Webb responded, but any more questions she had were hushed when he kissed her. He really kissed her. She tasted whiskey and felt a rush of pleasure when his fingers stroked the inside of her thigh. Dorothy's body tingled with anticipation. A warmth engulfed her and became pulsating heat. The cold night turned feverish.

With arms and legs intertwined, they made love in the tiny backseat of the old jalopy. It was not the love bed Dorothy dreamed of, but in that moment, she let herself give in. Dorothy surrendered her will and her body to Webb Bateman—all for love.

The Road

Webb rolled down the Chevy's window and hung his arm over the door frame. A coral wash on the eastern horizon brightened the snow-dusted landscape, bathing the gentle rise and fall of the plain in a promising glow. He could hear morning birds chirping. The smell of fresh, crisp air helped him stay awake, but the hope a sunny morning usualy brings didn't brighten Webb's thoughts.

He stared ahead at the road, looking, but not seeing what was there. Too much time to think and remember. He was nearing Sheridan, Wyoming, but still had another three hours of driving from Sheridan to Billings.

We danced right into marriage. I wasn't ready. I was just lookin' for fun, but got a whole lot more than I bargained for. Webb rolled the window back up. *Guess that wasn't the first time I danced into a situation that changed my life.*

1923 Ford Model T Touring Car

8

Coop, Giggler and the Model T

Almont, North Dakota 1924

Coop dropped ashes from the cigarette hanging out of his mouth as he bent over the pool table to make a shot. He straightened his burly frame and brushed ashes from the felt into a side pocket, glancing over his shoulder to see if Webb's dad, Jim Bateman, had seen what happened. He knew Webb didn't care.

Coop leaned over the table again to take his shot. "Hey, Webb. There's a Valentine's dance in Glen Ullin tonight. Wanna go?"

Things had calmed down in the pool hall since Tobias' murder the fall before. This morning the hall was empty except for the boys and a guy getting his hair cut, but it was still early and the place would be full by mid-afternoon. The Bateman Pool Hall was known for miles around.

Coop and his sidekick, Giggler, were in their teens, not much older than Webb, but already working on an extra gang, building a new bridge for the railroad near town.

Coop was the one who decided what he and Giggler would do in their free time. It was Saturday and they came into Almont to get cleaned up, spend time shooting pool and figure out how to get a ride to the dance in Glen Ullin that evening.

Shorter than Webb's six feet, Coop was thickset, muscular and had dark hair. He wore a stringy handlebar mustache that needed the barber's attention. It hadn't been waxed or curled at the ends and hung down either side of his mouth. With his squinty eyes, Webb told him more than once, he looked like a Chinaman.

Webb, almost thirteen, liked being pals with the older guys. "Sure, I wanna go to the dance, but it's too cold to hitch. Got a ride?" he asked, leaning against his cue stick, waiting a turn at the table.

"Nope. Thought maybe you had some ideas. You're the guy who knows your way around this town." Giggler tittered, showing off his trademark giggle while goading Webb with a little praise.

Giggler was Webb's height, but with his slouch, he always looked shorter. His shock of blonde hair needed a wash and attempts to grow a beard resulted in wisps of peach fuzz. There wasn't much the barber could do for Giggler, but he'd still be charged 75 cents.

When Giggler walked, he stuck his neck out and led with his chin. His weird laugh showed gaps where teeth should be. Webb thought he looked like a clown and told him so. "Stand up, Giggler. Ya' look like a dumb bunny lopin' round like that." Webb was merciless with his teasing. Giggler didn't seem to mind. He just giggled.

Webb would be thirteen in three months. From the time the family moved to Almont when Webb was ten, he'd made a lot of friends in the pool hall, most of them older and not always the best influence. Webb figured he could get along with anybody he met, whether it was a couple guys from the railroad gang or a local businessman.

"Looks like you know lots of folks in Almont, Webb. How is it you get in good with just about everybody you meet?" Giggler asked.

Webb took the bait. "You just gotta like 'em and find their good points, Giggler. You have to forget their bad points and talk to Joe, Tom, or Dick about Joe, Tom, or Dick and the things they know the most about."

Webb made it sound simple. But there were times like this when his friendliness was an open door to trouble.

"So you know anybody who'll loan us a car?" Coop took Giggler's lead and played on Webb's eagerness to be the good guy.

"We could take Ma's car." Webb's voice was lowered, even though he was out of earshot from his dad. He knew his mother would never give permission and he didn't want anyone telling her about the plan.

"Sure sounds good to us!" Coop responded.

"Yeah!" Giggler chimed in.

"We'll have to do this on the sly, though. Don't think Ma's goin' to appreciate us takin' her car. So we just have to make sure we have it back before too late."

"Hey, Webb. You can count on us." Giggler tried to sound convincing. "We wouldn't want to get ya' in trouble." Coop and Giggler both smiled.

The 1923 Ford Model T Touring car was stored in one of the bank's garages, a couple blocks away. Storage of Dena's car had been part of the deal with the bank manager in exchange for taking care of the manager's cows. Thanks to Henry Ford, Dena's "Tin Lizzie," as it was called, was considered the first affordable automobile in America.

Ford had created an efficient fabrication assembly line instead of hand crafting each vehicle. It made his cars something middle class Americans could buy.

According to Ford, the car was so low in price that "every man making a good salary would be able to own one and enjoy it with his family in God's great open spaces."

Ford may not have had Dena in mind when he advertised his car as "affordable" for every man making a good salary. Dena was not salaried. Her income was dependent on sweat equity running the hotel with the help of Elsa, her daughters, and once in a while, her sons.

Saving money for the Model T required hard work and planning on Dena's part. She got agreement from Jim that she could put away money for the car from what was earned in the hotel. After sixteen years of marriage, Dena still talked over decisions with Jim, but if she'd made up her mind, there was no need for much discussion. After all, Jim already had an old beater of a vehicle. He also had two businesses, the pool hall and the livery stable across the street from the hotel. And Jim had his own priorities— alcohol and gambling.

Dena's income came from the rooms she rented at the hotel for as many as ten boarders at a time. On Friday nights and Saturdays, there were additional cash-paying customers in the hotel for meals. Considering Dena had to pay for all the hotel food and supplies and provide for the family's needs, it took months to accumulate the necessary

393 dollars to purchase the 1923 Model T Three-door Touring Car. Dena called her Model T "majestic."

Ford had declared customers could have a car painted any color they wanted, so long as it was black. Dena's car was black and almost eleven feet long with thirty-inch spoke wheels and pneumatic tires. There were running boards on both sides and a fancy hood ornament out front. The leather seats were tufted and with the convertible top collapsed and extending almost three feet beyond the back of the car, the Model T's profile made Dena think it could take off on its own. That was unlikely, although there were occasions it would creep backward when Dena tried to hand crank ol' Lizzie to a start.

Because of the number of gas stations Jim and the bank owned in Minnesota, Dena had been around cars from the time they appeared on the roads. She was also woman with grit and determination and had insisted Jim teach her. She'd learned to drive before they moved to Almont, but it didn't mean driving was easy.

It was complicated because the car had three foot pedals and a lever mounted to the road side of the driver's seat. The lever was used with foot pedals to change gears and to put the vehicle in neutral. It also served as the parking and emergency brake. The throttle was controlled with a lever on the steering wheel.

The tires were a challenge, too because they required high pressure to keep them inflated. Horses still lost their shoes and the horseshoe nails on already bumpy roads, together with the high pressure, made flat tires a common problem. That didn't dissuade Dena from driving her "majestic." Dena drove to church with the girls most Sundays.

Toots, eldest at fifteen, rode with her mother in front. The younger girls, Vivian—nine and Blanche—six, rode together in the big back seat.

They dressed in their Sunday best. Hats, gloves, shoes shined and dresses unwrinkled, the Batemans knew how to make a statement on the day of rest. Dena couldn't help feeling proud when they rolled into the church's parking lot and saw heads turn.

It was understandable Dena did not want anyone else driving her Model T unless she was with them. That was the rule for Webb and Ray—and for anyone else who had an eye on her car. She had worked too hard to buy her pride and joy.

Webb's curiosity about the car had already gotten the best of him. Even before Coop asked about a ride to the dance, Webb had "borrowed" the key to the garage padlock one day, laid it on Dena's hot kitchen stove and then put it on a piece of canning wax. He took the imprint to a friend's house and they filed out a key—planning ahead for future joy rides. The keys for all Model T Fords were the same at the time, so it wasn't hard to "borrow" one of those.

That evening, Coop nudged Webb, who was taking a drink at the back of the pool hall. "We need to get goin' if we're gonna make the dance." Webb handed the bottle to Giggler, who put it inside his jacket. The place was crowded and noisy as usual. They sauntered out of the pool hall without anyone paying much attention.

Keys in hand, Webb led the way as they snuck over to the garage where the car was stored. Webb looked over his shoulder to make sure no one saw where they were going. After dark and off the main street, the neighborhood was silent.

"Okay you guys, we have to be real quiet and careful." He slurred a whisper and with a dramatic gesture, held a finger to his lips. His feet skidded from under him and he fell in a snow bank. Coop and Giggler tried to muffle their laughter at Webb's pratfall.

"I'm okay. I'm okay, but ya' know, if a car takes off in the snow after dark and someone sees us, the whole town will check right now to see who's havin' a baby or going to the doctor, or what's goin' on."

"Yeah, yeah. But you're the joker makin' all the noise!" Coop kidded Webb.

After they got into the garage, Coop slid onto the front seat and turned the key in the dashboard, put the car in neutral and Webb hand cranked the Model T to a start without too much ruckus. "Let's get the hell out of this garage before we gas ourselves to death," Coop yelled. Giggler and Webb pushed the vehicle outside and slid the big wooden garage doors back together, making sure they were locked.

"I'm drivin'." Coop was in the driver's seat, so Webb and Giggler piled in the back. "You two are too far gone for the job and I know where we're goin'." Webb and Giggler had managed to guzzle more than their share of booze at the back of Bateman's pool hall.

"I'm sure this girl who invited me will have some

friends. Not sure they'll want to dance with the likes of you two, though. You're so looped, you'll be dancin' with each other!" Coop laughed so hard at that one, he almost drove off the road. Giggler swatted Coop on the back of the head, giggled, and threatened to keep the booze in the backseat.

The dance was about an hour away. There was snow on the ground, but the frozen wheel ruts were almost clear—even if their heads weren't.

Webb loved to dance. Not long after they arrived, he did his own rendition of a jitter bug with some poor unsuspecting girl he'd grabbed on the way to the dance floor. Webb was sure his flailing arms and flapping feet impressed some of the other girls standing on the sidelines. They were smiling at him. That must have meant something. He was there for a good time and tried his best to entertain others.

A small band had been playing up-tempo songs. When the music slowed, Webb grabbed another girl from the sidelines and waltzed her around the floor. He wasn't a great slow dancer, but he had rhythm and little fear when it came to giving something a try.

"Hey kid. Don't you know how to ask a girl, nice?" Her question came with a smile.

He stopped in the middle of the floor. "Sorry, Ma'am." He gave a long, low sweeping bow. "May I have this dance?" He grinned. She laughed, pulled him back to her and they swung around the room, oblivious to others. They were having fun and at one point, wanting to impress her Webb said, "We're tripping the light fantastic!" His partner looked at him as though he was crazy. "I heard that in a song about dancing," he explained. The dance ended at midnight and the girls had to go home, but Webb, Coop, and Giggler found an open road house and continued to drink into the wee hours.

About 5 am, Webb remembered he had to get the car back before his mother found it missing. He didn't want to think what Dena would do, if she found out he'd borrowed ol' Lizzie. It was her pride and joy.

"Hey, Coop, Giggler, we gotta hit the road and head for Almont. This rig has to be back in the garage before Ma decides to go for a Sunday drive or I'm a goner."

They stumbled out to the Model T, just as the sun was coming up. With Webb behind the wheel and Coop on the hand crank, they tried to start the car. All they heard was the sound of the crank.

Lizzie's motor was silent.

"You guys jack up the hind wheels and I'll throw her into high gear," Webb ordered. "That's a trick that never fails 'cuz it makes the magneto stronger." Webb thought to himself, *If this car even has one.*

They jacked up the back of the car until the wheels were off the ground and all took turns cranking the handle. Each of the boys bragged he would get Lizzie started. No one did.

The sun was up and the boys were tuckered from partying all night and from winding the crank on Lizzie until they were blue in the face.

Webb sighed with fatigue. "Let's head to the train depot and get some shut eye. Then we'll figure out what to do." Since Webb was the one who would have to face his mother, Coop and Giggler shrugged. They didn't care and were happy to get some sleep.

The potbelly stove was fired up in the empty depot. It would be a while before any trains came through on a Sunday. Before long, they were all curled up on the floor in front of the warm stove, snoring up a storm.

About 9 am, a train whistle woke Webb up. He shook Coop and Giggler. "We gotta find a mechanic and get home. I'm gonna catch hell for sure."

Coop and Giggler yawned and stretched while Webb checked with the station agent about finding a mechanic to look at the Model T. They were in luck. He was just down the street.

When the mechanic heard the boys story, he sympathized. He'd sown his own oats as a young man. He checked over the car without charge.

"There was kerosene in the radiator for antifreeze and a top hose was loose. It let kerosene get on the spark plugs. I just wiped off each plug with a rag," the mechanic explained when Lizzie started right up. Grateful, they said their goodbyes. Webb took the wheel, while Coop and Giggler crumpled together, asleep in the back seat, sawing logs. It was 10:30 am and it would take him at least an hour to get home. There had been more snow during the night.

In Almont, Dena, Toots and the girls left the Merchant Hotel for church. With skirts hoisted to keep the hems clean, they carefully stepped through the snow for the two blocks it took to get to the garage. All dressed in their Sunday best: long dresses, jackets for warmth against the cold, hats on neatly coiffed heads, fur-lined gloves and high snow boots, they were ready for their time away from the hotel.

Dena unlocked the garage door. The girls helped her push the heavy wooden doors to either side along the overhead metal track.

They all stared at the empty space where the Model T was supposed to be sitting.

"Where's the car, Momma?" Vivian asked. Blanche held her hand and stared into the emptiness.

"What do you think happened, Momma?" Toots asked, just as surprised as the others. "Who could have taken the car?"

"Oh, that man! Your Dad must have taken off while we were in the kitchen. He knows I don't like anyone driving my car. He'll get a piece of my mind when I see him." Dena stomped her foot in anger and whirled around. Her skirt flew out behind her. She picked up the sides of her dress to hurry back. Maybe Jim had returned. The girls followed in single file. With heads lowered as if fighting a strong wind, the angry little parade pushed back toward the hotel.

Dena found Jim sound asleep where she'd last seen him. His snores were enough to rattle the windows. "Jim, wake up. The Model T's gone. Do ya' know who took it?"

"Whad ya' say?" Jim sat up, his head still swimming from the night before. "The car's gone?"

"That's what I said. You don't suppose the boys took it, do you? I'll have a look upstairs." Dena stormed up the back stairs and headed for the boys' bedroom in front. She burst through the door. One bed was empty and Ray lay snoring in the other.

"Ray, where's your brother?" Dena demanded. She got the same startled response from him as she had from Jim.

"What are you askin', Ma?" a sleepy Ray replied. He'd had a few too many at the pool hall the night before with Webb and the boys, and had begged off going with them.

"Oh, never mind. This is the last straw! Webb stole my car!"

As Webb sped toward Almont, he was thinking up stories he could tell his mother to calm her down. He knew she would be pretty darn mad.

'Well, Ma, these friends of mine had to get to Glen Ullin and they didn't have a way to get there. It was an emergency and I wanted to help out. I know I shoulda asked, but there just wasn't time.' How about, 'Gee, Ma, I just borrowed Lizzie 'cuz a guy was walkin' out of the pool hall and fell and hurt hisself so bad he couldn't drive home out in the country, so I had to take him. No one else could and...' Damn! The shit's gonna fly when I get home. No doubt about it. As soon as the car was back in the garage and the padlock in place, Coop and Giggler hightailed it toward Main Street. Webb was on his own with his mother.

He took his time going home. The pool hall was closed so he couldn't hide out there. A list of friends reeled through his mind, a list of possible hide-outs. He fiddled with the keys in his pocket, wishing he'd never gotten so curious about the Model T in the first place. *Guess I might as well face the music and get to the hotel.*

The back door made way too much noise for Webb's liking when he pulled it shut behind him.

"Webster Warren Bateman. Come into the parlor," Dena commanded.

Webb walked through the door of the parlor. The whole family was there—his siblings out of curiosity for what would befall their brother. As Webb entered, Jim and Dena were in their overstuffed chairs. Dena stood up, stick straight, chin elevated and hands clasped in front of her. Jim sat smoking his pipe.

All of the stories Webb had fabricated escaped him. He couldn't think of a thing to say, looking at his mother's reddened face.

"Do you know what you did was nigh on to horse stealing?"

Webb didn't respond.

Jim took the pipe from his mouth and blew a puff of smoke toward Webb. "Used to be a man could be hung for such a crime." Still seated, he put the pipe back in his mouth.

"But, I only…"

"Enough of your shenanigans, Webb. I work hard to keep this hotel going and I can't have you stealing and lying and causing me trouble, do you hear? And you know the rules about driving the car!"

"Yes, Ma, but…"

"You need to be taught a lesson. I called Dora. She and August need help on the farm. Maybe you'll learn something about what it means to work hard for what you get. You're leaving in the morning with the mailman."

Webb stood in the doorway, speechless. He wasn't surprised he was in trouble, but he hadn't expected to be sent away. He hadn't stolen the car, he borrowed it and even brought it back without a scratch—well, just one.

Dena had called her half-sister, Dora Johnson. She and August lived on August's parents' farm, twenty miles south of Almont. They had a one-year-old boy and could use the help of a strong young man.

Monday morning, wrapped in a horse hair robe, Webb found himself in the mailman's bob-sled, on his way to the Johnson's farm. The mailman made the route twice a week and on this day had more than mail to deliver.

It was a beautiful ride with sun glinting off new-fallen snow. The muffler over Webb's face grew frosty from his breath. The ride was smooth and silent except for the sound of the horse snorting and her hooves breaking the frosted crust. The shower kicked up by her back legs looked like diamond dust in front of the sled.

In spring, summer and fall this was a flat, featureless plain. Dirt, just lots of dirt. No one ever thought of this landscape as beautiful until a day like this one. Ice glistened on tree branches, frosty webs covered dried grass in a sparkling net. As breathtaking as the scene was, it didn't impress Webb. He was sad about leaving the pool hall and his friends.

Dad's gonna be sorry. He'll miss my winnings, he thought to himself. *And Ma's car wasn't any the worse for wear. Not sure why she was so mad. I didn't steal it. I brought it back.*

He paused, resigned to his fate. *Hell, just need to make the best of it, I guess. It's just for a while and maybe it won't be so bad.*

9

August Johnson
The Farm 1924

August pointed to a spare bedroom. "You'll bunk in there." It looked similar to the one Webb shared with Ray at the hotel, but smaller. "Drop your stuff and come outside. We've got work to do."

Twenty-eight-year-old August was square jawed with shoulders to match. He had the protruding brow and narrow eyes of a Norwegian and the attitude and stance of a man in charge. He'd heard about Webb's propensity for getting into trouble and he'd have none of it. August planned to work the kid's tail off and then some. Webb would know who was boss.

"I want you to milk the cows and clean the barn before supper. No meals around here until the work is all done. Got that?" August puffed out his chest and stood tall. Webb almost had him in height, but in that moment, he felt small. This may not be as easy as he had hoped.

With shoulders stooped and not knowing what to say, Webb followed August to the barn to start his chores. He'd been working for about an hour, when Webb's Aunt Dora called them in for lunch.

While serving the noon meal, she smiled and said, "We

can sure use your help, Webb. Dena wasn't none too happy with you stealing her car, but maybe getting you away from town will be a good thing for all of us." Webb didn't respond.

Dora was a couple years younger than August and Webb observed over the months to come that she was always busy with the baby or helping August's mother and father who lived a mile or so away. She didn't pay much attention to what August had Webb doing. She just appreciated another set of hands to get the farm work done.

At the supper table that first evening, Webb was about to explain to Dora that he hadn't stolen the car, just borrowed it. He thought better of it with August glaring at him.

"I didn't mean any harm, Aunt Dora. Just went to a dance."

"Well, you won't be goin' to any dances while you're here, Webb. There's way too much to do. No time for joy rides or gettin' into trouble." August had spent a lot of his jawin' time that afternoon letting Webb know what he could and couldn't do.

Webb knew from the outset he'd be doing farm work, but as months wore on, it became obvious August expected the same work out of him that a man would do. Unlike the pool hall, his stature wasn't an asset—he was expected to do more because he was tall for his age. He turned fourteen in May 1924.

Webb later told Ray, "I plowed fields behind a team of horses, pitched hay, built fences, cultivated corn, shocked grain and pitched bundles on a threshing crew. I got some muscle out of the deal, but that's the only good thing to come of it."

Webb also felt August's leather strap on his backside more than once, the same strap August used to sharpen his cutting tools. "Reform school would have been easier," Webb told Ray in all seriousness.

There was a small country school not far from the farm. Webb attended eighth grade during his time with the Johnson's and started ninth. There were other farm boys who attended, even bigger than he was.

One morning, after Webb started school, August yelled at him as he was heading out the kitchen door. "Webb, I want you to fight the Barstad kid after school," he ordered.

"Why? We're gettin' along just fine," Webb asked. "There's nothin' to fight about."

"You do what I say. Hear? It'll toughen you up. If you don't, you'll be feelin' the strap when you get home."

Many times after that, August told Webb to pick a fight with a certain boy. Webb fought, not one, but many of the bigger farm boys one at a time. He didn't always win, but his uncle and a neighbor always watched from the roof of the school's barn, making bets and laughing.

By October, 1924, Webb had been on the Johnson farm eight months. He'd grown in stature and muscle. August decided this was going to be another fight day, one he and his neighbor would lay bets on again.

August, eyebrows raised and a sinister look on his face, grabbed Webb's arm as he was leaving for school. "Get that Swenson kid today, Webb. Beat the crap outta him."

Webb jerked away without a word, picked up his books and stormed out the door.

After school, everyone filed out as usual. It had almost become routine. Get into a fight. Get beat up or beat someone else up. Get into trouble with the schoolmaster, and then get lectured by Dora about the evils of fighting. Webb never let on what August was doing. He knew that would mean another licking. It was crazy.

He didn't want to, but Webb pushed "Sven" on the way out the door. The Swede stood about a foot taller than Webb. The fight was on. Sven pushed back and Webb took a swing at him, hitting him in the chest. Sven clocked Webb a good one in the eye and followed with an upper cut to his chin.

Webb shook his head, but out of the corner of his bloodied eye, he could see a bottle of booze pass between the men on the barn roof.

I'm done! This is the last time that sonofabitch is gonna tell me what to do!

Webb spat blood out of his mouth and ducked another swing from Sven. The fight was short-lived when the school master came out and pulled the two apart. "Now get on home, the two of you," he yelled, "before I whip you myself!"

Webb took his time getting back to the Johnson's farmhouse. He'd made up his mind August wasn't going to force him to work like a slave or fight any more. It had been too long. He was going back to Almont. That was it. Webb was taller than August now. He could take the strap away from him—if he had to.

The Road

Webb pulled into a gas station in Sheridan, Wyoming. He shook off the memories of living on the Johnson farm. It was 8:30 am. He was still hoping to get to Billings by noon. He stretched as he got out of the car, then walked around and grabbed the handle from the lone gas pump with the large round globe on top with a sign reading GAS. He filled his extra cans, then the tank and headed into the station.

"Mornin'," the gas station owner greeted Webb as he came in the door. He was the station's first customer of the day.

Webb sighed and walked over to the nearest glass case, chest high with candy and cigarettes. He crossed both arms and leaned on it, road weary. "Mornin'," he replied.

"How are ya' doin'? You're lookin' pretty tuckered. What can I get for ya'?" The man's words and smile were sincere. "I just made a pot o' joe in the back room. Could ya' use a cup?"

"Thanks. Just need a pack of Chesterfields and somethin' to quiet the bear in my gut." Webb was brightened a bit by the owner's welcome. "I'm hopin' to get to Billings by noon." He looked at what the station had in the way of food.

"Well, you don't have much farther to go then."

Webb slowly shook his head. "Problem is I have to pick up family and then head for North Dakota to a funeral, so this trip's far from over." Webb explained.

"Sorry to hear that. I used to live in North Dakota. Went to school in Almont, but had to move west because of the Depression."

"No kiddin'." Webb cocked his head in interest. "What's your family name?" The two men exchanged surnames and spent a few minutes talking about the people they both knew.

Webb continued, "My family lived in Almont off and on for a number of years. Ran a hotel, livery and pool hall there between '22 and '27. I went to school there too—a couple times." Webb laughed. "Probably would have finished ninth grade in Almont if it hadn't been for a crazy professor at the school."

"Was that DeNoyer?"

"You have DeNoyer for a teacher?" Webb asked in surprise.

"Didn't have him, but heard the stories. Was never sure if they were true or not."

The gas station owner gave Webb his smokes. Webb stepped back from the counter he was leaning on, pulled out his wallet and paused, looking again at the candy through the glass. "Add a couple of the 3 Musketeers bars, would ya'?"

"Sure thing." The owner retrieved the candy bars from their resting place in the case and wrote up the total on a pad in front of him. "That'll be fifteen cents for the cigarettes and another dime for the candy."

Webb handed over the change. "My brother and I knew DeNoyer. Don't have time to tell you all the details, but the stranger the tales you heard, the more likely they were true." Webb put his wallet away and took the goods. "Gotta hit the road again." Webb headed toward the door. "Thanks."

"Thank you and good luck on the rest of your trip."

Webb left the station, climbed back in the Chevy and headed north—thoughts of Professor DeNoyer travelling with him.

Almont School

10

Professor DeNoyer
Almont, North Dakota 1925

When Webb came back to Almont from the Johnson's farm in late 1924, he didn't tell his mother about threatening August. He just announced, "It's time to come home and I'm not goin' back." No one argued with him.

Webb also figured he'd paid his debt with blood, sweat and tears for "borrowing" his mother's Model T and now all was good—or so he thought.

"DeNoyer's a strange one, don't ya' think, Ray?" Webb asked his brother after hearing DeNoyer talk to himself on more than one occasion in the hotel.

Twenty-five-year-old Professor Charles DeNoyer was a rent-paying boarder at The Merchant Hotel. The boys saw him almost every day. He was also a teacher at the high school Webb and Ray attended in late 1924 and early in 1925. At the time, teacher certification required a six-week training course at one of the "Normal" schools like the North Dakota State Normal School in Ellendale.

"I don't know how he ever got to be a teacher, but guess they had to hire somebody." Webb shrugged.

"Yeah, I don't think DeNoyer's all there. He may have

a wick, but there's no oil in his lamp." Ray threw his head back in laughter.

"That was a good one, Ray!" Webb slapped his brother on the back and laughed along with him.

Sixteen-year-old Ray was good looking. The entire Bateman clan was described by friends and other family members as a handsome group. The girls in the family, Toots, Vivian and Blanche, were beautiful, no doubt about it.

While the rest of the siblings had deep dimples when they smiled, Ray's cleft chin defined his good looks. He wore his hair slicked back with pomade and he liked bow ties. He was a ladies' man and knew it, but more often than not his head was in a book or he was tinkering with some gadget. Dena and Jim liked the fact he could fix things around the hotel and in the pool hall.

Even though Ray was two years older, sixteen to Webb's fourteen, Webb was a little taller and his shoulders were broader from farm work. Both were well-liked by town's folk and friends at school. Ray was glad Webb had come back to Almont. So was Webb.

The school was a mile from town, a three-story brick building opened in 1918 replacing a smaller two room school house. The area had grown. The elementary grades used the first floor. The high school occupied the upper levels. A barn behind the school kept horses used by students who lived miles away.

The roads were still poor and got even worse in winter, but the horses could get through. There were no snow plows and school was never dismissed early because of bad weather. The horses were trusted to take the students home. Many students "batched" with other families closer to school because of distance and weather. The Bateman kids lived a mile away. They were close enough to walk to school regardless of the weather. A school bell perched on the roof, its ring unmistakable. It let the whole community know when classes started and ended each day.

By the time Ray and Webb moved to the second and third floors of the school, there were two grade school teachers and two high school teachers. Charles DeNoyer was the high school teacher appointed by the Almont School Board to run the school, earning him the title of "Professor." He was respected in the community because of his position, not his personality which was considered strange by more than a few.

DeNoyer and the other high school teacher organized the Literary Society which met once a month. All high school students were members including Ray and Webb.

The meeting was conducted according to Roberts Rules of Order and there was always a program planned for the public. It included debate, skits and a musical program. Webb didn't mind being in front of the public; he had a good singing voice. What he sang in school was quite different from what he sang elsewhere. He'd learned many of his ditties at the pool hall:

> I've got a girl,
> She lives up on the hill,
> She won't let me do it,
> But her sister always will!

The Literary Society meetings didn't appeal to Ray. Even though he was an avid reader, he didn't find much to engage his literary taste. He thought it a waste of time and often skipped out, raising Professor DeNoyer's ire.

The boys were getting by in school and doing their homework when it didn't interfere with chores or time in the pool hall. They had separate class rooms. Ray's class had ten students; more than half were girls. He liked that and was known as quite a flirt.

DeNoyer had noted the way the girls in school glanced at Ray and giggled. If Ray looked back at a girl, it became fodder for school gossip. While other boys were rough housing at recess or lunch time, Ray could be found leaning up against a wall engaged in conversation with some pretty young thing.

In contrast, DeNoyer found it difficult to talk to a young woman, unless it was about school or some administrative matter. He moved with a stiff gait and stuffy attitude. Students whispered behind his back that he looked like Ichabod Crane, the protagonist in a scary, short story many of them had read called *The Legend of Sleepy Hollow.*

DeNoyer brought stares, snickers and speculation from students when, walking down the hall, he'd spin around and look behind him, as though he was being followed.

Ray had been chastised by DeNoyer multiple times for flirting with the girls and for skipping the Literary Society meetings. Ray shrugged off DeNoyer's scolding. He couldn't win with the man. If he attended the meetings and there was flirting, he was in trouble. If he skipped the meetings, he was definitely in trouble.

The class bell rang and Ray's classmates took their seats. The routine called for each student to get their notebooks and pencils ready for the class lecture. Ray was a little slower than usual. He sighed, as though put upon in the process of getting his notebook out, drawing the attention of the girls closest to him. They giggled.

"Bateman!" DeNoyer yelled across the room. "Didn't I warn you?"

Ray sat up straight. "Sir?"

"Yes, Ray, you. I've warned you before. I can't teach if you are going to disrupt the class and make all those strange noises."

"Uh, I didn't make a strange noise, Professor. I was just getting my notebook." Ray hadn't thought his noise strange—maybe a bit dramatic, that was all.

"I heard you, you disrespectful ingrate. You can't make those noises in my classroom and get away with it!" DeNoyer strode across the room, shouting and raising a fist. He was bigger than Ray and fueled by anger. Other students shrank back in their seats in fear. Ray froze. He'd never seen DeNoyer like this before.

"Stop making that noise, I tell you!" DeNoyer's voice was a shriek. He grabbed Ray by the shirt and yanked him out of his chair. Ray was in shock. Never good at defending himself, more a lover than a fighter, he stood there, staring into the maniac's crazed eyes. DeNoyer wrestled Ray to his back on the floor and clamped both hands around his throat. Ray kicked his feet and grabbed the professor's hands with little effect.

One of the girls ran out of the room to get help. She hadn't seen Ray do anything to provoke *that* kind of anger. The man was crazy. "DeNoyer's killin' Ray!" she screamed.

A janitor pushing a broom in the hallway dropped the handle and ran into the classroom. He found DeNoyer sitting on Ray's chest, hands still clinched around his neck, strangling the life out of him.

Yanking DeNoyer back, he broke his hold on Ray's neck. "What the hell happened, Professor?" The janitor was aghast. DeNoyer got up, walked back to the front of the room, brushed himself off and straightened his vest. He smoothed both sides of his hair with his hands. Ray lay on the floor trying to get his breath back and figure out what happened. He struggled getting up and when he did, ran out of the room. The professor just stood and watched him.

"Ma, I didn't do anything," Ray pleaded showing her the marks on his neck. "The guy is crazy as a shit house rat! Nearly killed me!" He was trying to convince his folks, but Jim and Dena had already heard the professor's story, which was quite different. Webb was listening to Ray's version even though he'd heard it from other students. DeNoyer had gone bezerk.

"If you boys don't want to go to school and behave, you can go out and go to work for your own living," Dena shook her finger at both of them. Webb looked surprised and crooked an index finger back at himself.

"I wasn't even in the room, Ma!"

"Doesn't matter. Figure out where you're goin' to work

and move on out." Jim stood off to one side with his arms folded. It was clear, Dena had made up her mind and Jim wouldn't argue. Life would be easier without the boys getting into trouble. Ray and Webb went outside the hotel to catch some air.

"I think they like the idea of gettin' thirty bucks a month from the Professor better than feeding us," Webb groused.

They shoved their hands in their pockets for some warmth. It was below freezing and they hadn't bothered to put on coats.

Ray paused, gazed across the street, then turned to Webb with a smile. "Hell, Webb, we can make some good money goin' to work." Spurts of Ray's frosty breath marked the enthusiasm of his words.

"Who needs school, anyway? We could do some farm work the rest of the winter and then join the circus in the spring! They probably need help and we could see some territory. They do these one night stands and we might even get back to our old stompin' grounds where we were kids in Minnesota. Let's get the hell out of Almont."

Since Ray seemed sure they could make it on their own, Webb was willing to go along for the ride. What did they have to lose? It would be an adventure. They'd make their own way and have some fun.

The Road

Webb was nearing Billings. He still wondered why his folks had believed DeNoyer instead of Ray, but if there was an explanation, maybe it was because they were just trying to survive.

Webb took a swig of whiskey from the bottle beside him and smiled to himself. *I wonder what they thought when they found out Ray's story was true. DeNoyer was crazy as a loon. After all, he ended his days in the North Dakota State Hospital for the mentally ill and criminally insane.*

But—by then, Ray and I were long gone. Joined the circus. We were gonna see some of the world.

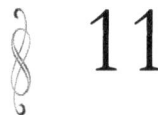

11

Honest Bill's Motorized Circus

Bismark, North Dakota May 1925

Hands twisting in her lap, Toots asked, "Dad, how can you let a sixteen- and fourteen-year-old take off like that? We won't know where they are or how they're doing. At least when they're working the farms, we know where to find them."

Webb and Ray had heard the circus would be in Bismarck in May, about 45 miles from Almont. They had no misgivings about leaving back-breaking farm work for the excitement of the circus. They gave notice and headed home to say goodbye.

At supper, the only one who worried about the boys' plan to hit the road was seventeen-year-old Toots. Born with a soft heart and given the responsibility at an early age to watch out for her younger siblings because her parents had businesses to run, Toots did the best she could. She cared about what might happen and couldn't understand why her parents would let them join a circus.

Jim didn't look up from his meal. "They're old enough to make their own livin'." Dena sat without a word. It was obvious, they'd made up their minds; it was time for the boys to be on their own.

"Hey, Sis, we'll be okay," Ray tried to reassure her. "If we can survive the farms we've been workin', we can make it just about anywhere."

"You got that right," Webb chimed in. "We've been workin' fourteen hours a day, seven days a week for fifteen bucks a month. I've heard we'll make at least four bucks a week with the circus and get to see some country at the same time!"

That didn't salve Toots' concern and she shed tears when they hugged goodbye the next morning. Jim shook hands with the boys. Dena was stoic and said little other than she wished the boys well. Ray and Webb laughed and joked as they headed down Main Street to hitch a ride to Bismarck.

When they arrived in Bismarck and found Honest Bill's Motorized Circus sitting on the outskirts of town, they were surprised at the rag-tag looking outfit. The circus had ten Model T trucks loaded with tents, poles, props, ponies, performers and one camel. The trucks, while built to carry equipment and performers, were weather worn. But from the chatter the boys heard as they walked through town, the thought of a circus had folks excited, regardless of what it looked like.

Times were good. Men had jobs and the economy prospered, due in part to Henry Ford and his manufacture of the affordable automobile. The huge demand for trucks and cars had led to the construction of all-weather roads, replacing trails established by wagon trains. Electric utility networks expanded, which meant places like Almont could turn on lights instead of using oil lanterns. People bought appliances, listened to the radio and talked on the telephone. Travel, movie theaters, and professional sports became major businesses and the 1920's were the heyday for circuses—at least some of them.

Long lines of rubes, towners, hayseeds, and hicks paid green money to see a showgirl in the center ring display her pretty legs, while local children watched her ponies dance to the music of the calliope. There was something for everyone, Honest Bill promised in every pre-show speech.

"You guys got any experience?" Honest Bill asked when they first approached him about a job. He wore a beat up fedora tilted to one side. Suspenders held up his trousers and an open-collared shirt was so dirty, the color was questionable. An unlit stogie hung from his mouth. Big and burly, his pants wide at the top, it was evident he hadn't missed many meals.

"I'm lookin' for guys who can do it all: drive a rig, put up the tents—and perform. No soft jobs here, if that's what you're lookin' for," Honest Bill warned out of the side of his mouth.

Ray shifted from one foot to the other. "We've been working on two separate farms near Almont this winter, doing whatever was needed, sir. We can handle just about anything you give us." Ray at sixteen, stood straight, fiddling with the brim of his own fedora.

Fourteen-year-old Webb stepped forward, chest puffed out and newsboy cap still on his head. "Where I worked didn't even have a outdoor toilet. I think the dogs had it better." Ray shot him a look. How was that supposed to convince Honest Bill to hire them?

Honest Bill grinned. "Sounds like you'll fit right in boys. You'll have to help setup and I need a couple drivers when we head out in the mornin'. You know how to drive a Model T truck?"

"Sure do," they both responded at once. They both knew how to drive their ma's car and farm equipment—that was true.

"Okay, two guys left the show this mornin'. You can take up their slack. Check over there with Clyde. He's the Boss Canvasman. He'll get you started on the sledge gang, setting up the Big Top."

The Big Top lay flat on the ground. Men stood over the seams, bent at the waist to lace canvas pieces together. Towering wooden poles, some distance apart, stuck up in the center, already flying Old Glory and looking like the masts of a clipper ship.

"Are you Clyde?" Ray asked as he approached a giant of a man, who they later found out performed as the Strong Man in the Spectacle, the Big Show. With a small crew, everyone except the cook did double duty.

"Yeah, who's askin'?" Clyde pushed up the brim of his battered straw boater and looked the boys square on.

"I'm Ray and this is my brother, Webb. Honest Bill told us to check in with you 'cuz he just hired us."

"Great. Not one, but two First of Mays. Don't know your ass from a hole in the ground."

"Ray, what's a First of May?" Webb whispered as he stood just behind his brother.

113

"Probably means we're new," Ray said under his breath. He didn't want to raise the ire of the muscled man in front of him.

"Here! See if you can handle this." Clyde tossed a sledge hammer toward the boys. Webb caught it in midair, but the fourteen pounds brought his arm to the ground in one fell swoop. Another hammer was tossed to Ray, who had seen what happened and prepared himself to catch and hold—which he did.

Clyde laughed. "You'll either learn to swing those things or die tryin'. This mornin' you're part of the sledge gang." Clyde pointed to two other roustabouts with sledge hammers who started pounding stakes in the ground at the perimeter of the Big Top.

Ben and Chief were happy to have help. Strong as an ox, Ben was a beanpole of a man with tattoos covering every inch of skin the boys could see and more they couldn't. He told them later, he'd been inking himself for years to make sure he'd have something more to offer to any circus he approached. Chief, better known as Chief Iron Tail in full American Indian regalia once the "spec" began, was no slouch with a sledge, either.

It took a while for Webb and Ray to get the rhythm needed to drive the tent stakes into the ground. They weren't used to swinging a fourteen-pound hammer, taking turns with three other guys in a circle. When one sledge hammer hit the stake, three others were in motion, hitting the stake one after the other. Chief started a chant to keep the action going. Ray and Webb didn't want to look like slouches, so they gave it their best.

With all the stakes in the ground, a block and tackle system was used to hoist the Big Top canvas. Without work animals to help, the hoisting was left to three crews of four men. The teams, with Ray on one and Webb on another, raised the canvas. They glanced at each other from time to time, shaking their heads at what they'd gotten themselves into. Clyde didn't cut them any slack. They knew they'd either keep up or be out on the first day. To create a rhythm for the men pulling ropes to hoist the Big Top, Clyde yelled, "Pull it, shake it, break it! Pull it, shake it, break it! Now down stake it!"

The cook tent had been put up before the Big Top, but the roustabouts sleep tent still had to be erected. That was nothing in comparison to what the boys had experienced with the Big Top.

"I thought I had some muscle, but Clyde may be right about this job killin' us," Webb moaned to Ray, as he bent over to stretch and rub his aching back.

"I think my arms are gonna fall off," agreed Ray, "and it's not even noon. Wonder when we eat."

Ben overheard the boys talking. "You'll get used to it. Now you need to suit up and do some training as the giraffe jargo for today's matinee and evening shows. The guys who left this morning had the routine, but now you're it."

"We're gonna do what?" Webb asked scratching his head.

"You guys are the jargo," Ben said in a louder voice and slower this time. "Shorty Sylvester, the midget, will show ya' what to do. He's the clown who'll be leading ya' around the ring and orderin' ya' to perform," The boys gave him blank stares in response.

"Jargo means, why pay for a real animal, when two guys dressed up like one will do. Look. What ya' do is put on this giraffe costume. One of you is the back end and the other is the front end holding up the neck and head. Ya' both wear pants with dots on them like giraffe legs. Then there's material with dots that covers you from front to back so just your legs show. Got it?"

"Yer kiddin' us, aren't ya' Ben?" Ray laughed thinking it was a joke on the new guys.

"Hell no. In this outfit, we all have to perform *and* be roustabouts or you don't have a job!" Ben was getting impatient. "Go find Shorty. He's at the prop wagon. Don't count on eatin' if you haven't gotten ready for the show first. That's the way things are 'round here."

"Okay, Ben." They headed for the truck with all the show props. Webb slapped his brother on the back and with a big grin on his face shouted over his shoulder toward Ben, "I'll be the front and Ray can be the ass."

Jenna and the Giraffe Jargo

12

Shorty and the Giraffe Jargo
Bismark, North Dakota 1925

They found Shorty rummaging through the props in the back of a truck. "I bet you're Shorty," Ray yelled through the back door.

Shorty Sylvester looked over his shoulder at the two young men staring at him. "Yeah, how the hell'd ya' guess," he responded with a twisted smile. He stood in the back of the truck as tall as his four-foot stature would allow. Looking up, Ray and Webb could see short legs attached to an oversized upper body with a big head stuck on top. The snarling face was anything but friendly.

Webb put up his hand and whispered behind it to Ray, "He doesn't have a neck. Never seen anythin' like him." Ray pushed him away.

"We've been told we're the giraffe and that we should see you to get some trainin' for the show."

Shorty grimaced and swore under his breath, but they heard him mutter, "Great, more greenhorns to train. Nothin' but turnover in this damn outfit." Shorty tossed their costume out the door. "Put that on and we'll see what you can do." He looked down at the boys staring at him, costume pieces drooping in their hands, the giraffe's head on the ground.

Shorty thought maybe he'd seen it all in his years with the circus. Here again were a couple of stupid kids looking for adventure, money, maybe just wanting to get away from home, but having no idea how hard circus life would be.

He'd seen the faces of lots of drifters, faces grim and bitter, quite at their wit's end, not that they had any to begin with. Some were just out of the county jail for doing whatever or had left a wife and family behind. Shorty never asked for details. These were men who drove the trucks, swung the sledge hammers, and put on clown costumes to make kids laugh, not that Shorty would trust them when they weren't in costume with anyone's kid.

Shorty knew how hard circus life was and yet he stuck with it. It was all he knew and the one sure way he had of making a living—if you could call it that.

"Well, don't just stand there. Get the damn thing on!" Shorty shouted at the boys.

Ray and Webb took off their shoes and put on the dotted pants. Before putting on the head and material covering for the back, they slipped on black shoes that were supposed to look like giraffe hooves. The shoes were too small for their feet, but they managed to squeeze them on.

"So what do I do with this head?" Webb asked. "How the hell do I keep it up?"

"Lift it up over your head and you'll find a couple handles on the inside of the neck tube," Shorty instructed. "Grab those and hold 'er up. Then you look out the holes in the neck so you can see where you're goin'."

"Yeah, but I can't see down, just ahead," Webb said a little frustrated. But he held the neck tube steady over his face with it extending five feet into the air. The head bobbed up and down at the top.

Shorty yelled at Ray. "Hey, you gotta bend over so the material from the head comes over the top of your back."

"Great, as if my back ain't aching enough as it is," Ray muttered.

Two hours later with Shorty still shaking his head at what he had to work with for the show, they headed for the cook tent. The matinee would start at 3:00 pm.

Webb, Ray and Shorty went through the chow line with the rest of the roustabouts. The cook served each a measured spoonful of hominy and what resembled stew and vegetables, but they couldn't be sure.

They sat down at roughhewn wood tables and benches. Webb took a bite. "What's that smell?" He wrinkled his nose and put the fork down.

"You'll get used to it or starve," Shorty responded. "Cookie's truck also carries the camel, so there's your answer. Everything he fixes tastes like the camel smells."

Webb and Ray had seen the camel unloaded, but didn't recognize the handler as the cook. They looked at each other and back at their plates. Still growing boys, they were starving, so the smell of camel wasn't going to stop them from devouring the little there was. Webb held his nose as he shoveled in the first few mouthfuls.

When they finished, Webb asked, "Shorty, what's the story with this circus, anyway? Why aren't some of the performers eating? I saw a woman with the horses and a guy with dogs. Aren't there some acrobats and other acts too?" Webb laughed, "Or are we the main act?"

"For a giraffe, you sure ask a lot of questions." With his mouth full, Shorty smiled a toothless grin.

"Honest Bill and his wife, Jenna, who is the equestrian act; Joseph, the dog trainer; Harry Barnes, the slack wire act; and Freddie and Felix, the acrobats—they all get fed first and better than us. They go back to their trucks where they also dress and sleep—and whatever else they do there. They're the main acts, the ones who bring in the crowds.

"We had a fat lady, but she ate a lot and took up a whole sleeping truck. I don't think Honest Bill was too unhappy when she keeled over dead. Wasn't that old, either," Shorty said.

"The rest of us are the clowns when we're not puttin' up or takin' down the show. When I'm not performin', I'm in charge of the props. I make sure they get where they're s'pose to go."

"But you have a…a special kinda talent, Shorty. Not everybody's as tall as you are. I mean…uh, short. I mean looks like you. Awe…ya' know what I mean. Shouldn't you be one of them? Get some kinda special treatment or somethin'?" Webb's attempt at diplomacy was met with a glare from his giraffe trainer.

Shorty's scowl softened. He burst out laughing, "This kid's a laugh a minute, Ray. How do ya' stand it?"

Ray smiled and roughed up Webb's hair. "It's not easy, Shorty." Webb gave Ray a playful shove.

"Was that Jenna working with the horses? She looks pretty young, if she's Honest Bill's wife."

Shorty cocked his head to one side and raised an eyebrow. "You better steer clear of her, Ray. She's the show's money maker and Honest Bill knows it. He found her on some farm awhile back and promised to make her a star. She fell for it and here she is, in a second rate motorized circus, but the crowds come to see her and she does know how to work her liberty horses."

"What's a liberty horse?" Webb asked.

Shorty took another bite and with his mouth full and fork drawing pictures in the air, he explained. "She commands the horses with words and the way she moves. No halter or reins. And she knows how to ride and perform on them bareback, too." He swallowed, but food was still hanging on his lip. "In fact that's why the horses are white. White don't show the resin from her slippers that helps keep her on their backs. She's too good for this show, but she doesn't know it."

"How old do you think she is?" Ray asked.

"You lookin' for trouble or are you just deaf?" Shorty shot back.

"Hey, I'm curious. Just wonderin'." Ray shrugged his shoulders.

Webb changed the subject. "What are you doin' here, Shorty? You seem to know a lot about this circus business."

Shorty paused and shifted his attention to Webb. "You really want to know?"

"Sure," both the boys responded.

Shorty swiped his mouth with the back of his hand. "I've been with the circus all my life, the one place I could fit in and get a job. A couple were train circuses, much bigger than this one, but they fell on hard times and I ended up here. This one is nothin' compared to a train circus. A train circus might have hundreds of animals and a midway with lots of freaks called 'sideshow exotics,' not just a midget like me and a tattooed guy like Ben. I've seen giants and bearded ladies, fire eaters, alligator men, a woman with no arms or legs, a three-legged man; you think of somethin' strange and you'll find it in a train circus like the biggest one, Ringling Brothers and Barnum and Bailey, or even Cole Brothers, or Hagenbeck-Wallace."

Shorty pointed a stubby index finger at the two of them. "And let me tell you, if you're caught messin' around with someone you shouldn't 'a been, you'd be red-lighted in a flash. And before you ask me what that means, I'll tell you."

"It's a way of gettin' rid of you; leave you in the dust without payin' you. All you see when you're tryin' to pick your ass off the ground, is red taillights disappearing down the road. Or if your circus travels by train, you'd be thrown off the back, maybe off a trestle above a fast flowin' river and left for dead!" Shorty hoped that made a point with Ray in case he was still thinking about Jenna. He shoved back from the table and swung his short legs off the wood bench.

"We got to get to it. The show starts in an hour and you two still need work on the act. Back to the giraffe suit," Shorty ordered.

The Big Top Matinee was about to start and the Bismarck crowd had on their Sunday best. All the ladies wore their fanciest hats, some with ribbons, others with flowers. Shorter hair was a 1925 fashion trend and mid-calf frocks had men in line ogling ankles seldom seen on the farm. The men wore fedoras or straw boaters, vests and suit coats with their work shoes or boots. The folks were wandering about or standing in line to pay their 25 cents for tickets.

The sounds of laughter, chatter, feet scuffling in the dirt, and children screeching with delight announced the crowd's excitement about the circus. Flyers posted around town before the show arrived promised a wholesome but unexpected experience viewing death defying acts and freaks of nature. Businesses closed early and kids tugged at their parents to hurry, afraid they might miss something either terrible or wonderful. There were visions of lions, tigers and elephants. Little did they know that horses, dogs and a camel would have to do.

Honest Bill stood on a platform beside the ticket booth. From there he could draw in the stragglers, get them excited about the show and keep an eye on the guy taking money from rubes willing to pay for something they didn't see every day.

"LADIES-S-S-S-S-S AND GENTLEMEN-N-N-N-N-N-N. ONLY TWENTY-FIVE MINUTES TILL THE BIG SHOW."

He continued in a loud voice, "More than enough time to get your tickets to the biggest little show on earth. You'll see wonders you've never seen before!" His voice was a practiced sing-song, moving up and down like a roller coaster, generating even more excitement in the crowd.

"There's still time to find good seats and there's somethin' for everyone! This is strictly a family affair." Honest Bill's chest puffed into his checkered waist coat. He wore black jodhpurs, and a black top hat. Swinging his cane in the air, his loud claims about the show made the performers and roustabouts snicker. But if it brought in money, that was all that mattered. Besides, if the show didn't live up to his hype, they could high-tail it out of town before sunrise.

Once ticket sales were finished, money put in the safe and crowds seated in the bleachers, Honest Bill ordered the music to start. A lone air calliope—an automated orchestra operating much like a player piano—provided a musical backdrop for the parade into the Big Top. It heralded the start of the show.

With the air calliope providing triumphant marching music, it was a parade—as much as thirty people could muster, led by the "freaks."

Chief Iron Tail was first, in his full Indian regalia: leather fringe flapping, bear tooth necklace rattling and tomahawk raised. Clyde, the Strong Man, followed with muscles flexed. Next Beanpole Ben showed all the tattoos decency would allow. A roustabout called "Elastic Man" did body contortions that made folks grimace.

One of the roustabouts had a retractable sword. He stopped here and there to "swallow," the shiny, sharp instrument, much to the delight of some. Ladies, on the other hand, covered their faces with hankies, afraid to view the anticipated blood-letting. Roustabouts-turned-clowns sprinkled themselves among the professional entertainers as they circled the Big Top. Cookie's one-hump camel was led by a clown who knew better than to let the dromedary get very close to the crowd. The camel had a nasty habit of regurgitating stomach contents and then spitting at its nearest victim, often the clown. It was the price paid for having an exotic animal—the only one—in Honest Bill's Motorized Circus.

Joseph and his dogs brought squeals of delight when they appeared. The pups pranced in on their back legs. They headed for Ring Number Three, while Freddie and Felix the acrobats, entered Ring Number One and began their foot-juggling act. On a platform on his back, Freddie extended his long legs straight up in the air and with his feet began spinning Felix like a ball.

The Center Ring had been set up for Harry Barnes, the slack-wire artist. At the appropriate time with the calliope music reaching a crescendo, the young man bounded into the ring with arms upraised. The crowd roared even before he began. His aerial act proceeded on a low slung, slack, swinging wire which made balancing nearly an impossible feat, or so the crowd had been told. Honest Bill couldn't afford the high wire acts found in the Barnum and Bailey Big Top with all the expensive rigging.

After Jenna, Harry was the show's biggest draw. The kid had talent, and fortunately for Honest Bill, no parents to interfere with contract negotiations when he'd been hired.

Harry had fine-tuned his skill on the clotheslines of an orphanage, until he was discovered. This was his first experience as a paid performer and Honest Bill was trying his best to convince Harry he'd found his family and he'd be part of the fold indefinitely.

Harry wowed the crowd with splits, somersaults and high kicks, landing handily on the wire each time. He received a standing ovation. Now it was time for some levity before the main act featuring Jenna and her Liberty Horses.

"I can't see a damn thing!" Ray, bent over and holding on to Webb's waist, complained as they headed into the Big Top. Shorty led the way dressed in a clown suit, big red nose and an oversized Stetson. He had a baton in one hand to direct his giraffe. Other clowns entertained around the arena.

"Well, neither can I! These eye holes aren't in the right place. I can't see Shorty, 'cuz he's so damn short!" Webb hollered, not sure Ray could hear him with the noise the crowd and the calliope were making.

They pranced into the Big Top, and a couple times, as they had been told to do, ambled over to a group of children on the sidelines, stopped, and did a little jig in front of them. The kids giggled with delight.

Shorty directed them into the Center Ring. They were the warmup to the star attraction.

Like a maestro, Shorty waved his wand and the giraffe bowed, requiring Webb to get down on his knees, and tip his giraffe head forward, leaving Ray with his rear in the air. The crowd laughed and applauded.

For a few minutes, the giraffe behaved and followed orders, sitting, kicking up its feet, and doing the best imitation of splits the boys could muster. But the whole idea of the jargo was that a naughty giraffe would follow orders only so long. Shorty gave directions to roll over. That was the cue to revolt and so they did. Webb tried to run one way and Ray the other. The result was the costume yanked them both back together and into a pile on the ground. Although the adults in the crowd knew this was slap stick, they roared with laughter anyway. The kids jumped up and down and squealed with delight.

Still unable to see where they were going, Webb took off out of the ring, stumbling over the curbing on the way. Again, they were in a pile with Shorty swinging his baton and feigning disgust. The boys, unveiled, grabbed their costume pieces and ran out of the Big Top. The crowd erupted in laughter again. The giraffe jargo had been a hit.

That was the cue for Jenna to enter, riding atop one of her six white horses. Ray threw off his portion of the giraffe costume and ran back into the entrance to watch her. She was a ballerina floating on the back of first one and then another of the horses. With ease and grace, she dismounted in the center ring. All eyes were on her as she put her ponies through their paces. It was magic and Shorty could see Ray was enthralled.

Shorty shook his head. He didn't see anything good coming from this.

Honest Bill's Motorized Circus

13

Ray's Jenna
South Dakota 1925

Shorty screamed as the truck careened over the side of the road and down an embankment, "Jeezus christ, Webb!" The load of big top poles leaned toward the ditch and strained against the tie-downs as the old Model T truck bucked like a bronco.

Webb's eyes flew open. He sat upright and clutched the spoked wheel. He'd closed his eyes for a second, but that was all it took for the truck to head off the road. Now alert, he turned the wheel slowly back to the left, shifted down and gave the unwieldy, top heavy rig enough gas to get her back on the road.

"Want to get us killed, kid? That's a sure way to do it. Good thing we're not hauling the dogs or ponies. They'd be kickin' shit about now."

"Hey, Shorty, good thing you don't weigh more or it woulda' been all on you. Get it?" Webb grinned and tried to make light of what could have happened.

"Look. I've been with a lot of these small time circuses and managed to survive. I don't want my headstone to read, 'Shorty, Mighty Midget, bought the farm at the bottom of a pile of Big Top tent poles.'"

"Awe, come on. I was just catchin' a couple winks. Can't blame me, can you, Shorty? We work from first light 'til past midnight. Get four, maybe five hours sleep a night, if we're lucky. How's a guy s'pose to stay awake under these conditions?"

Seeing the world from a circus roustabout's perspective wasn't what Webb imagined when he and Ray first got excited about the idea. The daily grind had become tedious routine. Up at dawn, pack up the circus, hit the road for the next burg, set up the big top, perform, tear down, get to bed late and repeat the routine the next day. Webb hardly had time to work in a game of poker now and then. However, the hours and hours of boredom could also be marked by moments of sheer terror, as he and Shorty had just witnessed.

Shorty shook a stubby finger at him. "You'll be awake alright when you and your brother are hitchin' it down the road without a job and without pay either. Good ol' Honest Bill's been known to leave roustabouts in the dust, if he doesn't like somethin' or somebody. Good thing we're the last truck or you would be hoofin' it in short order. Not a pretty thought in the heat of summer in the middle of goddamn nowhere, South Dakota."

"Yeah, I know, Shorty, but this is not what I expected when we left Bismark. Here we are headed for who knows where. I thought by now we'd be headed for Minnesota.

It's hot as hell and we've been doin' these one night stands all over North Dakota and part of South Dakota for two months. I thought we would be further east by now. Ray and I have friends in Milroy, Minnesota, and one of the reasons we joined this outfit was to get back where we grew up."

Shorty sat on a pile of blankets with his arm hung out the open passenger window to stay cool. "So you think you're all growed up, do ya'?" He asked with a crooked smile. Webb shrugged.

It was mid-August. Shorty had a soft spot for Webb. It wasn't surprising, since they spent so much time together on the road and Webb was a likeable guy. Shorty had become an ear for his complaints, most of which Shorty laughed at. The kid was still learning how tough life could be and maybe Shorty could teach him some lessons.

"We'll get there when we get there, kid. Honest Bill is his own advance man. He lays out the route in the off season and sometimes things change. He don't always know 'til we get to the town. Sometimes there's a new sheriff and he decides we can't use a lot that Honest Bill thought was a sure thing. That really pisses him off 'cuz more than likely, he paid off some guy to get the lot in the first place. Then we either have to find a new spot or move on. There's nothin' fair in this business, kid. You should know that by now."

Shorty squirmed on his perch. His legs were numb from dangling over the truck's bench seat. "Take those two guys back in Rapid City that got left in the dust 'cuz they gave their two weeks' notice the way they're supposed to.

What's Honest Bill do? He just tells everybody they didn't earn their keep and to take off without 'em. The only way you get paid in this outfit is to keep workin'. Is that right? Hell, no, but it works for Honest Bill and those of us ignoramus enough to stay with this two-bit circus. And then there's times when the money doesn't come in like it should and the roustabouts don't get paid. The performers do. Not me. I'm just the prop guy, but I stay with it thinkin' I'll get paid what's owed me next week."

"Hold your horses, Shorty. I got somthin' to ease your pain." Webb smiled and reached under the seat. "I got this jug of home brew just before we pulled up stakes from that last town. What the hell was the name of it?" Webb uncorked the jug, took a quick swig, wiped the neck with his sleeve and passed it to Shorty.

"Here, have a belt. May be your last since you're ridin' with the likes of me." Webb gave Shorty a wink and a smile.

"Kid, yer' crazier than a hootie owl." Shorty took a drink and gave a toothless grim. They rattled down the road after the trucks ahead of them.

Shorty knew Webb was just a happy-go-lucky Joe, itching for adventure, but when it came to Ray, that was different. Shorty waffled between worrying about him and not giving a damn. If Ray wasn't smart enough to figure out that he was playing with fire when he flirted with Jenna, why should he care? But then again, if Honest Bill booted Ray, Webb would go, too. Shorty would hate to see that happen.

Webb must have read his thoughts. "Hey, Shorty. What do ya' think about Ray and Jenna? He's sure spendin' a lotta time hangin' round her. Says he's in love and thinks she's in love with him."

"Your brother's just askin' for trouble, Webb. I figure she likes the attention, but sooner or later Honest Bill's gonna notice what's goin' on and then watch the fur fly." Shorty grabbed the bottle and tipped it back again. "He may have already figured it out, but maybe he can't afford to lose any more people from the show right now, performers or roustabouts. You know Harry Barnes left at the last stop. Was hired by a train circus for more money and better conditions. That left the show with one less main attraction, so Honest Bill might have his mind on other things right now. But you just wait…"

Shorty was feeling the effects of the booze in the heat of the day. The sun's glare was blinding. It blurred the landscape into a non-existent shimmering sea. Shorty's thoughts melted into wondering why he took so much interest in the welfare of Webb and Ray. At thirty, he knew better than to worry about anyone but himself. People disappointed him. They couldn't be trusted, women in particular. He'd been married to another midget and had a child. When the going got tough, his wife ditched him for some sonofabitch, wife-stealing, no-good low-life. They took off and Shorty hadn't seen them since. They could be dead, as far as he knew.

Getting close to Webb might be a mistake, but Shorty chalked his feelings up to the amount of time they spent together. When they weren't doing the jargo act, they were rolling down dusty roads. And yet, as much as he tried to squelch the feeling, he was getting used to having Webb around and tended to look out for him. Webb was always smiling and kidding – when he wasn't complaining.

Shorty's eyes closed. He smiled at how important Webb thought his complaints were: the food, the sleeping tent, his turn at the back of the giraffe, Ray spending time with Jenna instead of him, the food...

From Webb's perspective the chow hadn't improved one iota from the first day on the job. It didn't matter where they were.

"Hominy for breakfast, fried hominy for lunch and supper. Is that the only thing you know how to make, Cookie?" Webb railed at the cook, whose deadpan look said he'd heard the complaint before and didn't give a damn.

"Take it or leave it, kid. Makes no difference to me. Ain't gonna fry up the camel, that's for sure."

Both Webb and Ray had cinched up their belts a couple more notches since joining the circus in May. Laboring as they did and living on hominy and not much else was getting wearisome. They dreamt about their mother's good cooking.

"I swear my belt buckle is gonna meet my back bone the next time I have to cinch her up," Ray mumbled as he and Webb moved to a vacant table and sat on opposite sides. Flies buzzed around and landed on their plates. They were sweltering in the heat of another summer day.

"At least your shoulders are gettin' some muscle. Bet Jenna likes that," Webb wisecracked, swatting away a fly.

"Hey not so loud." Ray looked around at other roustabouts seated close by. "One of these guys might hear you and say somethin' to Honest Bill. I don't think he's noticed us together yet."

"That's a joke. Everyone but Honest Bill thinks there's somethin' goin' on with you two. And I'm not so sure he doesn't know, the way she grins every time she sees you. Maybe you should pay attention to what Shorty said about messin' with Jenna, Ray. Honest Bill might kick your ass, if he catches you."

Ray took a couple bites and then looked at Webb. "You ever been in love?"

"Well, uh…I kinda liked Alina and we…"

Ray cut him off. "You don't know about love. When you're in love…it's crazy. You just want to be with her no matter what. You'll find out one of these days."

When it came to girls, Ray wore his heart on his sleeve. If he was attracted to a girl, he made it known even when he tried hard not to. When Jenna performed, Ray peered inside the Big Top, mesmerized by her agility and grace. She was petite and lithe, dancing from the back of one horse to another before dismounting. Once on the ground, she worked wonders with her body signals and quiet commands that had the horses genuflecting, prancing, dancing and twirling around her. Ray had never seen anything like it.

"Have you kissed her yet?" Webb, with a lowered voice and foolish grin, prodded for more information.

"Well…maybe once or twice." Ray smiling, eyes on his plate, responded in almost a whisper.

"I knew it!" Webb howled.

Ray planted his hands on the table and started to stand

up in an effort to quiet Webb. His thighs hit the table edge and sent the tin plates bouncing. The clatter caused every roustabout in the tent to turn around and look toward Webb and Ray.

"Thanks a lot, Webb!" Ray stormed out of the tent.

Webb watched his brother leave the tent. He smiled and shrugged his shoulders at the gawking audience, then grabbed Ray's plate with its remnants of food and scarfed down the remains. As awful as it was, it was food.

Ray went looking for Jenna. He found her outside her horse tent. When Jenna saw him, she leaned back against one of the tent poles. Ray raised one hand above her to brace himself against the pole. He touched her arm with the other and gazed into her expectant, upturned face. "Listen, Jenna, I don't mean to cause you any trouble."

He felt himself drawn closer because of her beautiful eyes, dark hair and full lips. She was so small; he felt protective.

"You aren't causing me trouble, Ray. I enjoy our time together, but I'm not sure Bill would understand our...friendship."

"Friendship? Is that what this is?" Ray stood up straight, hiked his shoulders and raised his palms in question. Here he was, ready to proclaim his undying love regardless of the obstacles they faced, and Jenna called it a 'friendship.'

"Well, I have to call it that, 'cuz I'm married, Ray. Doesn't mean I don't have feelin's for you though. I like spendin' time with you...'specially when we're alone." Jenna tipped her head toward her shoulder and looked up at Ray. Ray stared at her. He couldn't believe what he was hearing.

"I told you I married Bill to get away from the farm and have a better life. I get to have people come and watch me perform and we see a lot of places I wouldn't of seen otherwise. And I meet nice people like you." Her voice trailed off and she gave him that look again.

"But do you love him?" Ray was still trying to get his bearings and understand what she was saying.

"Love's not everything, Ray. Getting away from my other life makes this what I want for now. You did the same thing, getting out of Almont. You just didn't get married to do it." Jenna laughed. "But I like havin' you around. You make me feel real special." She put a hand on his chest. "And you're real special too," she cooed.

Honest Bill walked around the corner. He stopped in a gorilla-like stance and stared at the couple in front of him. With hands on his hips, sweat dripping from beneath his stained fedora and a ruddy face about to explode, he hollered, "What the hell's goin' on here?"

Jenna responded wide-eyed. She clasped her hands in front of her, like a school girl caught doing something she shouldn't. "He was just wonderin' about the act, Bill. Wanted to know how I make the horses move the way they do."

Ray stuttered, "Uh…thanks for the information. I'm just on my way to the prop tent, Honest Bill. Got to get ready for the show."

As Ray turned on his heel to get the hell out of there, Honest Bill grabbed his arm and pulled him close. They were nose to nose. Ray could smell his cigar breath and feel his rage.

"If I ever catch you sniffin' round...these horses...again, you'll wind up as feed for the animals. Hear me? I didn't hire you to spend time talkin' to my wife. She don't need no distractions—specially from the likes of you!"

He let go of Ray's arm and shoved him away from Jenna. "You worthless piece of shit. Now beat it."

Ray raced back to the prop tent. He was sweating. It wasn't because of the heat.

Ray told Webb what happened with Jenna and Honest Bill as soon as he got back to the prop tent. "He scared the bejesus outta me, Webb. I thought he was gonna kill me for sure, the way he looked. Besides, she's not even in love with me! She was just stringin' me along."

Ray had gotten a clear message about not messing with Jenna any more, but after that feelings still welled up every time he caught sight of her.

"We're leavin' as soon as we get to Milroy, Webb. We're done with this flea bitten circus. I liked Jenna a lot, but I like livin', too, so best we get out while we can. I know we'll find some folks in Minnesota to help us head back to Almont."

Webb and Shorty bounced along the road at the back of the circus trucks as they had so many times before. South Dakota's early morning sun peeked over the eastern horizon. "We're finally going' to Minnesota, Shorty! We got a telegram from my sister, Toots, and she said there are folks in Milroy who know we're with the circus and they're comin' to see it just 'cuz they know the Bateman name. I haven't been to Milroy for five or six years, not since we moved to Almont."

For the first time in weeks, Webb was excited, but he hadn't told Shorty that he and Ray had decided Milroy would be their last stop with the circus. He knew it would be hard to say goodbye.

14

Sheriff Murphy

Milroy, Minnesota 1925

The circus pulled into Milroy around 9 am. The boys helped set up as usual and then went to find Honest Bill to let him know they were leaving the circus after the final show.

They found him directing setup of the ticket booth in front of the Big Top. His sweat stained fedora was pushed back on his head; a lit stogie hung from his fleshy lips.

"Honest Bill." Ray called the circus owner's name as he and Webb walked toward him. Ray stopped and stood spread legged, hat in his hand. Webb was a step behind, newsboy cap still on his head.

Honest Bill turned slowly. "Yeah, what the hell do you want? You're 'spose to be workin'."

"We're leavin' the circus after the show this afternoon. Need to get our pay for the week and we're givin' our notice."

Honest Bill scoffed. "You piss ants know the rules. You gotta give two weeks' notice. Now get the hell outta here and get back to work." He laughed. "I'm not givin' ya' a plug nickel."Ray moved closer and stood toe to toe with Honest Bill. He tossed his hat on the ground.

"Whadda ya' mean, you're not payin' us?" He was fired up, his fists clenched. Even though it was only mid-morning, heat bounced off the dirt and droplets of sweat appeared on Ray's forehead, every muscle in his body tensed.

A small group of roustabouts gathered around to see what was happening. They had a personal stake in the outcome.

Honest Bill snarled at Ray. "I'm not obliged to pay you. You can leave now for all I care or you can stick around for two weeks and get your final pay." Honest Bill inhaled his cigar and blew a cloud of smoke in Ray's face.

Webb snatched his brother's hat from the ground and waved it at Honest Bill. "Hey, we saw what you did to those two guys in Rapid City." Webb, mustering his bravado, moved closer to Honest Bill. "They gave their notice and you didn't pay them, either. There must be a law against that. We have friends in this town *Honest* Bill."

The circus owner laughed. "I'm the big dog around here. Now beat it." He turned to the gathering. "And the rest of you, get back to work or you'll be hoofin' it down the road, too."

The group dispersed. The boys went to the sleep tent, packed up their satchels, and started for the main part of town.

Webb grabbed Ray's sleeve and stopped him. "I haven't seen Shorty to tell him we're leavin'. Shouldn't I say somethin' to him? He's been good to us."

"We'll be back. We're gonna get paid. That sonofabitch ain't gonna get away with keepin' our money, Webb. We broke our backs for this outfit and I want what's ours." Ray's determination was unmistakable. Webb didn't know if he'd ever seen him so mad, but he knew it had more to do with Jenna than with the money.

As they walked into town, Webb asked, "S'pose anybody will remember us, Ray? It's been almost five years since we were here."

"Well, if they don't remember us, Toots' telegram said people remember the Bateman name. After all, Dad ran gas stations and livery stables around here for ten years. He knew a lotta people and Granddad and Grandma Bateman lived here a long time before that. Toots and I were little when we moved here to take care of grandma in 1910. You and Walt, Vivian and Blanche were born here. You know how small this place is, a couple hundred people maybe." Ray said without smiling. "So…yeah, somebody better remember us."

Dust devils blew swirls of dirt from the road onto the wood slatted sidewalks that fronted businesses on the main street. Euclid Avenue was also Highway 68, running north and south through town. There wasn't much more to Milroy than when they left five years before. The boys walked six blocks into town and by block seven they were on their way out again.

"Hey, there's the bank. The bank manager knows everybody. Let's go in there and tell the guy what happened. Maybe he'll figure out a way to help us," Webb suggested.

Mr. Arden, the bank manager, was a friendly sort who knew the Bateman name. He'd heard Ray and Webb were coming to Milroy with the circus. The boys told their story and Mr. Arden responded, "I think we can get this resolved, boys. Let me make a call."

He picked up his phone and called Sheriff Murphy. Murphy had been around long enough, he also knew the Bateman name and agreed to come to the bank. It was 1 pm.

"Boys, you're tellin' the truth about what happened, I hope?" Sheriff Murphy was imposing in height and his broad shoulders gave the impression he could handle just about anybody who gave him a bad time. He was also a man who didn't want to waste time with some kids out to pull a prank.

"Sheriff, we've been workin' our tails off since May. Yeah, we did get paid every week like we were supposed to, but we need this final paycheck 'cuz we're planning to head back to Almont and have to get some sort of transportation to get us there. The boys had managed to save some of their earnings, but late night poker games also took a chunk out of their combined eight dollars a week.

"A good meal wouldn't hurt, either." Ray explained.

Webb chimed in, "All we've had to eat for months is hominy. I've lost so much weight; my stomach thinks my throat's been cut." He pulled up his shirt to show off his ribs.

"Okay, okay." The Sheriff smiled. "I get the picture. There's ladies present. Put your shirt down, son."

Sheriff Murphy turned to the bank manager. "Mr. Arden, can you draw up some papers that the boys and I can take to good ol' Honest Bill that might change his mind?"

The bank manager pulled out some forms. One had big block letters on top that spelled, FORECLOSURE. Arden had his secretary type across the top of another form the words, JUVENILE FRAUD.

With papers in hand, Sheriff Murphy and the boys headed for the circus lot. People were already milling around, anxious for the matinee to begin.

Webb didn't see Shorty. He guessed he was working with other roustabouts on the jargo routine. They had left him in the lurch, but at this point, he didn't see there was much choice in the matter.

The show was about to start. Ray and Webb stood at the entrance to the Big Top, spread-legged and arms crossed, defying anyone to enter. Honest Bill, now in his Ring Master get-up, was told what was going on and came storming around the line of people.

"What the hell do you think you're doin'?" Honest Bill bellowed at the two of them.

Sheriff Murphy had been talking to the ticket taker with his back to Honest Bill. He turned around to face him, his Sheriff's badge flashing in the sun.

Honest Bill stopped short, startled by the appearance of the Law.

"Sheriff, I'm so glad you're here. As you can see, these two hooligans are causing my show trouble. I want them arrested right now and thrown in the hoosegow."

Ray and Webb grinned at each other from behind the Sheriff. They held their position. Sheriff Murphy put one hand on Honest Bill's shoulder and with the other, pulled papers from his back pocket. "Honest Bill, we have a little problem here that I'm sure can be solved real quick so you can get on with your show. These boys came to me with their dilemma. Said there's been some mistake about their final paycheck. I'm sure you don't want any trouble, but I have a couple legal documents here that you might want to take a look at."

The townspeople in line had quieted down and were leaning forward, so they could hear what was said.

"One of the documents talks about the illegality of juvenile fraud. These boys are still owed their last week's wages of four dollars each. This other legal document is about havin' to foreclose on your property—everything that's part of your motorized circus—if your obligations aren't met. Those obligations include payin' these boys what they are due."

Honest Bill grabbed the documents and gave them a quick glance. He didn't have time for the small print which carried no legal authority whatsoever. He had a show to run. Without further argument, he ordered the ticket taker to pay Ray and Webb the four dollars each they were owed.

The boys sprang to the ticket window, grabbed their cash, and as they walked off the lot past the line of potential ticket buyers, Webb couldn't help himself. He puffed out his chest and announced at the top of his lungs, "Hey folks. It's a lousy show. We should know 'cuz we were in it! Don't waste your money."

The townsfolk closest to the action began a chatter that telegraphed down the line. Money was hard-earned and if the Bateman boys said the show wasn't worth it, then people weren't going to waste their 25 cents. Most of the line dispersed, with parents huffing off toward town. They had to drag their children away, kicking and hollering about not seeing the circus.

Ray and Webb laughed and slapped their knees in glee when they heard a voice behind them. "Webb, Ray. Hold up a minute."

They turned around. It was Shorty. He strode toward them, his shoulders raised and arms a pumping. They could tell he was mad as hell.

"What did you idiots just do? Ever think about the rest of us who need to earn a livin'? Because of what you did, me and the roustabouts won't be gettin' all our money this week."

Webb tried to explain. "Hey, Shorty. We didn't mean you no harm. I thought I would see you before we left the lot earlier to tell you we were leavin', but Honest Bill changed our timin' and..."

"Doesn't matter, Webb. You didn't say a word to me and you screwed us all the same. That's what I get for makin' friends. The minute you trust someone, they crap all over ya'." He stormed off toward the Big Top.

Ray started walking toward Milroy. Webb, the cash suddenly cold in his hand, stood watching Shorty a while longer. He turned and caught up to his brother. The boys slow walk to town was quiet until Webb said, "I shoulda told Shorty we were leavin' and guess I coulda kept my trap shut. He was a friend."

They hitched a ride for the thirteen-mile trip from Milroy to Marshall in late afternoon and now, stood on the doorstep of one of their dad's old friends, John Halvorson. Jim had told them to stop in to see him, if they ever got to Marshall.

"Well, come on in boys. How's the family?" Ray and Webb were greeted by Mr. Halvorson who warmly welcomed them into the living room.

"Have a seat, boys." He noted their scrawny frames. "Mary, fix these boys somethin' to eat. They're skinny as a rail. What have you been up to? How's the family?"

Tales of the circus and some facts about the family unfolded as Ray and Webb devoured Mrs. Halvorson's chicken and dumplings. They left out the part about being told to leave home.

"Mr. Halvorson, do you know of a cheap automobile we could buy?" Ray switched the conversation to the reason for the visit. "We're planning to head back home to Almont and thought it might be easier to travel the 500 or so miles if we had a car. It doesn't have to be pretty, just reliable. We're hoping we can get home where we can find work and see the family again."

Halvorson stroked his chin. "I think I know of a vehicle you two could have pretty reasonable. We can take a look at it in the mornin'. Right now, you boys finish up eatin' and we'll find you a place to sleep for the night." The boys expressed their gratitude and slicked their plates clean.

Ray and Webb rose at the crack of dawn. They'd had a good night's sleep and Mrs. Halvorson fixed a filling breakfast to get them down the road. Excited about the prospects of a car and anxious to check out a buggy to get them home, they followed Halvorson to the backyard toward a dilapidated garage. The boys glanced at each other, not sure what Halvorson had in mind.

"She's right in here." Halvorson rolled back a barn door to unveil a 1914 Model T Ford. "Whaddaya' think?"

"Does it run?" Webb asked.

"Well get in and Ray can crank her up."

She ran. The tires were bad and there were no spares or tire pump, but for 25 dollars, the boys didn't complain. They loaded their few belongings, said their goodbyes and ground the gears north toward Fargo, North Dakota.

Flat tires stopped them in their tracks time after time. They would get out, pull the tire from the clincher rim and drive on the rim to the next town to get the tube patched, pumped up and put back on. What should have been a five-hour trip to Fargo took them a full day. They slept in the car that night.

Heading west from Fargo presented a new challenge. Highway 10, a main east-west route to the West Coast, was under construction. Mud hole after mud hole caused detours and delays. Nearing Jamestown, North Dakota, their headlamps went out. They weren't able to drive at night without the lights, so they pulled off the road and slept in a barn.

"Can we help you out by milkin' the cows? We borrowed your hayloft for sleepin' overnight 'cuz our headlamps went out," Ray asked the farmer as they walked up to his kitchen door. Webb stumbled behind rubbing sleep from his eyes. The farmer stood on the steps and held his screen door open. The sun was coming up.

"Sure thing. You get the milkin' done and we'll have some breakfast for ya'."

With the cows milked and bellies full, thanks to the farmer's wife, Ray and Webb headed west again. Home was four hours away.

Ten miles from Almont the motor overheated; steam hissed from under the hood. "What the hell? Unless it's bad, we don't have any luck at all." Webb pounded on the steering wheel.

"Let's get her into a farm yard. We're comin' up on the Sweeney's place and maybe he can help us out." Ray, weary from one trip mishap after another, was calmer about the latest setback. "We just have to figure out what to do instead of bellyaching about what's happenin'." He was becoming a philosopher at the ripe old age of sixteen.

Sweeney knew his vehicles. The soft plug had blown from the motor block and let all the fluid out of the motor, causing it to overheat. The fix was a new plug carved from a broom handle. When the boys checked the gas tank with a stick, they found it was empty too, but maybe their luck was changing. At least, they weren't driving down the road before they found out they were out of gas.

"I know you're almost home, so I can spare ya' a gallon of gas. It's on me," Sweeney said. The boys thanked him and drove off, grateful for the favor. As they neared Almont, they could see Lover's Leap, an outcropping on a bluff above the town.

Almont—they made it. The adventure hadn't made them rich, but they'd seen some territory, learned some lessons, and—home never looked so good.

Jim Bateman
Town Talk Billiards—Billings, Montana

15

Family

Billings, Montana 1939

Webb rolled into Billings around noon. For March, the weather was mild. He was home.

Guess I'm s'posed to make the funeral. The weather sure hasn't gotten in the way. It could of been a lot worse, but...I'm not there yet. Another half day of travel at least. We'll have to get goin' real early tomorrow mornin'. Wonder who'll be goin' with me or if I'll have to go it alone.

He lit a cigarette at a stop sign and then turned west on First Avenue, the main street in town from Highway 87. He could see the Rimrocks, sandstone cliffs rising 500 feet to the north of Billings, the stone faces etched over centuries by the Yellowstone River.

As he drove toward his folk's place, Webb's thoughts trailed back to the first time he came to Billings.

Hated the fact I had to leave Win Coman's construction outfit in North Dakota. He was the best boss I ever had. He gave me a break at age eighteen. Taught me how to run equipment. Had faith in me. I was even promoted to superintendent with the company after Dorothy and I got married in the spring. But the Depression got him too. The work just dried up, and according to Walt, there were truck drivin' jobs to be had in Billings. And the rest of the family seemed to settle in and find work. I thought Dorothy and me might as well head west with the rest of 'em in the fall of '35 after LaReta was born.

Webb glanced up again at the wall of stone north of town. The Rims were a popular spot to watch a sunrise or a sunset and spoon. Webb enjoyed the Rims after the move to Billings. He and Dorothy watched a couple sunsets from there. And after Dorothy left for North Dakota, there was another woman.

Webb shook his head at the thought. *I haven't even been to Dorothy's funeral yet to say my goodbyes and I'm thinkin' about Julia. I need to talk to her.*

He stopped at an intersection stop sign, rolled the window down, stuck his arm out to signal, and turned right onto North 33rd. *I didn't have much time to talk to her on the phone before I left Nebraska. I hafta see Julia before I leave for North Dakota.*

Webb pulled up in front of a two-story, box-shaped, white house. It wasn't his folks' first residence in Billings since the move from North Dakota in 1935, but for now it was home.

Two separate front doors, each with its own address, 407 and 409, faced the street. Steep stairs to the second floor were visible through the screen door on the left, 409. To the right, a screened porch spanned the rest of the first floor with an entry to 407.

Webb admired his mother's business sense, even though Dena wouldn't call it that. Webb laughed to himself. *She'd call it "common sense."*

His mother had learned from past experience. She was

the one who provided for the family when Jim didn't. The house in front of him with a sign that read, "BOARD AND ROOM," was one more example.

Webb turned off the Chevy, swung his weary body out of the vehicle and flicked his cigarette to the sidewalk. His work boot gave it a grind as Dena swung open the porch screen door.

"Glad you made it safe, Son. Sorry your dad's not here. He's at the billiard parlor with Ralph." Webb noted Dena's Norwegian lilt, even after all these years. Most of her words had two musical notes, instead of the flat tones Webb used. He liked the sound of her voice and smiled. That wasn't always true when he lived with the family in Almont.

Webb walked through the open door and onto the porch. "That's okay, Ma. I'm not in the mood for a lot of folks right now. I'm dog tired. I've been drivin' since I got the news." Once through the screen door, Webb stopped to wipe his feet on a small rug at the entrance to the living room and Dena patted his back as he walked into the house. Webb understood there wouldn't be hugs from his mother. Her Norwegian heritage didn't encourage displays of affection, even among family members, but he knew she understood just the same.

He entered the living room, small but comfortable. An overstuffed brown couch and two big chairs took up all the space. Dena's crocheted doilies adorned the arms on each piece of furniture; her large, multi-colored rag rug circled its way to fill the space between the couch and chairs. Knickknacks filled a couple corner shelves and family photos hung on the walls.

Dena closed the door behind them. When she turned to him, Webb noticed she'd put on some weight. His mother was heavy, but not fat, thick with childbearing and work. Her light grey hair, tinted slightly blue, was short and set with finger waves. Webb later learned the shop where Vivian worked told Dena the rinse was the latest thing to brighten grey hair.

She wore wire-rimmed glasses and her face was fuller than it had been the last time he was home, but in recent years her countenance was different. When she smiled, there was a kindness he hadn't known as a child. Living in Billings wasn't always easy, but it was nothing like the burden of running a hotel, a restaurant, raising six children and dealing with Jim in earlier years.

"I understand you're tuckered out, Webb, but just so you know, Vivian and Blanche will be home for supper. They're both working these days. Blanche was able to get a couple days off from Dr. Sun's clinic, so she'll go with you to Dunn Center. You won't see Walt or Ray till you get back. Walt is on a long haul for a couple days and Ray headed to Miles City to help somebody with their radio equipment."

Dena moved toward the kitchen door. "What can I get you to eat, Son?"

"Anything's fine, Ma. I haven't had much since leaving Ogallala yesterday. Could eat a horse, but what I need is a couple hours' shuteye."

Webb ate lunch, leftover lefse smeared with lots of butter and sugar and then rolled into a tube which he picked up and devoured. Sausages from the morning's breakfast disappeared just as quick and he wolfed down a piece of his mother's apple pie. A strange combination, but just what he needed.

"Sorry I didn't fix something else, Webb, but I wasn't sure when you would get here. We'll have a better supper. I was able to pick up a nice roast from the grocer yesterday, just for your homecoming."

Webb appreciated the effort. His relationship with his mother had improved over the years, much different from the challenging relationship of his youth. After lunch, Webb headed into the girls' bedroom to get some sleep.

He sat on the edge of his sister's bed and looked around the room. A Bible lay open on a side table. *One of the gals must be reading,* he thought. *Maybe that comes with being confirmed. You get in the habit.*

Webb flashed back to the hours he sat with other kids in an Almont church basement going over Luther's teachings and wishing he were at the pool hall.

I never did get confirmed in the Lutheran Church. Ma made sure all the others did. Guess they all got confirmed in North Dakota, except me. I did start the classes, but that stopped when Ma sent me to live with August Johnson…that sonofabitch.

Webb chuckled. Here he was thinking about Confirmation and calling his uncle names. *Guess I need a refresher on 'How to Forgive and Be Forgiven.' Probably need a refresher about lots of the things the Bible has to teach.*

Webb flopped back on the bed and fell asleep in minutes. Exhaustion from driving thirty hours, almost non-stop, caught up with him. Sleep soon twisted into a dream, deep inside the caverns of the earth. *Pitch black.*

Webb reached out and felt the cold, damp roughness of a coal room wall against the palm of his groping hand. His rubber boots sloshed in water up to his ankles. He hurried to relight the carbide lamp fastened to the cap on his head. He was alone, so alone.

He unclipped the small lantern from his cap, unscrewed the top of it and added some water from a flask at his hip.

I hope to God it just needs water and not more carbide, 'cuz I'm almost out, Webb's dream world spoke to him.

He hit the striker wheel on the reflector shield with a small piece of metal. The spark lit the acetylene gas coming from the front of the lamp. He adjusted the length of the flame with the lever on top and clipped the lamp back onto the front of his cap. A warm light filled the cavernous space.

Dorothy's face. He could see her face, like a portrait on the far wall. She looked worried, her brows knit together and her eyes followed his every move.

Dorothy can't be here! Webb panicked. *I'm seventeen years old, the youngest miner in the mine…and I'm 300 feet underground. What's she doin' here? Am I dead too? Is this what it's like?*

He saw he had on the same dirty, crusty, long-handled underwear and overalls he'd worn every day in that hole. Maybe that was his shroud…if he was dead.

If he could just get his cut of coal out, they would haul him up and he could get cleaned up. He'd know he was alive. *Just one more cut and I'll have my quota, ten one-ton car loads a day.*

Webb took his auger in one hand and pounded it into

the wall with a hammer in the other. There…he made the shot hole. He was cold, but sweating at the same time.

I just need to get powder in the hole, light it, let her blow and shovel the coal into the rail car. The mules will haul it out…and then I can get outta here. I need to get outta here. Damn, my headlamp's out again.

He could still see Dorothy's face in the darkness. *What the hell?*

She was saying something this time. He grabbed the lantern from his cap to relight it and heard her words, "No one knows darkness like a miner and you, Webb. Make your lamp work in total blackness and from now on, you'll know no fear of anything."

What's she talkin' about? Light in the darkness. You're damn right I want light in this hell hole!

Webb woke with a start. He stared at the ceiling to get his bearings, slowly sat up on the side of the bed and put his head in his hands.

Dear God…wasn't there somethin' in the Bible about hidin' a light or somethin'? I didn't hide my light. The damn thing just went out. That wasn't my doin'. I had to get 'er lit again.

He rubbed his forehead, confused. *What's she tellin' me? Am I livin' in darkness or somethin'? Not thinkin' clear and don't know what to do?* He shook his head to get some clarity. *Well, if that's it, she's sure as hell got it right!*

Late afternoon sun streamed through the window. Webb stood up and went into the bathroom to throw water on his face and clean up before supper. He checked his watch and realized he'd slept five hours. He felt almost human again. Webb knew the family would have a lot of questions. He wasn't sure he had answers, but he was still alive.

Webb walked into the living room and found his dad and the girls were home. They'd been quiet so he could sleep. Jim sat smoking a pipe and didn't get up when Webb came in.

Jim took the pipe out of his mouth by the bowl and shook Webb's hand. "Glad you made it home safe, Webb. Never know what the weather is gonna be like this time of year. Real sorry to hear about Dorothy. We liked her a lot. Nice girl." Mixed with the sweet aroma of Jim's pipe tobacco was the musky odor of whiskey. It was familiar; Webb knew he was home.

When they heard conversation, Vivian and Blanche popped through the doorway to give Webb a hug and say how sorry they were about Dorothy. After a quick welcome, they hurried back to help Dena with supper.

"How's Town Talk Billiards doin', Dad?"

Jim still had his ample belly, but looked much older than he had last year, older than his 56 years. A shock of dark hair swung to one side of a high forehead, but he was greying at the temples, just above his protruding Bateman ears. The Bateman children had inherited his deep set eyes, his ears and his rounded features, but Jim's face sagged now, as though weighed down by worry. Alcohol and smoky pool halls had taken their toll. He looked tired, worn out.

"The billiard parlor should be doin' pretty good. It's right on a thoroughfare, Montana Avenue, next to The Stockman's Bar. You know, Ralph and Toots moved from

North Dakota last year so we could partner. There's four partners total in the business now." The pipe glowed as he inhaled and blue smoke escaped out the sides of his down turned lips as he exhaled. "But there's not enough profit for two."

Jim removed the pipe by the bowl and pointed at Webb with the other end. "Ralph's worried I'm not holdin' up my end of the bargain. He tries to say it real nice, but I know what he's gettin' at." He took another aggravated puff and pointed at Webb again, his voice louder this time. "I've been in this business a hellaova lot longer than he has, so what does he know?" Jim's face flushed.

Webb shrugged his shoulders and didn't comment. He remembered all the times Jim had gone on binges leaving behind the pool hall or whatever business he had at the time. Dena was left to pick up the pieces. Maybe Ralph was feeling the same way.

As Webb sat down on the couch and crossed a leg, thoughts of the dream flashed back. He'd been the sole support for the family at age seventeen when they moved to New Salem, North Dakota and he worked in the coal mine.

Small talk continued with his dad. Webb knew he'd have to bring up the topic of money to go to Dorothy's funeral, but Dena needed to be part of the conversation. She was the one whose opinion carried the most weight in the family.

The men could hear sounds of the women bustling in the kitchen, pots being stirred and soft whispers of conversation. The smell of roast beef and vegetables wafted through the doorway. This *was* a welcome home dinner and Webb's mouth watered.

"Supper's ready," Dena called from the kitchen. These were words the men didn't have to hear twice.

One thing never seemed to change—his mother's skill in the kitchen. As she dished up from a large pot, steam rose and clouded her glasses. She took them off and rubbed each lens with the hem of her bib apron, then let it fall back over her house dress. Brown stockings and tie up black shoes with a small heel grounded her in the kitchen. This was where she reigned.

Webb sat at one end of the table, his dad at the other. *Some things don't change,* Webb thought, *while others are changed forever.* Dena and the girls dished up and placed plates on the table, first for the men, then for themselves. They all ate for a while without saying a word. Webb sensed they were giving him a chance to eat and holding their questions till later.

"Pass the potatoes?" Webb asked for another helping. "Good meal as usual, Ma. Never could complain about your cookin'," he said with a smile.

There had been no mention of what happened to Dorothy or the funeral the next day. Webb wasn't ready to bring it up. It meant he'd have to ask for money. He set the bowl down and smiled at Vivian. "I hear you're gettin' married, Viv. What's his name?"

Her face brightened. She was excited. "Harold Burnett. We're getting married this summer and plan to move to Portland. Lots of opportunity for us in Oregon."

Vivian was beautiful. She had the Bateman's soft round

features, high cheek bones, dimples and a pretty smile. She turned 24 in February, the month before. Never one with much interest in school, Vivian had left North Dakota before graduation and moved to Billings at the suggestion of friends who were already there. Ray followed not long after while Dena and Jim were still in North Dakota.

Vivian was 'discovered' in Billings by Kodak and was asked to model for their ads. She was thrilled by the offer, but later went to work at the Northern Hotel as a waitress. Now she was working in a beauty salon, which explained her defined eyebrows, red lips, rouged cheeks and finger-waved coiffure. In spite of her beauty, Webb thought she lacked confidence and he wondered if she knew what she was getting into. "Just make sure you get married for the right reason," he warned.

"Of course I'm getting married for the right reason. We're in love!"

"I shoulda known by the grin on your face, but there's different kinds of love, Viv."

"I know which kind this is, Webb." Vivian replied with indignation in her voice.

"I'm just sayin' be careful." Webb cautioned.

Vivian's tone softened, "You'll see, Webb. You'll like Harold. The rest of the family met him. He's a cosmetic salesman who's been coming into the salon for the past year. A gentleman and very nice. Good looking, too!"

Blanche interrupted, "Webb, I can't wait any longer to know." With one finger, she nudged her eye glasses up on her nose. "What happened to Dorothy? How did she die and what are you going to do about LaReta?"

Webb was taken back by her direct questions. He'd spent little time with his sisters in past years so he was surprised that as a young woman, Blanche had the same directness he remembered about her as a child. He thought her serious approach to life might also be the result of what happened to her in North Dakota. Dena had written she was the "no nonsense" Bateman in letters. Webb knew after the family moved to Billings in 1935, Blanch had gone to business college. Now, she had a bookkeeping job and was helping Jim and Dena by paying rent, along with Vivian.

"We're still going to Dunn Center in the morning, aren't we?" Blanche continued to question.

Webb cleared his throat and pushed back from the table. He felt himself getting defensive and reached in his chest pocket, pulled out the pack of smokes and took his time lighting up before he answered. "Yup, that's the plan. Have to leave about 5 in the morning to have any hope of getting to the funeral by 1 pm." There was a long pause. "And I need to see what I can do about gettin' some trip money."

Webb took another long drag to disguise his nervousness. He hated asking the family for money and could never bring himself to ask directly.

Jim, Vivian and Blanche looked at Dena who answered the unspoken question. "We all talked it over yesterday when you called, Webb. Dorothy was part of our family. We spent a lot of time with her when you were out of town and before she moved back to North Dakota. We want to do what we can to help. I got ahold of Ray and Walt and the girls pitched in. We have some money for you. We think it will be enough to get you there and back again."

Webb breathed a sigh of relief, cigarette smoke filling the room. "Thanks, Ma. I hated to ask, but I'm flat broke. Used every last dime to get here and I wouldn't have made it this far, if I hadn't collected on some debts before I left. You know I'll pay you back just as soon as I get work again."

Webb believed he would pay them back. He also knew he had a way with the family. While he was still prone to partying, poker and impulsive decisions, he knew the family looked up to him. He always managed to get a job somehow, somewhere, and he wasn't around much for them to judge. He'd heard about what the women frequently saw: Jim, Ray and Walt drinking—a lot—and not always working. He'd heard about Jim staggering in late at night, sometimes with Ray. Dorothy had even written him about some brouhaha they'd gotten into and the shiner Ray had to prove it.

Jim remained quiet throughout supper. Webb wondered if he was still brooding over Ralph's comments about the billiard parlor or about the family giving him money.

From his shirt pocket, Webb pulled two thin sheets of stationary. He'd taken them from the shoebox in the backseat after he arrived in front of the house, knowing there would be questions. The pages were written on both sides in pencil.

"Thought you might want to see this. It'll answer some of your questions." Webb smoothed the pages on the table.

"Dorothy sent me this letter from the hospital. I got it last week on the 5th. I don't know what happened just two days ago when she died, because from what the letter said, she was gettin' better and would be goin' back to the Baileys where she and LaReta were boarding. Maybe Blanche could read her letter out loud. It'll be easier than me tryin' to tell you what she said."

He handed the letter to her and Blanche began reading. She had to stop a couple times. Webb wasn't the only one who couldn't believe she was gone.

Dickinson Hospital, North Dakota
February 27, 1939

Dear Webb,

Well, I guess life has just handed me another kick in the pants. Some of these times I think I'll just give up instead of coming back for more.

I s'pose you would like to know what it's all about. Wed. night coming home I got about a quarter mile from Baileys. I simply fainted dead away and pitched head first off my horse. My horse ran on home. Richard came tearing back. I was just coming to a little bit but couldn't talk or move for quite a while. He went home and got the car and took me to the house. At first I was completely paralyzed then after a while it was just from my hips down. That was a pretty terrible feeling to look down at your legs and think maybe you could never use them again. I just went wild. I guess I scared LaReta and everyone else nearly frantic.

We called Dix [Dickinson] Dr. and he wouldn't move me unless some member of my family gave them permission. He was afraid of my heart. My brother, Laurel, came. He stayed here at the hospital all night with me.

I got your letter and check some time ago and should have written sooner but I'm so slow.

Arlis left for Oregon the nite before I got hurt. I miss him such a lot. I know he would have been in here nearly every day and it would have helped pass the time away.

Myra & Randeen tried to come but they got as far as Dunn Center and had to stay there because of a blizzard. They were in all day Thursday.

I talked to them all day and afterwards didn't even know that they had been here. I was plumb batty. I have a slight concussion. It might have been pretty serious but I guess I'll be all right now.

You didn't know how close you came to having a daughter all of your own.

They closed my school for me until I get well so I feel pretty lucky. I'll be back later in the spring but I'll need the money so much worse now.

Well, Webb, please write.

Love,

Dorothy

Webb had gone to get an ash tray from the living room, but could still hear Blanche reading the letter. He came back into the kitchen. "It musta been much worse than she thought," Webb said, clearing his throat.

"And who's Arlis?" Vivian asked.

Webb leaned against the doorframe and flicked the end of his cigarette into the ash tray. "Arlis is the older of two sons in the Bailey family where they were boarding in Gladstone, North Dakota. He had just left for Oregon to find work the day before Dorothy got hurt, like she said in her letter. Richard is the other son who found her in the snow."

"What are you going to do about LaReta?" Dena asked this time. "Looks like Dorothy thought you would be the one to take care of her."

"I don't know, Ma. I'm not sure she'll even recognize me. You know how I move around a lot. How can I take care of a three-year-old girl? I just don't know."

Blanche spoke up. "Isn't that why I'm going with you? To bring her back here? She's not just a girl, Webb. She's your daughter." She looked Webb square in the eye. He put the cigarette back in his mouth.

"I left something in the car." Webb turned and headed out to the Chevy. There were still a few drops left in the bottom of the whiskey bottle in the front seat.

Webb, LaReta, Blanche and Dena
1938

16

The Road

March 10, 1939

The day of the funeral and still long before light, tree branches answered to the wind and tapped mercilessly on the side of the house next to the living room. Webb was trying to sleep on the couch. He needed to get some shut eye for the trip ahead. It was 2 am.

She's your daughter.

It was going to be a long drive with Blanche and her judgements in the front seat beside him.

What Blanche had said brought the picture into focus. He wasn't going to Dunn Center just to pay his respects. He was going to get his daughter. He had known that was a possibility when he left Ogallala, but it wasn't why he wanted someone to go with him. He couldn't face Dorothy's family alone.

Maybe we shouldn't go. The Boes will take care of LaReta. She doesn't know me. If I bring her back here, Ma and Blanche will end up takin' care of her for a while 'cuz I'll have to get a job.

Webb thought back to the previous evening. He'd left the house again on the pretext of going to buy cigarettes, but found a phone booth and called Julia. He wanted to

170

talk to her alone.

"Yes, of course I can meet you," she said. Julia was living with her parents in Billings and knew they would care for her eight-year-old son, Raymond, while she was gone.

Lying in the dark, Webb thought about their conversation in the front seat of the Chevy.

It was good to see her in person. Talkin' to her on the phone wasn't the same. Said she would do whatever it took to help me. If there's ever been anyone in my life to marry for the right reasons, it's Julia. S'pose I could get a truck drivin' job local or figure out a way to take family with me.

Webb paused to let what he was thinking sink in.

My god, no wonder Dorothy looked sad in my dream. I'm thinkin' about doin' what she wanted me to do all along and she's not even buried yet.

He sat up on the side of the couch, angry and confused.

Hell, but what do I know about bein' a father to any kid? Look what I had for an example!

Sleep eluded him and he got up at 4 am. Dena and Blanche got up soon after. Blanche packed food for the trip while Dena boiled coffee on the stove and made breakfast. Webb drank a couple cups in a hurry to help him think, while Dena poured more in a thermos for the road.

"Ma, has Dad got a pint I can have for the road? I may need it."

Dena looked askance at Webb, but pulled a bottle of whiskey from the cupboard and handed it to him. Blanche's eyes met her mother's in agreement with Dena's distain about Webb drinking on the road. Blanche turned to Webb, "And I can drive, when you get tired."

They left Billings at 5 am heading east on Highway 12 toward Miles City. With luck and no car trouble, they would get to Dunn Center for the funeral at 1 pm. Webb had called to let Dorothy's family know he would be there.

Blanche wore a two-piece black suit she'd been able to buy with earnings from her bookkeeping position in the doctor's office. She wanted to look professional on the job and hadn't imagined she'd be needing this suit for a funeral. The shoulders of her jacket were padded, the fashion of the day. Together with her nylon stockings and pumps, she looked more mature than her 21 years. She brought along her overnight bag and warmer clothes, not knowing what the weather would be like in North Dakota. A small pill box hat sat off to one side of her pretty face. Never without her glasses, she had the look of one who knew what she wanted and was capable of getting it.

Webb wore his one dark suit, the same one he'd worn for his wedding. He knew he'd likely have to fix a tire or work on the motor, so he wore his work boots and brought along a warm coat and gloves. The well-worn fedora sat on his head at its usual jaunty angle. A few extra clothes were thrown in the back seat along with the jumble already there: tools for the Chevy, a spare tire, and the oil lantern from the previous trip. The shoebox sat by itself in the corner.

"Sorry if I sounded off at supper last night, Webb."
"No need to apologize, 'Honey Bunch of Onion Tops'," Webb teased Blanche with her childhood nickname.

She figured he was trying to lighten the mood. "You remember that? And do you remember what I said to someone who called me by that name?" Blanche smiled.

They both laughed, and in high pitched childish voices squeaked, "My name is Blanchie May Bateman and nossen nelse!"

They relaxed in each other's company and were quiet for a while watching the sun come up on the eastern horizon. It disappeared, hidden by clouds, soon after. There was a light dusting of snow on the ground and a dense shroud of grey sky threatened more before long.

Webb passed a slower moving car with a family inside. Blanche could see children leaning against one another asleep in the back seat. She thought about Dorothy and LaReta, how she'd seen LaReta lean against her mom and fall asleep.

Blanche said, "When you were gone, I spent a lot of time and even stayed overnight with Dorothy and LaReta because they were just down the street from Mamma and Dad. And you know they moved in with us for a short time before Dorothy and LaReta left for North Dakota for good."

Blanche had always wondered why Webb didn't make the effort to spend more time with his wife and daughter. Blanche was only six years old when he and Ray left to work on farms and then for the circus. Once they came back, the boys worked away from home. She knew Webb was a hardworking, fun loving guy and that Dorothy's parents expected a wedding when Dorothy got pregnant. She believed Webb always wanted to do the right thing, even when it didn't turn out that way, but Blanche didn't understand why Webb would get married and then not keep his family together.

She liked Dorothy a lot and it didn't take long for her to love little LaReta. Thinking back, she smiled at her memories. "LaReta was so cute. She was so blonde; it didn't look like she had hair at all. I got to see one of her first smiles, when she rolled over, and sat up for the first time..." Blanche's voice trailed off. "I got to see a lot of her firsts."

Webb pulled at his collar. Blanche saw the discomfort on his face. "You saw a lot more than I did, Blanche. Maybe she'll remember you."

"I hope so, Webb." Blanche straightened her skirt and then looked at Webb. "And I still can't figure out why you and Dorothy didn't get back together when she was in Billings last summer. What happened? Seems like you two were getting along just swell."

Webb tried to sidestep her question. "I'm glad you're comin' with me, Blanchie Mae," He teased again. "It would be pretty quiet in this ol' Chevy without all your questions."

Blanche was determined to get some straight answers in spite of Webb's attempt at levity. "I'm serious, Webb. Why didn't it work out for you and Dorothy?"

"You're sure the nosy one. Tryin' to get some advice so you don't make mistakes in life?"

Blanche thought he was still avoiding the question, but replied, "I've already made mistakes, Webb. You know that."

"Whaddaya' mean? The baby?"

Blanche didn't respond.

"You were a kid and it wasn't your fault. I'm sorry I wasn't' around. I still think about wantin' to kill the sonofabitch for what he did to you. You were seventeen, for Christ's sake! Sorry about the language, Blanche. I just get riled up thinkin' about it."

"I've heard worse, Webb. I try not to think about what happened, but if people in town had found out I was pregnant, it would have been so much worse for the family than when you and Ray got girls pregnant."

Webb avoided her gaze. He stared at the road ahead. Blanche continued, "Ray was married, had a child and then got divorced. Then he got another girl pregnant and he didn't marry her. You got Dorothy pregnant... No one said much about that because you boys were off working in other locations, but I was at home with the family. If people had known I was pregnant, 'specially since Mamma was running a restaurant, there would have been a lot of whispers and people talking behind our backs."

Blanche folded her arms in front of her to keep feelings of resentment from spilling out. She sat straight and rigid; she was cold. "Doesn't seem fair that men don't have the same burdens as women."

Webb looked even more uncomfortable. "Sorry Blanche. I didn't realize it was so hard on you. Guess life just isn't fair sometimes."

"Blanche gazed out the side window at the grassland and barbed wire fences as they slipped past. Her thoughts returned to Fargo, North Dakota, four years before.

The Crittendon Home for Unwed Mothers in Fargo, a big, three-story building. It looked like the school house in Almont, except it was made of grey stone. Mamma drove me there. We walked up to the front door along a path that had rose buses on either side of it. A man was cutting them way back, the way Mamma did to our bushes later in Billings. Funny the things you remember, but I can see it so clear. I was scared to death.

"Did you know our cousin Ruth gave birth to a baby at the Crittendon Home the same time in 1935 that I did?"

Webb gave his trucker's wave and a nod to a vehicle passing in the opposite direction. "I'd heard something about that."

"When Mamma got back, she had a lot of questions from people. You know how small the town is. She just said I'd gone to Montana to visit family. So when I came back and the questions started coming at me, I talked Mamma into going to Billings to see Vivian and Ray. Once we got there, I didn't want to go back. There was nothing there for me but bad memories. Guess Mamma felt the same way, so we stayed. Then Dad, you, Dorothy and the baby, and Walt came, too. Of course the Depression had a lot to do with all of us moving west, not just me having the baby."

"We had to find work. We could have gone separate ways, but we do stick together, don't we? Even with family troubles," Webb chuckled.

"The problem with moving, Webb, is there are some troubles you can't leave behind. I know I have a baby boy out there somewhere. He's six months older than LaReta. That's one of the reasons it meant so much to see LaReta's first smile, Webb. I never got to see his."

Blanche turned her gaze out the passenger window and watched the scrub brush and fence posts slide by. They were both silent except for the thumps, hums and clatter of the Chevy.

From the north, the Yellowstone River snaked in and out of low lying valleys making itself visible every few miles. Green scrub trees and grass gave life to either side of the highway in contrast to the leathery plain stretching beyond. They passed Hysham. "In '37, Hysham was one of my construction sites," Webb said, breaking the silence.

Blanche was still deep in thought about the past. She turned her steady gaze on him. "Why did you get married, Webb? Ray didn't get married the second time."

"There you go again... Okay—guess the only way you'll give up on the questions, is if I answer a few." Webb gave Blanche a crooked smile.

"I felt responsible and I wanted to be a stand-up kinda guy. Some called ours a shotgun wedding. Mr. Boe didn't have a shotgun, but he made it clear we'd be gettin' married. Dorothy wanted to. So we did."

Highway 12 was busier than the ones Webb had travelled the days before. He pulled up behind a slower moving pickup truck and the driver, out of courtesy, pulled over so Webb could speed ahead. They nodded at one another in passing.

Blanche wasn't finished. "You had the letter Dorothy wrote from the hospital. I know she wrote you other letters because I was with her several times when she was writing you. Did she write to you very much?"

"Yup. She did. I kept most of 'em. Sometimes I needed scrap paper to write on and would grab one of her envelopes to make notes on, and toss it out by mistake, but for the most part I kept 'em. Now I'm thinkin', someday,

I should give 'em to LaReta."

"You should." Blanche nodded in agreement. "When did she start writing to you?"

"Started in the spring of '36 when I moved from Hysham to Miles City for another construction job. I'd been hauling crude oil in and out of Billings all winter and was home on a regular basis the first year we were married, although Dorothy went home to Dunn Center a couple times. You know all that. But when a better paying construction job came along, I left trucking and went back to being a Cat Skinner for Colleson & Dolven. Anyway, all the letters are in a box in the back seat."

Blanche looked at him wide-eyed. "They are?"

"If you want to know what happened, her letters pretty much tell the story. We were already havin' trouble when she started writin'." Webb reached under the seat for the whiskey bottle. "This is goin' to be a long ride. Feel free to get your answers."

Blanche reached into the back seat to retrieve the beat up shoebox sitting by itself in the corner. The ribbon around the box was frayed from having the knot tied and untied many times.

Webb took a drink, put the bottle back beside him. He watched Blanche slowly untie the knot on the shoebox and lift the lid with reverence. Inside she counted twenty-nine letters from 1936 to 1939. Envelopes protected all but a few of them. While the back seat and Webb's life seemed a shambles, the letters were all lined up as if in a filing cabinet, with the oldest one in front.

"She must have loved you, Webb, to write all these

letters," Blanche almost whispered and thought, *And you must have felt something to keep them all this time.*

Webb chuckled and grabbed the bottle again. He took another drink. "You'll see. They aren't all professin' her love for me."

PART TWO
The Letters

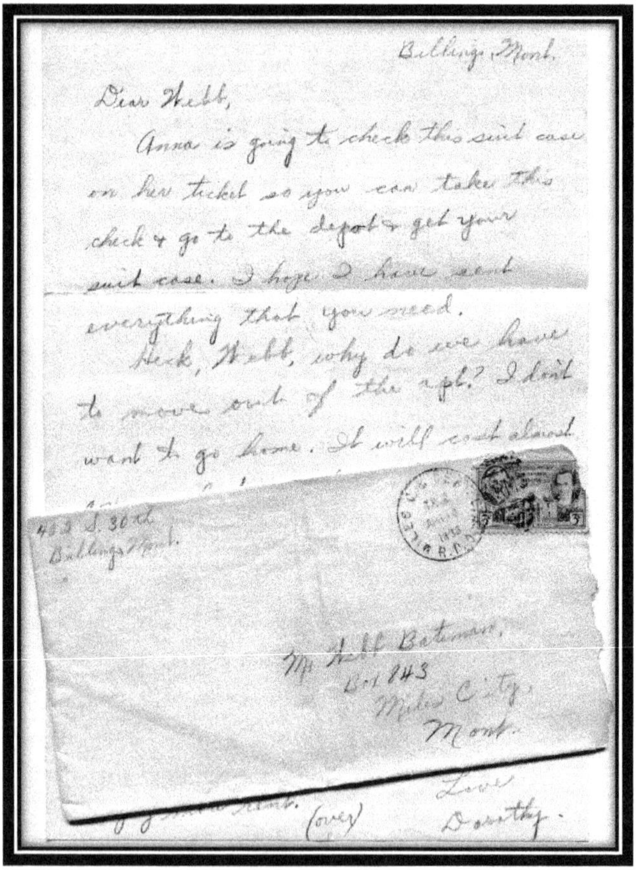

Billings Mont.

Dear Webb,

Anna is going to check this suit case on her ticket so you can take this check & go to the depot & get your suit case. I hope I have sent everything that you need.

Heck, Webb, why do we have to move out of the apt.? I don't want to go home. It will cost almost

432 S. 30th
Billings Mont.

Mr Webb Bateman,
Box 843
Miles City,
Mont.

(over)

Love
Dorothy.

17

Another Move
Billings, Montana 1936

The car motored onward, while Blanche took care in opening the first envelope. There were two small pages, folded together in thirds. She opened the letter and smoothed it against her lap, exposing penciled handwriting on both sides of the pages. Dorothy's cursive penmanship was neat, as you would expect from a school teacher. Blanche began to read and remember.

April 1, 1936

Dear Webb,

 Surprised you were going to Miles City so soon. How come? Is the other job in Hysham all thru? Thought you would be coming back here before you went to Miles City., but I guess it doesn't make any difference.

 Blanche staying with us all the time. Getting along just dandy. Too cold to go to your mother's for supper and take LaReta out, so they brought supper to us. Went to a show up town, Ruggles of Red Gap, because your mother insisted it was so good. I paid the rent (one weeks) today. Only paid up to Monday, so you better try and let me know what to do before next Monday as I think she would ask us to get out if we got behind at all. She much as said so today.

You will be moving around all summer most likely, won't you? I am all for buying a trailer house. We could be paying for that the same as we pay rent I should think. Then when we got it paid for we would have it. It would be pretty hard to be moving around every month or few months with LaReta and all the 'junk' we have. I saw a trailer house advertised in the paper the other day and had a notion to answer it.

Dorothy put the pencil down to watch Blanche playing with LaReta. They were on the floor. Blanche was teasing and tickling the baby.

LaReta started laughing out loud. The baby stopped to take a breath and then she started again, laughing harder and harder. Her whole body bounced up and down. Dorothy and Blanche couldn't help themselves and started laughing too. They held their stomachs and tears of glee ran down their faces.

"I've never heard her laugh out loud that long before, Blanche. She's so darn cute! I can't believe she's eight months old already." Dorothy wiped tears and stopped to take a breath. "And thanks for babysitting Reta last night so your mom could take me to the show."

"Which one did you see? Mamma didn't say." Blanche scooped LaReta off the floor and gave her a snuggle.

"*Ruggles of Red Gap.*"

"I haven't seen it. What's it about?" Blanche was still smiling from LaReta's antics.

"It's a comedy about this rich Englishman who

gambles away his manservant in a poker game. You know who Charles Laughton is?"

"I think so. Doesn't he have kind of big lips and a double chin?"

"That's the one. Anyway, he plays the servant who ends up with new masters, American millionaires, who take him to Red Gap, Washington. Once he gets there, folks think he's a wealthy retired Englishman and he becomes a celebrity. He learns about living in this rough community and how to live life the way he wants to. I liked it a lot. Maybe I should move to Red Gap." Dorothy was smiling, a hint of sarcasm in her voice. "Not sure what I'm going to do, Blanche…but that's not your problem. I may just have to move home to North Dakota again, if we can't afford it here."

Dorothy was upset and angry. She had hoped her marriage would provide love and stability for her and LaReta. Instead, she and Webb had moved soon after the wedding to Stanley, North Dakota because of Webb's construction job. That's where LaReta Lois Bateman was born on Dorothy's 23 birthday, August 8, 1935.

With no medical care before the baby's birth and Dorothy's own health issues, a carry-over from her childhood bout of rheumatic fever, it wasn't a surprise LaReta was premature. A local Stanley doctor delivered the five-pound baby, but reassured Dorothy when they first heard her cries: "She appears to be healthy and you don't have to worry about a bed. You could put her in a shoebox."

Dorothy was exhausted from the pain of childbirth and

Webb frazzled from worry about the birth. He'd been pacing the small living room of their rental for hours, while the doctor was in the bedroom with Dorothy. But once he was allowed in the room, Dorothy saw tears of joy in Webb's eyes when he looked at her and the baby. In that moment, they were the family she'd hoped for. They smothered LaReta with coos and kisses and Dorothy hoped the feelings would last. Their stay in Stanley, North Dakota did not.

Webb was proud he'd been promoted to superintendent with Win Coman. Win had taken Webb, at age eighteen, under his wing and taught him how to run every piece of equipment the company owned. When Webb first met Dorothy, he'd been promoted to timekeeper, but hoped he'd soon be a 'super.' The promotion came, but was short lived. The Depression caused money for road construction and maintenance to dry up and Webb lost his job. With better prospects and family already in Billings, he moved Dorothy and LaReta to Montana. Webb got a truck driving job, but once he was able to get back into construction, he moved out of town, leaving Dorothy and LaReta behind.

Dorothy tried not to complain about Webb to his family. The Batemans all knew Webb's shortcomings. He preferred to play poker with the boys on Friday and Saturday nights when he was home, instead of spending time with Dorothy and LaReta, but the family also knew he'd helped them out of tight financial spots. During the first winter in Billings, he paid his parent's utility bills. The Batemans didn't admonish Webb for not taking better care of his own family, even though Dorothy wished they would.

A week after the letter to Webb and the day before Dorothy's rent was due, she got a letter from Webb. Around noon, Dorothy carried LaReta four blocks to the Bateman's home, shifting the baby from hip to hip. She needed to talk to Dena. It was still cold out and Dorothy's thin coat didn't keep out the chill of the wind, so she snuggled LaReta even closer to keep them both warm. LaReta was wrapped in a couple blankets. She didn't have a warm coat.

Dorothy smiled when Dena opened the front door. "This little one is getting heavy," she said. Dorothy's strength was depleted because she wasn't eating enough. Dena welcomed LaReta into her arms. Dorothy was grateful to have the burden lifted. They stepped into the warm living room. Vivian was in town looking for work and Blanche was in the kitchen fixing lunch. Jim was at the billiard parlor.

Dena put LaReta on the floor with a few toys they kept for her visits. Her bright blue eyes got big and she giggled when she spied Floppy, a white, cotton-stuffed rag dog with droopy, black yarn ears. He was LaReta's favorite with his sad black embroidered eyes, a triangle nose, and crooked mouth. He was soon getting hugs and kisses and more giggles.

Dena, Dorothy and Blanche made small talk. When Blanche volunteered to take LaReta into the bedroom to put her down for a nap, Dena handed Dorothy a check. It was made out to Dorothy's landlady for ten dollars, a week's rent.

"Webb's letter said there would be a check here. I hope he didn't borrow money from you. I know you can't afford it with Vivian losing her job."

"We always seem to get by somehow, Dorothy. We get a little rent from upstairs and there's still some income from the billiard parlor."

Dorothy hesitated and then handed Webb's letter to Dena. "He said I should let you read this because we may have to move in with you for a while. I'm embarrassed to even think about it. I know you haven't had it easy since he left and stopped paying your lights and gas. He said in this letter he wasn't able to do that now. I'm so sorry."

Dena opened the letter from Webb, but took only a moment to read it. "I had a call from Webb the other day, Dorothy. When he suggested you move in with us, I told him he shouldn't be movin' you around so much."

LaReta napped while the women continued to chat. Around 3 pm, Dorothy, with Blanche's help, carried LaReta back to the rental.

Walking back, Dorothy made small talk with Blanche while pondering the conversation with Dena.

It sounds like I won't be moving in with the Batemans any time soon, not that they have much room for me anyway. Now what am I gonna do? And I know they don't need another couple mouths to feed, even though I'm not eating much. Dena doesn't know that I just snack here and there, but I probably look it. I have to keep my costs down somehow and still have food for LaReta. Blanche must understand I don't have anything to spare, 'cuz she always goes back to the Bateman's to eat.

187

That evening, realizing she may have given Dorothy the wrong impression, Dena brought supper to the rental.

"Dorothy, you know you can move in with us, if you don't have a place to live. I was tryin' to make it clear to Webb, he shouldn't be movin' you and little Reta around. I know how that is. I've had plenty of experience with it." Dena smiled and patted Dorothy's hand.

Without the burden of a full-time business and children underfoot, 51 year-old Dena had softened over the years and did understand the desperation of not knowing where the next meal would come from. Jim had kept her guessing for years until she took matters into her own hands. Perhaps Dorothy would have to do the same.

Dorothy wrote Webb again the end of April, angry that she and LeReta did have to move in with Webb's folks.

April 20, 1936

Dear Webb,

Well, we are back with your folks again. We moved down here Wed. So I s'pose you are satisfied. Webb, I am wondering if you will ever grow up and realize that you are a man with a family that you are supposed to support. All I have done ever since baby came is go back and forth between your folks and mine.

It wouldn't be quite so bad if you weren't making about twice as much as either one of our folks. I would kind of like to know just what we are going to do. Do you plan on getting a trailer house pretty soon? You must realize that I couldn't bring LaReta and all our things up to Great Falls. I should think the best way would be to come here and buy a trailer house, move our stuff into it and take it and us to Great Falls or wherever you are going. I suppose you are about there aren't you?

I spent that money you sent as I had to have some new clothes, LaReta had to have shoes and I have been buying her feed here of course. I can't very well go home broke, can I? Ten dollars doesn't go very darn far.

Viv is working at a new enamel shop in town—$10/week. Walter working part time driving a great big gas truck. Ray hasn't anything yet, but another black eye. (It is a honey. Bar fight.) They have all three (your dad, Walt & Ray) been celebrating pretty often lately. It's surely not nice for your mother and I.

Reta is so cute. She holds out her arms to come to you all the time now. She rolled over on the bed quite a few times last night and sat up alone today for quite a while. I am giving her cod liver oil now.

Write soon. You might try writing a letter once instead of just a little note all the time.

As ever,
Dorothy

The Road

Webb was lost in thought while Blanche read Dorothy's letters. He had taken a sip now and then from the pint bottle beside him. Although Blanche's questions were annoying, he knew he had to figure out answers to hers and his own. *Guess there's a reason she's the sister who came with me.*

The sun was above the eastern horizon, but hidden behind a high, flat layer of threatening snow clouds. They were driving straight toward them. The Yellowstone River continued to slip in and out of view to the north. It would still be a couple hours before they reached Miles City, a little more than a third of the way to Dunn Center.

"Webb, Dorothy's letters sound so desperate. One minute she's asking for money and the next she's giving you heck. And then she's telling about how cute LaReta is. Why weren't you able to buy the trailer or send her money on a regular basis? Once you started the construction job, it sounded like you were making good money."

Webb looked at Blanche, straightened his right arm, bracing it against the steering wheel. He retreated, against the door. "I had some things I had to take care of—money wise."

Blanche didn't hold back. "What was more important than sending money to support your wife and daughter?"

"Look, Blanche. I appreciate you goin' with me, but you're puttin' me on trial here."

There was silence again for a few miles. Blanche busied herself reading the letters.

"Okay, I had some poker debts to pay every once in a while. And I didn't buy the trailer even when I did have money 'cuz it just wouldn't have worked out. She would have been alone except for LaReta. The jobs meant a move every couple months. She would have been stuck in that trailer without any family at all. It wasn't a good idea and I tried to explain that to her, but she still kept askin'."

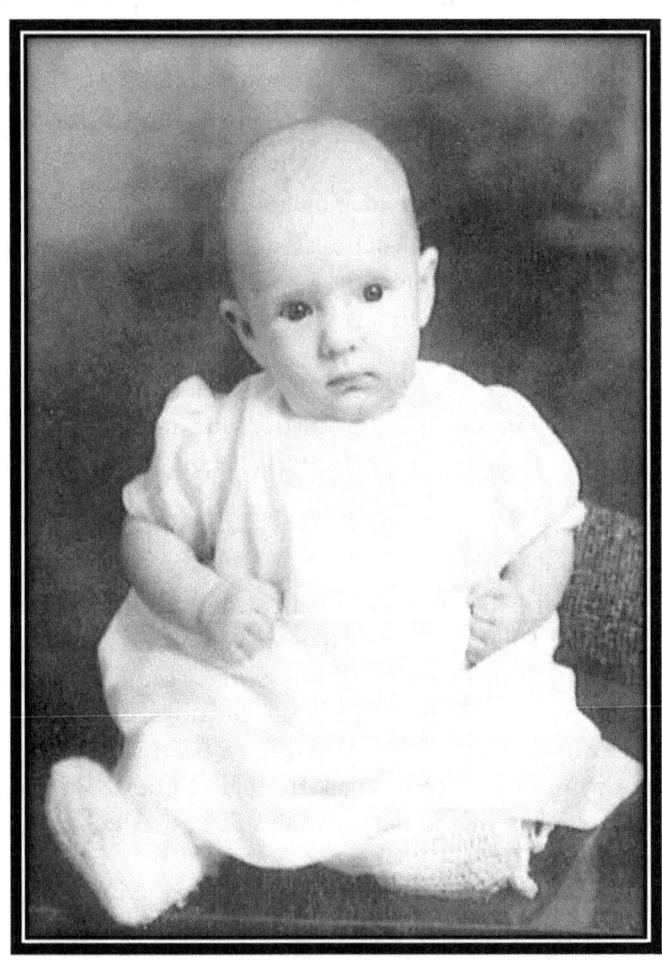

LaReta

18

Not Ready

Dunn Center, North Dakota 1936

B lanche glanced down at the next letter in her hands. "Dorothy went back to her folks in Dunn Center at the end of April. She said a friend of yours offered her a ride since he went that way on occasion. Did she stop to see you on the way?"

"I saw them for a short while on the way through Miles City, but I was still workin' and they had to beat a storm, so it was hello and goodbye and not much else." As an afterthought, Webb said, "I did send her some money again once I got to the new job." He said under his breath, "It was never enough."

Blanche looked at him, a scowl on her face, and then read the next letter without a word.

April 30, 1936

Dear Webb,

I got your check this morning so guess I better write a line. It is a pity you couldn't have written or did you break your arm or something?

LaReta has been so darn kranky lately. I guess she is cutting teeth. I hardly know what to do with her. We just came out to the folks' place from Dunn Center today. Have been staying with

Naomi since Sunday. Naomi and Paul met us in Dix. It was snowing like everything. I didn't even have a coat for Reta and only two little blankets but she didn't even catch cold so guess she must be tough. Mom says she looks just like you when she laughs.

The brother-in-laws are making trailer houses. Paul and Randeen claim the material will cost only about $50. That surely is cheap, don't you think?

Randeen says you should have them build ours rather than pay so much for one. I should think you could spend most of one month's check for it. Of course it is just up to you, but I thought we might as well save that much if you intend to get a trailer house anyway. Ours would have to be a little larger than theirs on account of the baby.

Well behave yourself and write pronto.

Love,

Dorothy

A walk to the mailbox in May lifted Dorothy's spirits. Spring was in the air and the letter she received made her even happier.

"I got a fifteen dollar check from Webb, Mother!" Dorothy waved the check as she entered the farm house kitchen, the same kitchen she'd known since childhood. As much as Dorothy wanted to be with Webb, if there was anywhere else she'd rather be, it was with her own family. It was home. After Ed and Laura Boe's children were born in their first home—a little sod house, a two-story building was moved to the land they homesteaded years before. The building, an old hotel from Dunn Center, was wheeled out from town, pulled by a team of work horses. When the building was delivered, there was a wide, open-air porch on the front, but it was on the second story. Ed, with the help of other farmers in the area, removed and lowered the porch to the ground and reattached it. Over the years, there were add-ons and other changes, but the kitchen was still the heart of the home.

A large, single-oven, cast iron, Home Comfort range stood on one side of the room. Its stove pipe stood at the back of the metal cooking surface with two warming ovens elevated on either side.

When Dorothy walked into the kitchen, the oven door was open, waiting for Laura to slip in a pan of chicken pieces, already breaded and seasoned. That same chicken had been pecking grain in the front yard a couple hours before. All the Boe children had been taught as youngsters how to wring a chicken's neck and use an axe to finish the job. Dorothy's younger brother, Aaron, had done the chicken-wringing, axe-wielding honors today.

Still holding the check in her hand, Dorothy sat down at the kitchen table with Webb's letter. She saw the chicken waiting for the oven and smiled.

"Mother, do you remember the time I tried to wring a chicken's neck, but I swung my arm around like a windmill instead of a quick twist of my wrist? That bird flew out of my hands and ran away with her head turned around looking back at me." They both laughed at the memory.

"And I had to finish the job," Laura added. "But you eventually got the hang of it. All you kids eventually learned." She slid the pan into the oven. Laura didn't laugh often. Her angled features, high cheek bones and a strong chin were testament to a life without excess and, at times, without necessities. She and Ed always got by, but barely. Add to that the deaths of four of their children when they were babies or toddlers and it gave her reason to be serious, often sad. Her shoulders were bent with the weight of being a farmer's wife and life in general.

Still smiling at the memory of the chicken with its head screwed on backward, Laura added a few baking potatoes to the main dish. A firebox was on one side of the stove with removable lids and a door in front, so wood, corn cobs or coal could be added for fuel. The stove was designed to heat the cooking surfaces, the oven and a ten-gallon reservoir filled with water. It also heated the whole room in winter when it was needed, and summer, when it wasn't. Today was a day when the kitchen was toasty but still bearable.

Laura turned back to the sink. It had a hand pump and counters on either side. A large cupboard sat against the same wall to hold dishes, pots and pans. A long dining table filled the rest of the room. When the Boe family was all together, all ten of them, there was still room for another guest or two.

Dorothy, beaming because of the letter and check from Webb said, "With this money, I'll be able to help a little with food. I know it's been tough on you and Dad, having me at home again with Melva, Aaron and Vernetta here too." Dorothy was excited to be able to contribute instead of being a burden to her family. The farm wasn't producing like it had when they first homesteaded. Dust storms took their toll, blowing away the livelihood of hundreds of farmers in North Dakota. The Boes weren't spared. Dorothy's siblings, Myra, Laurel, Naomi and their spouses helped the Boes when they could, but her brother, Miland, had already moved to Oregon to work in his uncle's shoe store.

Laura, a soft look in her eyes and a smile on her face said, "We love havin' you and LaReta here, dear." She looked back to the sink and the vegetables she was cleaning. The corners of her smile turned downward when she asked, "How's Webb?" She was glad her daughter was happy, but wasn't sure it would last. Webb was unreliable from the time the family met him. He was handsome and had a way with words, but Laura saw Dorothy in tears too often because of him. Her daughter and the baby had been back and forth between Dunn Center and Billings ever since the wedding.

"He's fine. Said he has a new job in Roundup, Montana, and maybe there's a place we can stay there for a few months. I sure hope nothing happens so we can't. I suppose LaReta and I should be in Billings when he moves, so he can pick us up on the way. Roundup is just north of Billings about an hour or so."

"Will you be able to stay with his folks until he picks you up?"

"I don't know. Webb's brother, Walter, and Juliet may be there by now. I got a letter from Juliet saying they were leaving for Billings in mid-May because Walter has to get back to his truck driving job."

"When did they get married? Wasn't there some trouble about the wedding?" Laura asked.

"Wasn't too long ago. Had a big wedding dance and everything. Juliet said she's so happy." With a bit of sarcasm, Dorothy added, "I should think she would be, after having Walter put in jail for a couple days. Her folks must have known the sheriff in Mandan or something to throw him in jail for not wanting to marry her. Walter didn't believe the child she's carrying is his. Everyone around here says they feel sorry for Walter and that if he'd fought it, they never would have gotten married. I need to write back to Webb right away to get the details straightened out so we'll know when to meet him and where."

Dorothy was happier than she'd been in a long while. "I want to tell him about Reta trying to walk. She gets cuter every day trying to lift her feet so high."

LaReta crawled into the kitchen to see what was going on. Short wisps of white blonde hair nested on her head. Her chubby cheeks and sweet bow-tie lips added to her cherub look. Dorothy bent down and scooped her into her arms. "Let's see those teeth of yours. Are they ever going to come in? You poor thing."

Laura watched Dorothy and LaReta go into the living room. She smoothed her apron and turned back to her work, gazed out the window and wondered what good could come out of her daughter's marriage to Webb Bateman.

By the end of May, Dorothy's hopes were dashed again. In her next letter, the greeting was a reminder to Webb of his family responsibilities.

May 26, 1936

Dearest Daddy,

This is just going to be a note as the folks are all gone to church and LaReta wants to go to bed, so I guess I'll go too.

I wish you a happy birthday the 28th. I thought sure you would send for us so we could be with you before then, but I guess you don't want us so there isn't much we can do about it, but stay here is there?

Even if you didn't get to go on that other job you might write so I'll know where you are and what you are doing.

We were in Halliday a couple days this week. My brother Laurel's kids are getting big. He and Ada have just painted, kalsomined and varnished their whole house. They sure are lucky to have such a nice place.

The happiest kind of a birthday to you. Celebrate some but not too much. Ha. Taken some snap shots of LaReta but haven't them back yet.

Well, Reta is crying so good night.
Love,
Dorothy

It was a long summer for Dorothy without Webb. In late October, 1936, Dorothy and LaReta caught a ride to Billings and stayed with the Batemans. Webb was between jobs again and living with his folks.

On a beautiful evening, Webb took Dorothy for a drive. LaReta stayed with Blanche who was always happy to spend time with the one-year-old. She was busy during the day attending business college.

Webb pulled into a parking spot on top of the Rims, overlooking Billings. He was hoping for a pleasant evening. Dorothy was more interested in their future.

The sun was going down and the chill of fall was in the air. Webb lit a cigarette and rolled down his window; the smoke floated away. He had one arm on the back of the seat and an elbow hung over the sill. He motioned Dorothy to move closer to him. She stayed on the passenger side of the bench seat.

"Webb, I don't understand why we can't buy a trailer house. You know Paul and Randeen would make us one for a reasonable price. It wouldn't even take a month's paycheck. Then I could go with you wherever you have to move."

A car with another young couple pulled in next to them. The necking began as soon as the ignition was turned off.

Webb inhaled his cigarette and sighed. "We've been over that before, Dorothy. It just won't work. What would you do in a trailer house in some town where you don't know anyone?'

"I have LaReta to worry about. She keeps me busy. And I could fix meals for you and we could spend time as a family, like we're supposed to. We'd have evenings together." Dorothy looked at him in earnest.

The lights of Billings flickered below them in the distance. "There are times I have to work at night. In fact, I never know from job to job what shift I'll be on. Every job is different."

Dorothy was frustrated and angry. "I wish you would

just be honest with me, Webb. Are you sure it's not because you want more time to play poker with your cronies? If you don't want us in your life, just say so."

Webb took his arm off the back seat. Dorothy was ruffling his feathers like no one else could.

"Look, Dorothy. I'm doin' the best I can. I send you money when I have it. You're askin' for somethin' I'm just not ready for."

"What do you mean not ready for? We're married. We have a child. Remember the vows you said in North Dakota? Don't they mean anything to you?"

"You know as well as I do, we're different. You want a place of your own, a place to call home and family and nice things. I have to go where the work is, and that won't get you what you want."

Dorothy fired back. "It's time to grow up, Webb, and be responsible. You're married with a family who depends on you."

Dorothy had a way of pushing Webb into a corner. His way out was to push back and get control. Webb took another drag on his cigarette. He threw it to the ground and grabbed the steering wheel with both hands. He sat straight, his knuckles white. Dorothy backed against the passenger door, startled.

Webb's words were measured and forceful. "I like what I do. I'm good at it. I get respect on the job. I run jobs. I like movin' around and seein' the country—always have. You knew that about me when we met. What I do is who I am."

Dorothy folded her arms in front of her. "I thought I

knew who you were when we met. You've changed…" Dorothy glared at him.

Webb wasn't done. "We might not even be together, Dorothy, if it wasn't for the baby. Ray and now Walt got divorced when their marriages didn't work out. Maybe that's what we should do."

Webb thought what he was saying was evident, but it knifed Dorothy in the heart.

"I can't believe you just said that. Maybe divorce is a solution in your family, Webb, but it never has been in mine. Take me back to the house." Tears streamed down her face. Her anger changed to a feeling of betrayal. She'd held on to hope for a year and a half.

A couple days later, Webb was called back to work in Big Timber. He left Dorothy in Billings with his folks. Nothing more was said about the relationship.

Dorothy became ill. The stress of the visit with Webb took its toll. She'd planned to go back to Dunn Center right after Webb left, but instead came down with a sore throat, headache and abdominal pains. Her initial bout of rheumatic fever as a child left her at risk for subsequent episodes. She was told patients with rheumatic fever could also develop long-lasting heart problems. Dorothy knew all that. It made getting sick even more stressful.

She and LaReta got a ride back to Dunn Center on November 18th. Dorothy still wasn't ready to let Webb go and wrote to tell him so.

November 25, 1936

Dear Daddy,

I guess it is about time I am writing so you will know where your family is and how we are getting along. I was waiting to get some photos of Reta that I had taken the day we left Billings, but they must not have sent them as soon as they were going to. I'll send them next time. They should be good as we got her to smile.

We left Billings Wednesday night. Got to Dix okay. Naomi had to hire a lady to come in to meet us as they broke the Ford down the day before.

Reta slept almost all the way so it wasn't hard traveling with her. I got terribly tired out, but didn't get worse. I am getting quite a lot stronger and eat pretty well but am a long way from well, but I guess I'll make it in time.

I don't s'pose you work Thanksgiving? I am wondering what you will be doing? Mom has to furnish a turkey for church supper so they all plan to go up there. I don't know just what I will do as I probably won't feel like going up there.

I hope you will write to us and let me know what you plan to do. I guess you know how I feel about all this and that we would come to you no matter where you are or under any circumstances if you want us. There will never be any other man in my life. But of course that is entirely up to you as you were the one that was going to walk out on us.

All our love,

Reta & Dorothy

LaReta and Scout
Dunn Center 1937

Webb and his Pontiac
Fall 1937

 19

Silver Service and the Schoolmarm

Dunn Center, North Dakota 1937

By summer, Dorothy, although saddened at the thought, accepted that Webb would never be the husband and father she wanted. But she left the door open just in case he changed his mind. Her health issues continued.

June 28, 1937

Dear Webb,

I just got to wondering where you were and how you were all getting along so thought I'd write a few lines.

The folks are all in church. My younger brother, Aaron, was confirmed today. LaReta and I went too this morning, but Reta doesn't like to go to church any better than her daddy does so I wouldn't take her again tonight.

I am still doctoring my throat. I have to go in twice a week for treatments. I don't know how long I will have to keep going. I only hope that I will be all right in the end. It costs so darn much. I would surely appreciate some money from you. If you can

just help me out now so I can get OK. I have a teaching job for
this fall so I can take care of baby and myself without any more
assistance I hope. I know it is tough on you, but just put yourself
in my place and think what you could do about it.

Of course I am still hoping that you will change your mind
about us someday.

Well I hope you are all well. You might write even if you
can't send any money.
As ever,
Dorothy

By August, Dorothy's sore throat improved, but lack
of money was still a worry.

"What should I do with this silver service?" Dorothy
asked her sister Myra, who was visiting the farm in Dunn
Center. Myra rocked her baby, Kenton, who was sleeping
soundly in spite of the heat. "Webb's mother sent it to me.
It was a wedding gift from a friend of Webb's. I left it in
Billings when LaReta and I came back here because Webb
had said something about it was more his than mine. I
don't want it and will never use it...I don't s'pose."

Myra and Dorothy sat at the big kitchen table chatting.
It was late morning on another hot August day. Two-year-
old LaReta and Myra's three-year-old daughter, Donna,
were playing outside with the Boe's dog, Scout, a German
Shepherd who was just as good at herding kids as he had
been herding cows—when the Boe's still had some.

Dorothy could hear LaReta giggle and the girls
jabbering about who could ride Scout the farthest before
falling off. She glanced out the window to see LaReta,

blonde-haired, blue-eyed and fearless, chasing Scout around the yard. He was having none of it. It was a relief to see LaReta, chubby-cheeked, happy and healthy after her sick spells cutting teeth.

Myra and Randeen lived about 60 miles from Dunn Center in Watford City. They had come for a weekend visit. Randeen was still building trailer houses, but he and Myra made additional money painting grain elevators. That work was becoming scarce because of farms failing all over North Dakota. Today, Randeen was in town working on another trailer house.

Dorothy got up and moved to the stove to pour herself and Myra a cup of coffee. "I know I owe you money for helping me get back and forth to the doctor in Dickinson. Maybe if Webb agreed, I could give you the silver service as one way to repay you. Webb did send a check last week and I can pay part of what I owe you, but I also need to pay some of my doctor bills. I should be able to pay all my bills once I start teaching in another month."

She finished pouring coffee from the pan in which she'd boiled the grounds. "I'll be making about sixty dollars a month, but I would surely like to help pay for Melva to go to Normal School in Ellendale for six weeks. I want her to get a teaching certificate when she turns eighteen so she can support herself." Dorothy also thought, *I don't want my little sister to have to depend on a man to support her.*

"If Webb doesn't want it, *you* should sell it, Dorothy, and maybe get some money."

Dorothy laughed. "Who's going to have any money around here? Times are tough for everyone. If it helps settle my debt with you and it's okay with Randeen, you should have something nice."

Myra smiled and put her hand on her sister's arm. "You deserve nice things, too, Dorothy, but if Webb doesn't want it, then I would love to have the silver service."

"I'll write Webb and find out. If I want nice things, Myra, I'll have to figure out how to get them for myself," Dorothy responded.

Webb sent money the end of August and okayed Dorothy giving the silver service to Myra, but by her third week of teaching in September, Dorothy was again desperate for money. She wasn't sure when she would get her first check from the school board. During the week, Dorothy lived at school where she taught, while LaReta stayed with Dorothy's parents in Dunn Center.

September 27, 1937

Dear Webb,

Here I am starting on my third week of school. I like my school just awfully well but there aren't enough pupils. I only have eight and it isn't enough work to keep me busy.

I don't get a check until the month is up and don't know whether I will get it then or not. If possible at all, I wish you would send me some money right away as I am broke and need some badly. It is so cold already that Reta should have her winter pajamas and underwear and a few other heavy clothes. I have been having a toothache every once in a while and know that I should have a couple teeth pulled but can't until I get some dough. Please try and help us out this time and I will try not to bother you again. LaReta is OK again now. She had a sick spell the first week I was gone and was sick almost all week. I don't see what can be wrong with her. She won't eat anything and has a fever and just wants to lie down and sleeps a lot. I guess I will take her to the clinic and have her examined after a while.

She is so darn cute. It is a shame that you can't see her. She is always talking and writing letters to her daddy. Last week she wrote on a paper and she told ma she was writing to her daddy, so ma told her that her daddy's name was Webb and he lived in Montana. When I came home Friday night she said, "Daddy Webb went to Montana."

She talks all the time and so plain. Everyone remarks about her talking so you can understand everything she says. She always cries when I go and that makes it so much harder for me. She says "Friday night, go to get mommie."

I am wondering if you are still working or what? I haven't heard from any of your folks since the first of August.

Well write once in a while so I'll know that you are alive anyway.

As ever,

Dorothy

As the only teacher in a small rural school, Dorothy was expected to teach and maintain the building. Fortunately, before she started at the school, school board members mowed the tall grass in the yard, cleaned spiders out of the storm cellar, and ordered a load of coal and a barrel of sweeping compound. Wives of school board members freshened the schoolroom and gave Dorothy a large key for the front door.

Dorothy was an experienced teacher. She had taught when she was nineteen, before she went to Oregon to business school and before she married Webb. But in August 1937, she turned 25 and it seemed she was starting all over again.

The schoolhouse was a small clapboard building with a bell hanging near the front door. Dorothy rang the bell promptly at 9 am each morning, at recess during the day and again at 4 pm when school was dismissed.

In the morning, Dorothy would stand at the front door with a smile and a kind word for each student, but her demeanor told students she expected good behavior.

"Welcome, children. Proceed in an orderly fashion, as always." Dorothy's voice was high and clear. "Good morning Ingrid…Marie…Wilhelmina…Rolv…Sig… And so it would go with each student.

They would respond, "Good morning, Mrs. Bateman."

Students marched up three short steps and into the coatroom, one side lined with book shelves, the other with coat hooks. The smell of the coal fired furnace, chalk and the oil-sawdust floor cleaning compound met their nostrils. The large sunny, interior room had a desk at the front for Dorothy. Rows of individual wooden desks sat facing the front, seats attached with decorative wrought iron.

The desks showed evidence of previous students' mischief with initials and hearts carved into the hinged, slanted tops. The pencil well at the top of the desk was dark from students running their pencils back and forth in the trough. They wanted to make their mark on the school, to leave a reminder for future students that they'd been there.

Damage to school property was not something "Mrs. Bateman" encouraged or condoned. She made it clear early in the school year, there would be consequences for such behavior.

Aisle ways ran up the middle and on both sides of the room. Slate blackboards ran along the east and south walls, with posters of the alphabet—upper and lower case—and multiplication tables above. The other walls had large windows, under which were low shelves filled with more books.

With the pull of a string, Dorothy could unfurl a colorful map of the world on the wall. If students knew something about the country their parents had emigrated from, they were asked to find it on the map. Maintaining a link to their homeland was important to families in the community.

Dorothy's eight students ranged in grades from third to eighth. The State Course of Study provided a specific plan for each grade, but to make things easier for her and the students, she combined grades into groups for instructional purposes. Each group studied arithmetic, language arts, reading, spelling and writing appropriate for their ages. Dorothy and the older students helped the younger ones progress.

Eight students was not much of a challenge for Dorothy, but because she stayed at the school in a small apartment during the week, there were other things to keep her busy. She had to keep the furnace burning around the clock with a lot of coal and ashes to shovel during the long cold winter. Older students carried coal from an outside bin into the furnace room to keep the fire going and Dorothy made sure there were corn cobs soaked in kerosene for fire starters, should the furnace go out.

Prior to the students' arrival each day, Dorothy filled a large crock with fresh-pumped water for the children to drink. She also wrote the blackboard assignments ahead of time, positioned artwork, and made sure her lesson plans were ready.

After school, a couple of students stayed to help erase chalk from the blackboards and dust erasers by banging them together outdoors. The floors were swept every afternoon. By hand, Dorothy broadcast a sweeping compound under the heavy desks. She or one of the students would sweep up the oil and sawdust mix and dump it outside. The oil and sawdust combination assured that dirt, mud and manure from the shoes of students who rode from nearby farms was sent back outside where it belonged.

Occasionally, if the weather allowed, she would walk a half mile to the home of one of the school board members, just for company. The evenings were lonely. When she wasn't visiting, it was time to light her oil lantern, eat a light supper, correct the day's papers and write letters to Webb.

He finally responded to her September letter. The thought of his little girl shivering with cold in a North Dakota winter must have been enough to make Webb send money in October. He also sent a picture of himself with a newer car, a Pontiac. He gave Dorothy the option of burning the picture, if she cared to. She didn't burn it, but couldn't resist a poke at Webb when she responded. She underlined the word, "flattering."

November 10, 1937

Dear Webb,

I received the picture, letter and money some time ago. I was so pleased. Thanks a lot. I know I should have written before but please excuse me as I have been so busy.

The picture is good of you but rather <u>flattering</u> don't you think?

You don't need to worry about me burning it. There just isn't anything that can change my feeling for you. If you ever change your mind and want to try over again, we will be here waiting for you. I am not planning on that you know but just hoping.

When I go home on Friday LaReta thinks that I should just play with her all weekend. She will hardly get away from me at all. Mom says she is so good all week too! She sleeps with my youngest sister Vernetta but you couldn't hire her to sleep with anyone but me when I am there.

Last Saturday there was a State Dr. in Halliday to examine preschool children. I took LaReta down to him. He said that she seemed to be OK and he thought her sick spells were from cutting teeth.

I promised her a big doll for Christmas. The other day, my nephew was up home and had his tricycle along. LaReta liked it so well. She wanted one so badly. I asked her which she wanted the doll or the tricycle. She said "Bose (both) of them." You should see her take the catalog and pick out what she wants. She says, "I would like to have <u>red</u> pajamas." Every color is red to *her.*

You said you would like to see Reta so much. Well I guess there is only one way of doing that and that's coming down here. Of course you know you are welcome to come and stay as long as you like… and <u>no strings attached.</u>

Why don't you come down for a few days? Bring your mother along if you wish. I bet she would like to see LaReta too.

Well my light is going dry so will quit. Take care of yourself. I hope that your job lasts all winter. Write.

Love,

Dorothy

20

The Road
March 10, 1939

Blanche and Webb were an hour beyond Miles City, nearing Terry, Montana. At Miles City, Highway 12 became Highway 10, the main route from the West Coast to Minnesota. This was the challenging highway Webb and Ray drove in North Dakota on their way home from working in the circus.

"Good ol' Highway 10," Webb smiled, remembering the detours and the nights in hay lofts along the way. "At least there aren't as many mud holes as there used to be when it was under construction." He took another drink of Jim Beam. Blanche noted the diminished level of liquid left in the bottle.

"Want something to eat, Webb? I packed a lunch and there's coffee in the thermos."

"Nah, I'm fine. Ate a lot at breakfast. Should be good for a while. We'll need to stop in Terry at Four Corners for some gas and maybe take a breather."

It was 9 am. They still had another four hours of driving to get to Dunn Center. Blanche poured coffee into the cup she unscrewed from the top of the thermos. The road still had stretches of wrinkled asphalt from winter

214

freezes so she only filled it half full. Road repairs wouldn't be made until summer. Blanche held her cup with both hands to prepare for the next bump. She'd set the letters aside in the shoebox.

"Did you threaten a divorce in the fall of '36?" Blanche asked. She hadn't known anything about the discussion on the Rims. Maybe Dorothy said something to Dena about the conversation, but she never let on to Blanche.

Webb glanced at Blanche. "I don't recall sayin' that exact thing—then. I think I was just talkin' about what happened with Ray and Walt.

Webb gestured toward Blanche, "You know how it is sometimes when you get mad and say the first thing that comes into your head. That happened a lot when Dorothy and I were together. She had this way of gettin' me so lathered up, I could swallow a horn-toad backwards." Webb tried to make light of the evidence in Dorothy's letters.

Blanche spoke in a soft voice, "It didn't seem to matter what you said, she was still willing to come to you wherever you were to try and make it work."

The liquor Webb had consumed was starting to loosen his resolve to stay strong, get to Dunn Center to the funeral, pay his last respects and get back home without having to think too much more about the past and the future. Blanche wasn't helping. He took another drink.

"I said some things I shouldn't of said. I did some things I shouldn't of done. I didn't mean to hurt Dorothy and then when we were apart…." Tears welled in Webb's eyes. "Things were better. You know what they say,

'Absence makes the heart grow fonder.'"

He swiped his sleeve across his face. "I wrote to Dorothy to say I wanted to see her and LaReta and had good intentions, but somehow they just didn't pan out."

Webb cleared his throat, embarrassed he'd let his sister see him cry. "I'm gonna pull in, Blanche. Gotta get gas and I need a smoke break."

They pulled off the road into a miserable looking gas station at Four Corners. If it hadn't been for the OPEN sign in the window, passersby might have thought it was abandoned. The station was weather worn and dilapidated with one pump out front. There were no other cars. The main part of town was several blocks away.

Wind blew cold from the east when they opened their doors. Webb got busy with the gas pump. Blanche pulled her coat around her and a cold gust of wind flicked the hem of her skirt as she headed for the station door to get the key to the ladies' room. Webb relieved himself where he stood. There was no one around.

When Blanche returned, Webb was already waiting inside the car with the Chevy's motor running. She saw him take another drink before she got in.

Blanche hadn't been back to North Dakota since 1935, when they moved to Billings. She had her own feelings about the trip and Webb's drinking worried her. She grabbed the lapels of her coat to keep the chill from her neck and looked east. The end of the road met the horizon line, flat and low, straight ahead. Slate grey, low-hanging clouds looked like dirty dish water, a sure sign. It started to snow.

She got in and shut the door. "You know I could drive, if you want to get some sleep in the back seat."

"I'll be fine. We got to keep goin'." He reached for the gear shift.

"Wait a minute, Webb." To stop him from shifting, Blanche put her hand on top of his.

"You're my big brother, but you're coming apart and the liquor isn't doing you any favors. Can we just hold up here a little? I'll give you some coffee and something to eat. We need to get to Dunn Center in one piece and back again with your daughter."

Webb exhaled long and deep. "You think we're bringin' LaReta back with us?"

Blanche stared at Webb. "That's why I'm going with you, isn't it? Mamma and I both asked you that question last night at supper, but you didn't answer."

Webb shifted into low and rolled the Chevy to a stop at one corner of the gas station lot. A truck had pulled in behind them. He put the stick shift in neutral again and left the motor running.

"I can't, Blanche. I can't do this. I don't know how to be a father. LaReta doesn't know me. You know it would be you and Ma lookin' after her, not me. I have to get another job and who the hell knows where that will be." He crossed his forearms on top of the steering wheel and rested his forehead.

"Webb, you have a choice about your daughter." Blanche's words were forceful, but her chin began to quiver. She laced her fingers together in her lap and looked at the floor boards. Her words came in spurts. "I didn't have a choice, Webb. I had to give up my son. He's out there somewhere and I'll never know him. I don't know how to find him. I don't know his name. I've never seen him smile. I've never heard him say 'mommy.'" Tears spilled down Blanche's face.

Silence enveloped them except for the whine of the wind blowing around gaps in the doors and the unsteady throb of the car's motor. Blanche squared her shoulders and turned toward Webb. "You have a daughter who knows she has a daddy. She writes to you. She said, 'My daddy is in Montana.' Dorothy talked to her about you and asked you over and over to come see them. She wanted you to have a relationship with LaReta." Blanche took a handkerchief from her pocket and dabbed her eyes. "We can figure a way to make this work, Webb. LaReta just lost her mommy. You want her to lose her daddy, too?"

Webb returned her gaze. His eyes were red, his face twisted in pain and self-doubt. His words were flat. "It's not that I don't want to…and I even think Dorothy wants me to, but look at me…"

The strong, self-confident man Blanche knew disappeared in front of her. She had seen Webb drink too much before, but he was known as a happy drunk, dancing and singing, even more self-assured than when he was sober. This wasn't the man beside her now. Webb was wallowing in self-pity, shame and regret.

Blanche unwrapped and handed a sandwich to Webb. He took it. She poured him a cup of coffee, now cold. While he ate, Blanche opened her door and poured the rest of the whiskey out of the bottle. It made a large dark circle beside the Chevy devouring what snow there was on the ground. Webb didn't object. He looked ragged and beaten.

They were quiet while he finished eating. He asked for another cup of coffee and then stepped out of the Chevy. The clouds were spitting more snow and the temperature was still above freezing, but Webb wasn't feeling much of anything.

He shook himself to get control of the strange man he'd shown his sister. *Who is that guy anyway? Not someone I want to admit to.* He lit a cigarette, took a long puff and got back in the car.

"Listen Webb, you need to sleep off the whiskey. I can drive to Glendive and you can take over after that when we head into the Badlands," Blanche suggested.

Webb nodded. He got out, flicked away his unfinished cigarette, opened the back door, pushed everything to the floor and folded himself onto the bench seat using his satchel as a pillow. Blanche climbed in the driver's side, shifted into low and headed northeast on the straight-as-a-stick road toward Glendive. There were black clouds in the distance while Webb's whiskey-induced sleep led him to his own dark place.

Webb floated above two horses trudging around a merry-go-round platform. He could see himself on the ground with three other people. The auger in the middle of the merry-go-round-like contraption dug out a three-foot hole. Ten feet, twenty feet...seventy feet, ninety feet, the auger descended into the earth. The muffled sound of metal scraping rock told Webb the well digging operation had come to a standstill. The auger hit rock instead of water. Dorothy stood twenty feet away on the other side of the platform holding LaReta's hand. A metal, arched sign beyond them read, Dunn Center Cemetery. There was a small cross on top of the arch.

What the hell are Dorothy and LaReta doin' here anyway? Well diggin' is dangerous, no place for them. I'm crazy as hell to be here myself. We're in a cemetery and I'm supposed to go down that damn hole and drill rock for a dynamite shot?

The other man motioned Webb to get roped-up so he could let him down the hole with a winch. Webb thought the man looked like an old boss he'd had, but maybe he looked more like his dad, or was it August Johnson?

I'm crazy workin' for this guy, but we gotta hit water. I need the money. Seems like I always need money.

One moment Webb was floating in the clouds and the next he felt himself inching toward hell with his back against one wall and his bent knees forced against the other. Dirt crumbled with every move. He could feel silt sift down on him from the side walls above.

Shit! This whole shaft could cave in on me. What the hell am I doin' here?

A burning lantern on a rope hung above him. *If that lantern goes out, he better get me air or get me outta here!*

Webb was already gasping. His body blocked most of the light from the lantern hanging just above him when he bent over to place the chisel between his legs. He struck it with his hammer and the sound echoed in the hole. More strikes resulted in a small hole in the wall. With each contact between hammer and chisel, the hole in the wall deepened and the shaft above Webb rained more dirt. He was sweating and breathing hard even though it was cold. The lantern went out. There wasn't enough oxygen to keep it lit.

"Goddamn it! I need air!" Webb felt woozy. He was going to pass out in that well and no one would get him out. *I'm down here and Dorothy's up there with LaReta.*

Webb straightened his body and put his feet on the rock he hoped to blast. He tipped his head back against the wall. Perspiration trickled into his eyes. *I just helped dig a hole that could be my grave. That's the way it should be... 'cuz of the way I treated her.*

Lengths of inner tube joined together appeared in front of him. A black smith bellows pumped air into the shaft. Webb could breathe better, but he couldn't see a thing. Webb had to finish the job in total darkness, just feeling his way.

In darkness again and, this time, in a cemetery. There's payback. Dammit! I'm not ready. I gotta see some light. When I'm outta this hole, I quit, money or no money. Things are gonna change.

The winch was cranked and Webb brought to the surface. "You're gonna get me killed," Webb yelled at the man in his dream.

He watched himself walk toward the cemetery gate. Dorothy and LaReta stood nearby. As Webb approached, Dorothy smiled and held out LaReta's hand to him.

The Badlands

Glendive was in the rearview mirror. Webb and Blanche were headed into the Badlands of eastern Montana. Webb was behind the wheel again.

221

"Thanks for the break, Blanche. I needed it."

"Hope you're feeling better."

"Had the strangest dreams the last two days." Webb glanced at Blanche. "Dorothy was in both of them even though they were about work I did in North Dakota when I was seventeen and eighteen. Remember when I worked in the mine in New Salem and later for Wilbur Sharff digging wells? You were about eleven years old."

Now that Webb was driving, Blanche had the shoebox with Dorothy's letters in her lap once again. "I remember you were always off working someplace. I didn't always know where or what you were doing."

Webb ran his fingers through his hair. "These dreams had me in the dark in the mine and in a well at the cemetery. All I could think about was gettin' out."

"They say dreams mean something, if you can figure out what it is." Blanche gave Webb a sideways glance.

Webb was staring straight down the road. "Do you think when people die, they come back in dreams?" Webb was thinking out loud more than looking for an answer. "If they do, I think I'm startin' to get the message."

Blanche smiled and went back to reading Dorothy's letters.

AUCTION

At my place on Sec. 4-144-94, two and 1-2 miles south and one mile east of Dunn Center on

Tuesday, Apr. 5

The following described property:

Livestock

3 head of Horses, ages 8 to 9
4 Cows from 3 to 9 years
4 Calves from 6 mos, to 1 year.

Farm Machinery, Etc.

1 wagon with box.
1 wagon with rack.
1 two-horse cultivator
1 gang plow.
1 sulky plow.
1 four-section steel drag with cast

1 ten-foot drill
1 five-foot McCormick mower
1 ten-foot Deering binder
1 ten-foot disc
1 Emerson fanning mill
1 stock saddle
1 spring wagon
1 ten-foot McCormick rake
1 bob sled
4 sets of harness

Poultry

2 turkey hens
1 gobbler

24 chickens

Household Goods

1 cupboard
1 Home Comfort range
1 sewing machine
3 dressers
1 gas stove
1 dining room table
4 beds
Chairs
Dishes

Other Articles too numerous to list

Terms: C A S H

Sale Starts at 10 o'clock. Lunch will be Served at Noon by Group of Lutheran Ladies

ED BOE, Owner

ABE PORTER, Auctioneer   RANDEEN HOOVESTOL, Clerk

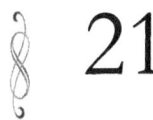

21

It's All Over

Dunn Center, North Dakota 1938

Dorothy's folks were gone. Blanche thought Dorothy's next letter to Webb only skimmed the surface of emotions they must have felt. The Depression and drought had defeated Ed and Laura's efforts to stay on the land they had worked and loved for over 30 years.

April 13, 1938

Dear Webb,

Well, it's all over, the folks are gone. They sold everything and left Sunday nite. S'pose they get to Oregon sometime this fore noon. Ma's brother, Will, has them at his ranch in Scappose until they find their own place. My youngest brother, Aaron 15, and sister, Vernetta 12, will stay here till the end of school. Miland was old enough to ride the rails to Oregon and Melva is staying here to get her teaching certificate.

Such a time as we did have all last week. Just one continual round of going. Tuesday was the sale. I went over after school Wed. nite. They hired the hall and gave a dance and card party in honor of the folks. Thursday the family went to Ada's, Friday nite to Folklers, etc. until the last minute before they left.

Myra and Randeen came down from Watford City and stayed until Thursday. It was pretty tough to say goodbye and break up the home after living here for 32 years. It was hardest for Myra and Naomi as it is hard telling when they will ever see the folks again. They are staying here with their families as they can still make a living.

I am trying to get a job here and if I can LaReta and I won't go west at all. Everyone says there just isn't any work of any kind to be had out there. So I am rather scared out as I just have to have a job.

Naomi has LaReta here while I finish up teaching. I don't know just how she will stand it as she hasn't gotten very strong yet after the baby came. There are about 5 other people around here that offered to keep her for me so guess she won't want for a home. Everyone makes so much over her. Mrs. Pelton was half angry at us for not letting her have LaReta during the week.

We had to give Reta's kitty away and sold some of her things on the sale (her rocker, table, etc). I kept her tricycle tho' and will take it along with us. I will have Aaron and Vernetta with me if I do go west. If it's O.K. with all of you we can stop over there. I thought just one day as there are so many of you. I guess your mother wouldn't want to bother with us any longer.

I finally got my new glasses. Everyone says it makes me look like a new person. I wish you all a Happy Easter. Take good care of yourself and here's hoping you find a job soon. Write.
Lovingly,
Dorothy

Dorothy stayed at school during the week, but since

the Boes had moved to Oregon earlier in the month, she and LaReta lived with her younger sister, Naomi, and brother-in-law, Paul, in Dunn Center. Dorothy helped pay the rent.

Dorothy and Naomi were sisters, but they were also best friends and Naomi would have figured out a way to let them stay, even if Dorothy couldn't pay.

Naomi picked Dorothy up from school on Friday evening. LaReta was always along, whether it was Naomi or her husband Paul driving to and from the rural school house on Sunday and Friday nights.

"Give mommy a kiss and a hug, Reta." LaReta ran to throw her arms around Dorothy's neck. Dorothy bent down to scoop up her daughter and give her a squeeze. The two clung to each other in the car all the way back to Dunn Center.

"Who's taking care of the baby?" Dorothy asked. LaReta snuggled closer to her mommy.

"Paul is getting practice changing Bill's diapers. It's good for him." The girls laughed at the thought of Paul struggling with wiggling, two-month-old baby Bill.

"And I need a little break, even if it's just an hour or so."

"I do appreciate you taking care of Reta, Naomi. I know it's not easy with a new baby and Paul trying to figure out how to make ends meet."

Naomi took her eyes from the road for a moment and smiled at her sister. "You know, Dorothy, LaReta is a much better girl when you're at school. She does what we ask and gets me things for the baby. We just don't have any trouble with her."

Dorothy gave LaReta another squeeze. "I know I spoil her. I can't help but baby her along when we're together on weekends. I miss her so much during the week and we have so little time together."

"What are you going to do for a job when school is out?" Naomi asked.

Dorohty looked out the car window. "I've been trying to get a job teaching night school in the C.C.C. camp out of Watford City. They wrote that I would have to get on with the W.P.A. You know I went to Killdeer to find out about getting on with the W.P.A, but guess I can't do that, either. They said as long as Webb and I aren't divorced, I couldn't get on. They did take my application and said they would see about it. I'm hoping to hear soon."

Operated from 1933 to 1942, the Civilian Conservation Corps (C.C.C.) was a public works relief program for unemployed, unmarried men as part of Franklin Roosevelt's New Deal. It provided unskilled manual labor jobs related to conservation and development of natural resources on rural land owned by federal, state and local governments. The program provided men between the ages of 17 and 28 with shelter, clothing, and food, along with a small wage of thirty dollars a month. Twenty-five dollars had to be sent home to the men's families. They sometimes hired women as teachers, but it wasn't surprising the agency was reluctant to hire Dorothy. She was still a married woman.

The Work Projects Administration (W.P.A.), another New Deal agency, employed millions of people, most of them unskilled men, to carry out public works projects, including the construction of public buildings and roads.

"I heard from Mother that when Miland got to Oregon, he got a part-time job with the W.P.A. He's doing maintenance on trails and benches at Mount Hood," Naomi informed Dorothy.

"Well, at least someone in the family is getting government help. I just hope one of those agencies will help me find something."

They pulled up in front of the house. Naomi shut off the motor. "What do you hear from Webb?"

"Last time he wrote, said he's out of work again and living with his folks in Billings. He had a nice car that he bought last year, but couldn't make payments, so they took it back. He wants to talk about us, so I'm going to try to get to Billings in a few weeks. We need to get together face to face. I don't know what's going to happen."

The end of May, Dorothy wrote to Webb she was "down in the dumps" because she received a letter from the W.P.A.—no job in Killdeer. "I'll tell you about it when I see you," she said. Plans were still in the works to go to Billings. At the same time, living arrangements for Dorothy and LaReta changed again.

Naomi, Paul and the baby moved into one of the trailer houses Paul and Randeen had built and moved the family to Oregon. Dorothy wrote to Webb about it.

May 26, 1938

Dear Webb,

We are all to go to Watford City and spend a week with Myra and Randeen. Then we plan to come west. My youngest brother and sister, Aaron and Vernetta, will go through to Oregon by train and Reta and I will stop off in Billings for a few days.

I hadn't planned to go to Oregon because I thought I had a job. Now I just don't know what to do for a home for myself and Reta. If I could just find anything to pull us through for a few months we would be O.K.

Here's hoping you make good at your new job. If you want to write us send it to Watford City in care of Randeen next week. I'll write again and let you know just when we are coming.

As ever,

Dorothy

LaReta and Webb
1938

22

Oregon?

Billings, Montana 1938

The first week in June, Dorothy, LaReta and two of Dorothy's younger siblings travelled to Billings. When they arrived, Dorothy made arrangements for Aaron and Vernetta go on to Oregon by train. The Bateman's made a fuss over LaReta and they all spent time getting reacquainted. Vivian and Blanche were still living at home and Ray came for supper Sunday afternoon. It was a full house.

Tuesday evening after the meal, Webb pulled Dorothy aside and asked her to come and sit on the front porch. "I know things didn't go well for us the last time we were together. I want to try to make it up to you. Maybe you and Ma could go shoppin' for a dress for you tomorrow and you could find somethin' for LaReta too. I'll pick up the tab. This local delivery job I got drivin' truck has given me a few extra bucks. Whaddaya' say?"

"I'd like that, Webb. We haven't had something new for a long time. Sure you can afford it?"

"Let me worry about that. You go and pick out something nice," Webb responded giving her hand a squeeze.

Dorothy wasn't sure where all this was leading. Was Webb willing to try the relationship again and provide a home for the three of them or was something else going on? She wasn't sure. When Webb left to buy cigarettes, Dorothy tried to get clues from Dena.

"Dena, thanks for the nice presents for LaReta. You can tell she just loves everyone so much. You've made us feel at home."

"We've missed you and having little Reta around. Blanche talks about her all the time." Dena wiped her hands on her apron. She was cleaning up the kitchen after supper. Dorothy had come in to help and Vivian and Blanche went back into the living room to play with LaReta. The two women were alone for a few minutes.

"Dena, I'm worried that LaReta didn't make up with Webb right away. She knows she has a daddy, but I don't think she remembers Webb from last fall. She won't kiss him or anything and I think it hurt him. Now he's not paying much attention to her."

"Well, what could he expect?" Dena asked flatly. "How could she remember him? She won't be three for another two months." Dena stacked a plate in the dish drainer on the counter. "They just need time together." Dorothy wiped the dish dry and put it in the cupboard.

"Has Webb said anything to you about his plans for us? I know I should be asking him…and I will, but thought maybe I should be prepared, if you have some ideas about what he's thinking."

Dorothy twisted the dish towel. "I'm not sure what Reta and I are going to do. I don't have a job yet in North

Dakota and haven't decided if I should go to Oregon either. I don't know about Webb and me."

Before Dena could respond, Webb strode into the kitchen with a smile on his face and a lit cigarette. "You gals goin' shoppin' tomorrow?"

Before they could answer, he continued. "Some friends want to go for a ride downtown tonight and it looks like the girls are havin' fun with LaReta in the livin' room, so you want to go, Dorothy?"

They left to spend the evening with friends at the Stockman's Bar and his dad's Town Talk Billiards. That night, there was no mention of the relationship—once again.

Richard, Augusta, Arlis, and James Bailey
LaReta
1938

23

The Road

March 10, 1939

Webb thoughts about the previous summer faded and he focused on the landscape in front of him. The rugged terrain was eerie, strange and yet, beautiful. The sandstone outcroppings, sculpted grain by grain by wind and rain, were miniature and giant toadstools, castles, balancing rocks, and sentinel-like spires.

The formations provided a break in the monotony of low-lying, furrowed hills, covered in white and shaded by a formidable grey sky overhead. The snow wouldn't keep them from getting to Dunn Center, yet. The road was manageable, but desolate.

Highway 10 from Glendive to Dickinson snaked eastward through the Badlands and small, quiet towns: Wilbaux, Yates, Beach, Sentinel Butte, spots on the side of the road. The landscape, a desert created over thousands of years by the destruction of vegetation, water runoff and erosion, was now covered by a shifting blanket of snow.

Webb looked at Blanche with her head down still reading Dorothy's letters. She was oblivious to the scenery. There was something Webb had to tell her, but he wasn't sure how to bring it up.

"Are you gettin' the answers you're lookin' for?" Webb broke the silence.

Blanche placed an index finger on a sentence in one of the letters and looked up. "No, not all of them. After her time with you in Billings last June, I thought I would find out something I was wondering about, but Dorothy didn't say, so I'm still reading." She paused. "But there's a lot here I didn't know about. Dorothy didn't write details in the letters she sent to Mamma. Maybe she thought you would fill us in." Blanche glanced at Webb to see if he would defend against her remark.

"It's been a while since I read the letters, Blanche. I don't remember all the details, either," Webb said. He seemed preoccupied. Blanche thought maybe he was concentrating on the road. It was snowing harder and sticking.

"You know she went back to North Dakota and got another teaching job last year near Emerson, north of Gladstone. She worried about finding the right place for LaReta, if teaching required her to be gone all week. Blanche thumbed back a couple letters and read out loud to Webb:

"I wonder how LaReta is going to do now. I am afraid I'll get in some place where they won't be good to her. She is so darn spoiled and mean that I can't do anything with her. It sure is tough to be kicked around from one place to another. The poor kid never has anything of her own and always has to give up everything. I think that makes her worse than ever. I get so darn disgusted. I think what is the use to try to do anything."

"But she did find a boarding house for herself and LaReta in Gladstone." Blanche lowered the letter into her lap. "It was lucky Dorothy found the Bailey's boarding house. Mrs. Bailey watched LaReta during the day, while Dorothy was at school. They even loaned her one of their horses, Sweetheart, to ride to school during the week."

Webb added, "It did sound like a good setup for them, from what she wrote. I remember Dorothy said she and LaReta were gaining weight. Dorothy seemed pretty happy there. Her letters may not have mentioned it, but when I moved to Nebraska in November, I did start sending her some money again." Webb felt he should set the record straight about the financial support he *did* provide for Dorothy and LaReta.

Blanche, ever one to correct people when she felt a statement didn't quite hit the mark, added, "Dorothy also mentioned she was glad she didn't have to depend on your checks to support them."

She moved on to another letter.

"I didn't know about the grasshoppers. Dorothy wrote that she and Myra drove out by their parent's homestead and the 'hoppers cleaned it all up.' She was glad her parents weren't there to be disappointed all over again. Guess the vegetation was just coming back from what happened during the dust storms and then the grasshoppers ate everything. That's so sad. But you're right, Dorothy did sound happier in her letters. Do you remember about the finger waves?" Blanche asked.

"Read it to me," Webb prompted and Blanch

continued:

>*"We all went to Dunn Center Sat. Mrs. Bailey and I and*
>*Reta got finger waves. Nina fixed LaReta's too. Was she ever*
>*proud. She sat under the dryer with a net on so big. The next*
>*morning, she said, 'I am going to town and get a finger wave every*
>*day.'"*

Webb and Blanche laughed. "She sounds like quite the kid. I can't believe she'll be four in August," Webb chuckled.

"In November, Dorothy wrote about the snow suit, stocking cap, snow shoes and lamb skin mittens she bought to wear while she was riding back and forth to school. She got a snow suit for LaReta, too. Said she took some pictures of them in the suits. Did she send them to you?"

"Nope. Didn't get em."

"A couple of her letters in December and January mentioned moving to Oregon after school was out in the spring. She said Naomi and Paul had moved to Oregon in the fall and that before they headed west, her folks wanted LaReta to come to Oregon with them. Dorothy said her folks 'wanted her so bad.' I'm sure they still do..." Blanche's voice faded and she went back to reading the last few letters.

Miles slipped by.

"There are missing pieces, Webb. What did Arlis mean to Dorothy? Her letters to you mention him a lot. I know he's the oldest son of the Bailey's, about a year younger than Dorothy, and was living with his parents where

Dorothy was boarding. Dorothy talks about going to dances and shows together. Arlis loaned her his C.C.C. coat to wear over her snow suit, he gave her a manicure set for Christmas, and they were out on New Year's Eve together. Remember? Dorothy wrote:

> *"Arlis decided to stay home this winter, instead of working some other place. I go with him all the time. He is such a crazy kid we have such a lot of fun. We go to a dance about every week. To Dickinson nearly every Saturday and generally a show Sunday. So time just flies by."*

Blanche waved the letter at Webb. "I don't understand, Webb. You two were still married weren't you? Why is she dating another man and telling you about him? And she still called you 'Honey' in her February 1st letter, the one where she told you that LaReta got whooping cough from her cousin."

Webb smiled. There was a lot Blanche didn't know.

They crossed a bridge over the Little Missouri River. Medora, North Dakota was within sight, but Dunn Center was still a couple hours away and it was snowing harder. Webb pulled into Medora's roadside gas station. He put the car in neutral, shut off the motor, set the hand brake and glanced at his wrist watch. They were going to be late to the funeral, unless the weather got better and he knew he couldn't push the Chevy much harder.

Webb also knew Blanche wouldn't let up until he told her what she wanted to know, but decided to keep his sister in the dark a little longer. He changed the subject and proceeded to give Blanche a history lesson. "You know what Medora's claim to fame is, Blanche?"

"Is it important for me to know?"

"No, but in case you ever need to know…" Webb grinned at Blanche, "This place was visited by President Theodore Roosevelt, good ol' Teddy, in the early part of the century. He came on a train and claimed that the entire population of the Badlands, down to the smallest baby gathered to meet him, and that they all became good friends even though he was just here an hour or two. According to him, he shook hands with every one of them. But that wouldn't of been too hard since there's barely a hundred people in this town now. The same year, a local hotel even changed its name to the Rough Riders' Hotel." Webb grinned. "So what do you think of that?"

"You were right. I didn't need to know." Blanche returned his smile. She buttoned her coat and got out of the Chevy. Webb grabbed an overcoat from the back seat, put it on, and settled the fedora on his head. He gave the brim a two fingered tug to keep snow out of his face and headed for the gas pump.

Blanche rounded the front of the car and shouted to Webb through snow flurries, "When we're done here, you have some explaining to do. No more history lessons." She walked toward the gas station and then turned back around to shout, "Unless they're about you."

They headed east toward Dickinson, North Dakota. Webb had bought a couple snacks and a refill for the thermos at the gas station in Medora. Snow was still falling, but not as much as before. They could see dry patches of highway. Blanche was not about to let her questions go unanswered. "Okay, Webb, so I asked whether you and Dorothy were still married before she died or did you get a divorce and not tell anyone?" Webb took a deep breath and leaned toward the steering wheel as though he was bending into a headwind.

He began the story about the evening nine months before in Billings, when Dorothy surprised him.

Dorothy, Webb and LaReta
1938

24

Time to Let Go
Billings, Montana 1938

On Thursday evening, another balmy June night, Webb and Dorothy sat in separate wicker chairs on the front porch of the Bateman's home. They had been on the go ever since Dorothy and LaReta arrived the Saturday before. Dorothy sent Aaron and Vernetta by train to Oregon to join their parents During their goodbyes, Dorothy shed many tears. She had no idea when or if she would see them again.

Tonight, LaReta was in bed and the rest of the family was inside. Since Dorothy and LaReta arrived, sleeping arrangements dictated that Dorothy share a bed with LaReta, not Webb. He was bunking with Ray in the back of his radio repair shop. This evening was the first time the two of them had been alone long enough for an intimate conversation.

"Thank you again for paying for the clothes yesterday when Dena and I went shopping. It's so nice to have something new once in a while."

"I'm glad you had fun, Dorothy. We had a good time this week. Thought maybe we could go downtown again tomorrow night after I get back from a local delivery run.

Friday nights there's plenty of action in town."

"Webb, we need to talk about what we're going to do…what I'm going to do." Dorothy's voice was low and steady. Her direct gaze caught Webb off guard.

This was the conversation she knew had to happen. Even though she had given it a lot of thought, her heart was racing.

"Dorothy, I'll do what I can and send money when I can, but as soon as I get a construction job again, I'll be on the move. That hasn't changed, so…"

Dorothy interrupted him. "It's okay, Webb. You know how I feel about you. That won't change any time soon, but I have to do what's best for me and for Reta." Dorothy gripped the arm rests of the wicker chair, feeling roughness against her palms.

"I've learned something about myself, Webb. I found out this past year I can take care of LaReta and I don't have to depend on you." Dorothy smiled and reached for Webb's hand. She gave it a squeeze. "That doesn't mean you shouldn't send us money."

"I know, Dorothy." Webb squeezed back. "I know."

Dorothy withdrew her hand. "I still don't have a job for this fall. I may go to work for Paul, if he and Naomi open their store in Dunn Center. That would be great for LaReta because she could stay with people she knows during the day and I wouldn't have to be away from her. But if that doesn't work out, I'll try to get another teaching position."

Dorothy was nervous, not because she thought Webb would object to her words, but because she was making a decision about their relationship. She was a strong woman in so many ways, but she had been taught to be dependent on the man in her life. That was about to change.

"I have to tell you something." Dorothy cleared her throat. She had an empty feeling in the pit of her stomach.

"I've decided we need to separate for good and get a divorce."

She took a quick breath and continued before she changed her mind. "It doesn't make sense staying married when we can't be together. It may even be better for me because I could get a job with the W.P.A. or the C.C.C." Dorothy looked at Webb with tears in her eyes and a pained expression.

"This is not what I wanted, Webb, but it's the deal life handed me and I guess I need to figure out how to make the best of it."

Webb didn't know what to say. He stared at her as she got up and walked back into the house. He hadn't expected Dorothy to be the one to decide what would become of their marriage.

The following Saturday, Dorothy and LaReta caught a ride back to North Dakota. She'd made up her mind to let go.

The Road

"So, Dorothy was the one who decided the two of you should call it quits?" Blanche asked after Webb told her the story. "Did you get a divorce and not tell anyone?"

"We did decide that's what we would do, if it would help Dorothy. But she got the job teaching and wrote about going to Oregon, so there didn't seem to be a rush. We knew it would happen in time," Webb explained.

"From what she wrote, it sounded like she was falling for Arlis. They were sure having a good time. And then he went to Oregon to look for work just before she had her accident. Maybe they thought they would get together out there." Blanche paused and shook her head. "I can't imagine how he must have felt when he found out Dorothy died and he wasn't there. It's enough to make me cry all over again. Boy…life did give her a kick in the pants, like she said in her letter. Will Arlis be at the funeral?"

"I don't know, Blanche. I talked to Mrs. Bailey on the phone from Ogallala. Dorothy had given me their number because that's where they were staying. Mrs. Bailey said she was at the hospital last Saturday, with her son Richard, when Ed and Laura Boe arrived from Oregon. She didn't say anything about Arlis.

"From what she said, I guess Myra brought LaReta to the hospital to see Dorothy on Sunday. LaReta wanted her mother's food table tray because she thought it was her size." Webb smiled at the thought, but grew serious again, staring straight ahead at the endless road. "I'll have to make sure she gets one."

He reached for the cup of coffee Blanche poured for him. "At least LaReta got to see her mother before she passed, but I'm sure she doesn't understand what happened."

Blanche glanced at Webb and wanted to ask again what he was going to do about LaReta, but decided not to. Webb didn't need extra pressure from her right now.

"Mrs. Bailey said Dorothy died at 9:40 pm Tuesday night." Webb took a drink of coffee and exhaled slowly. "Seems like a long time ago now, but it's only been three days."

"Was anyone with her when she passed?" Blanche asked.

"According to Mrs. Bailey, Dorothy was gettin' ready to leave the hospital the day she died. She was waitin' for someone to take her to the Bailey's when she had another stroke and collapsed. She died later that night. Her parents were with her and so was her older brother, Laurel, and two of her sisters, Myra and Melva. I'm sure they're all still in shock. It's not real for me, either." Webb shook his head in disbelief. "I keep thinkin', what if we'd been together? Would it have been different? Would she still be alive?"

They were silent for a few minutes and then Blanche commented, "She seemed so young to have a stroke."

"I'm not a doctor, but I know she had rheumatic fever as a child and she told me one time that could lead to heart trouble. And then when she fell off Sweetheart the end of February on her way home from school, Mrs. Bailey said she landed on her head and shoulders, suffered a concussion and laid there in the cold and snow for a long time before Richard found her." Webb paused. "It makes me angry and sad all at the same time." Webb took another drink of coffee.

"Mrs. Bailey said it took time for them to fetch a doctor and he wouldn't move her 'til a relative came. She was even paralyzed for a while, couldn't talk or walk." Webb choked up. "I can't imagine how she must have felt bein' like that and then it took Laurel time to get there. He lives in Halliday." Webb pounded his fist on the steering wheel. "Damn! Maybe if I'd been there…" Webb focused on the road.

"Webb, there wasn't anything you could have done. Even if you'd been there, it may not have made any difference," Blanche said.

Webb took his eye off the road and looked at Blanche. "We'll never know, will we?" He was silent for a few more miles.

"Anyway, once Laurel got there, they moved Dorothy to the hospital. Then she had those horrible headaches. Maybe the doctor shouldn't of had her up and walking around so soon. Guess there were too many strikes against her to make it. Sure doesn't mean she didn't deserve to live as long a life as anybody else. She had a child to raise."

The snow let up, but the landscape was as forlorn as before. The sky set the tone for the funeral. Grey, sad, heavy and grieving. They drank the strong coffee in silence, each absorbed in thought. It was noon and they still had sixty miles to go at 45 miles an hour. "Do you think we'll make it on time?" Blanche asked.

"Doin' my best, but we might be a little late," Webb responded. There was still something he had to tell Blanche before they got to their destination.

"Do you remember Julia?" Webb asked.

It wasn't a question Blanche expected. "Julia? The woman you brought to the house a couple times last fall before you left for Nebraska? That Julia? I thought she was just another one of your dates."

"Yes. That Julia. I'll tell you her story and then there's something else I want you to know before we get to Dunn Center."

John Skates, Julia Skates Whitney, Ina Skates and
Raymond Whitney

 # 25

The Other Woman

Billings, Montana 1938

Ray took Julia to the Windmill Club on First Avenue South in downtown Billings for an evening of dancing and fun. It was mid-August and their second date. Webb spied the couple as soon as they came in. It didn't take long for him to cut in on his brother and stake out territory, soon after Ray and Julia started dancing.

At the end of his first dance with Julia, Webb boasted, "Sorry Ray, she's my gal now. You're outta luck. Done missed the boat. One dance with me and she knows which Bateman brother's she's goin' home with tonight." Webb had a playful grin on his face and an arm around Julia's waist.

Ray shot back, but with a smile, "Wait a minute, Webb. Julia might have something to say about that."

Julia was grinning ear to ear. "I may not want to see either one of you Batemans after tonight," she joked. Getting attention from two handsome brothers was making her happier than she'd been in a long time. It had been all work and no play for the last six months. "Who wants to dance again?"

Average in height, with a slight build and a slim waist, Julia had short, soft, and wavey, dark hair. She wore the typical wire rimmed glasses everyone wore. She wasn't quick to smile, self-conscious about her teeth, but tonight with Webb was an exception. She couldn't stop smiling. When she did, her girlish dimples had Webb holding her even closer. In many ways, Julia reminded Webb of Dorothy. He was drawn to a particular type of woman.

He grabbed Julia's hand and pulled her onto the dance floor. Her skirt flared as Webb whirled her around the room. Ray turned back to the bar and ordered another drink—for himself. It was one of many that evening. Webb moved in and took over. It didn't seem to upset Ray. He easily found other female company for the evening. Whiskey and women kept him occupied the rest of the night.

Webb was a wonderful dancer. He took big, swirling steps. His lead was firm, but gentle and he sang in Julia's ear the words to almost every song. Charming and funny, Webb made a definite impression on her.

"So you're still married?" Webb asked Julia when he took her home after midnight. "Ray said something about it." Webb wasn't ready to tell Julia his story. He'd wait to see if this went anywhere.

"I'm separated. The divorce is supposed to be final the end of September. My seven-year-old son, Ray, and I are living with my parents right now and have been for about six months." As she talked, Julia focused on her hands; hands that had already seen years of hard work. They were clasped in her lap.

"So you have another Ray in your life," Webb said with a grin, "but your separation is nothing to be ashamed of. Sometimes things don't work out." Webb spoke from experience.

"I know I shouldn't be, but it's something I never thought would happen when we married eight years ago. I'm the youngest of eight kids. My five brothers and twin sisters are all still married."

"Maybe it's not my business, but what happened?" Webb was interested in Julia and had been from the minute he laid eyes on her.

Julia smiled. "It's late, Webb. I need to get home and get some sleep. My son doesn't sleep in and that means I can't either. My folks watch him for me before and after school and other times, but I don't want to trouble them any more than I have."

"Can I see you again?" Webb asked and reached for her hand. "I'm driving truck local now and have at least one day off. We could 'trip the light fantastic,' if you want. We seem to be pretty good dance partners."

Julia grinned at the man who enjoyed time on the town. "I'm working all week, so I'm pretty worn out come Friday, Webb, but a Saturday night might work. I have to check with the folks though, about watching Ray." Julia gave Webb a big smile, but pulled her hand away and got out of the car before Webb could make a move.

Webb thought a lot about Julia from the time she closed his car door. He didn't want to seem too eager, so he'd waited until Wednesday evening to call her about the date. When she answered the phone, she was breathy and upset. "Oh my gosh, Webb, you won't believe what happened to Mom and Dad. They could have been killed!"

"What are you talkin' about? Are you okay? What happened?"

"Mom and Dad run a grocery store, you know, and we all live here. Well, this morning there was a robbery!" Julia paused long enough to correct herself. "Well, a guy tried to rob Mom, but she wouldn't give him the money. They told me about it when I got home from work. It could have been so bad, Webb. They're pretty calm about the whole thing. The police were here. Lots of people were talked to, but I can hardly breath, thinking about it. I was at work and Ray was in school, but what if …."

"Calm down. I'll be right over."

By the time Webb got to the Skates Grocery Store, Julia was calmer. They sat on the back steps as she told Webb what happened. "The folks work so hard to make ends meet running this grocery store. This guy came in and stuck a gun right in Mom's face, told her to open the till and give him all the money."

Julia chuckled and Webb asked what was so funny. "He didn't know my mom. She holds on to what's hers and she and dad need that money. Mom grabbed his arm and yelled for Dad. He was sitting in the living room reading the paper. When Dad came out with the shotgun, the fella hightailed it. Some neighbor kids said he drove away in a black, muddy sedan with Montana license plates, but no one got the number. Could have been fifty vehicles with that description, but they actually caught a guy and think he's the culprit. A newspaper reporter was even here getting the story. Now Mom has to go identify the robber and everything."

Webb was impressed, by Ina and John Skates story of bravery and by Julia. He saw how much she cared about her family. It was a trait she shared with Dorothy, but there was something different about Julia. He wasn't as hesitant about his feelings for her, as he had been with Dorothy. She was fun, but serious, supportive but not demanding. He appreciated her caution in their relationship; it increased his interest.

Saturday evenings on the town became a regular thing for Webb and Julia. Her parents were happy to watch Ray. They were glad she had some fun for a change. Her life hadn't been easy. At age sixteen, she left school to help care for her dad who was then ill. She was the last one at home and it was expected. Julia was the one entrusted to give her father his medicine, a prescription so powerful that if not given in precise dosages, it could have killed him. When she wasn't helping with her dad, she worked as a dishwasher to help pay family bills.

It was understandable Julia had welcomed marriage in February 1930. She turned eighteen a couple months later. Her husband, Raymond Hackett Whitney—everyone called him "Hackett"—was 24 years old on Valentine's Day, the day before the wedding. In December of the same year, Julia's son, Raymond Francis Whitney, was born.

But eight years later, the end of September 1938, Julia's divorce was final. Julia let Webb read the divorce decree:

That for a period of more than one year last past and

*preceding the commencement of this action, and extending up to
the time of the filing of the complaint herein, the defendant has
been guilty of a course of conduct in his treatment of the plaintiff
by the infliction of grievous mental suffering upon the plaintiff by
the defendant, which justly and reasonably is of such a nature
and character as to destroy the peace of mind and happiness of
the plaintiff and entirely to defeat the proper and legitimate objects
of marriage and to render the continuance of the married relation
between them perpetually unreasonable and intolerable to the
plaintiff.*

Julia and Webb were alone in the living room at the
back of the Skates store. Ray was tucked in bed and his
grandparents followed not long after, to give the young
couple time alone.

"What does 'infliction of grievous mental sufferin'
mean?" Webb asked.

"It's still kind of hard for me to talk about. We didn't
have a good marriage the last couple years. After we moved
to Billings from Pierre, South Dakota, where we got
married, my husband started gambling—a lot. It's legal
here and it wasn't in South Dakota.

"He would lose all his money and demand my money.
He was always going to make it big, but instead he lost
more than he ever won. I worked the entire time we were
married as a telephone operator, house keeper, dime store
clerk, a waitress, and now I'm a seamstress. I make fur
coats downtown, at Gordon Ray Furs." Julia chuckled. "I
guess I wouldn't know what to do, if I wasn't working
somewhere." Her smile faded. "There were plenty of times

he wasn't working and I supported the family" Julia sighed, "but it didn't stop him from gambling."

"At first I gave Hackett money, but as time went on and he wasn't working, I couldn't give him money we needed for food and rent. I just couldn't. The final straw came about a year ago." Julia's face was pained at the thought of retelling what happened, but she confided in Webb.

Billings 1937

Hackett sat in an old overstuffed chair in the living room of their small rental house. The armrests were worn through to the stuffing, seat cushion springs long gone.

When Julia walked in the door from work, carrying a bag of groceries, Hackett didn't look up. Six-year-old Ray played with a toy car on the floor.

"Ray, why don't you go outside to play for a while," Hackett commanded more than asked.

"It's getting late. He should stay inside while I cook supper," Julia countered.

"He needs to do what I tell him." Hackett's voice was raised. He glared at Julia.

Julia hurried into the tiny kitchen, visible from the living room, and grabbed her apron. Ray took his toy and went outside. He glanced at his mother as he hurried out the door. He had seen his dad mad before, felt the man's grip on his arms and the pain of hitting a wall. There had been nights he cried himself to sleep from unwarranted spankings. Julia was afraid of her husband, too, for good reason.

"Stay close to the front door, Ray," Julia cautioned. She started putting groceries away and took pans out of the cupboard. She had seen her husband in these moods before, a storm cloud brewing.

"I stopped by Mom and Dad's to pick up a few things at their store. I put them on our bill. They know we have to pay rent this week."

Julia had a hunch about the discussion she and Hackett were about to have, one they'd had too many times before, times when she had given into him and other times when she'd been able to reason with him. She shivered with dread at the thought of his foreboding posture and dark face, even though she had her back turned to him. Julia pushed an envelope into the pocket of her dress and covered it with her apron.

"You get paid today?" Hackett asked. He stood up from the chair and walked into the kitchen.

"Yes, but you know we have to pay rent and then have enough for gas and groceries for next week until I get paid again."

"Well, I have to have some money tonight. I've got a big game going. I've beat these guys before, so it's a sure thing. I don't want any argument from you. Hand over your pay envelope."

"Hackett, we can't keep on like this. If we don't pay the rent, we'll be out on our ear. The landlord has let us slide a couple times, but the last time he talked to me, he said he wasn't running a charity and that we had to pay. There are other people who could move in here at a moment's notice. You have to understand that." Julia's voice was shaking, but her resolve was solid. She was not going to hand over the envelope.

"Where'd you put it?" Hackett demanded. His voice escalated with every word.

"I can't give it to you. Think about Ray. We have to have a home for him," Julia pleaded.

"Give me the envelope, damn it, or you'll be sorry." Hackett raised his fist and pushed Julia back against the wall with his other hand. Her body made a loud thumping noise against the thin, insulated outer wall. Her hand hit cans on the kitchen counter top. They crashed to the floor.

"Stop it, Hackett. You don't want to do this." Her voice shook with fear. Julia put her head down and jerked her arms up to protect herself.

"I won't give it to you. We need the money, Hackett," Julia screamed at the top of her lungs. Tears streamed down her face and she tried to turn away from him.

"Give me the goddamn money. I'm not going to let you ruin my chances" Hackett grabbed Julia's shoulders and whipped her around toward him. Her glasses flew off and onto the floor. He grabbed her wrists, pulled her arms down and thrust his face into hers.

He seethed. His hot breath engulfed Julia with fear. Sweat dripped from his brow. He was on fire with anger. Julia struggled to get away from his grip, but he shoved one hand into her midriff and slammed the other against her throat, pinning her to the wall. Julia clutched at his forearms, but she couldn't breathe or yell. The room was growing dark. She was blacking out.

Ray came screaming through the front door. He pulled

back his small arm and threw the toy car at his dad. "You stop hurtin' my mommy! You stop!" Ray started kicking the back of Hackett's legs.

Caught off guard, Hackett released Julia and started toward Ray. He grabbed his son and tossed him in the overstuffed chair. Ray was screaming and crying. "Don't hurt my mommy!"

A neighbor walked in the open front door. "What's going on here?" he said in a voice that got Hackett's attention. "I heard screams from next door."

Hackett squared his shoulders toward the man, straightened himself and swiped a hand through his hair. "This is a family disagreement, fella. None of your business, so move on outta here."

Julia pulled herself away from the wall and staggered into the living room.

"Are you okay, Ma'am?" the neighbor asked, ignoring Hackett.

"No, I'm not." Julia was still crying and shaking. "If you could please stay while I get some things for my son and me. We have to leave and go to my parents. It's not safe here."

"Wait a minute," Hackett's tone was threatening. "You ain't goin' nowhere."

"I think the little woman knows what she needs to do. Either you let her get her things and leave or the police will be the next ones through this door." The man's size made Hackett pay attention.

Hackett pushed past the man in the doorway, got in the car and drove away.

"Can I give you a lift wherever you need to go, Ma'am?"

"Yes, please. Thank you so much. I'm forever grateful. You saved my life." Julia packed suitcases for herself and Ray. The neighbor took them to her parents' home.

The Road

They were within sight of Dunn Center. It was 1:20 pm. Webb had turned north on Highway 22 out of Dickinson and then east on Highway 200 to Dunn Center. They made better time since the snowfall subsided, but they were still late.

"Julia and I were gettin' serious by November," Webb said, looking straight down the road. "We'd been seein' each other as often as we could, at least once a week since August. I had a short-haul truckin' job, but she knew I wanted a better payin' Cat Skinner position."

"Did you tell her about Dorothy?" Blanche asked.

Webb looked at Blanche. "Of course, I did. I told her about Dorothy and Arlis and how we'd decided to separate and get a divorce." There was indignation in his voice. "Shared that with her on the second date." He turned back to the road. Dunn Center's city limits were in view.

"When I left in November for Nebraska, Julia and me stayed in touch. We called each other and had a short visit when I was home at Christmas."

"Why didn't you say something more to the family about her?" Blanche asked.

"I figured you all were still thinkin' about Dorothy and LaReta, especially from all the Christmas gifts you girls and

Ma sent to North Dakota. Ma even found a gift for me to send to LaReta, a toy car pulling a trailer. I think Ma was tryin' to give me a message with that one. So the timin' wasn't right to talk about Julia and me. I thought I had 'til spring when the Nebraska job was done and I could come home for a visit.

"So you didn't get a divorce." Blanche stated, more than asked.

"Nope. We didn't get 'round to it."

There were a few rolling hills, but for the most part, Dunn Center on their left was flat, about ten square blocks of small houses on big lots. Every house had a garden, not yet roused from winter. The trees were still bare.

Webb remembered the location of the church. The Normanna Lutheran Church was where he and Dorothy were married on March 20, 1935. Ten days from today would have been their fourth anniversary.

"I don't know what to expect, Blanche, whether they want me here or not." Webb picked up his fedora from the seat beside him and put it on his head as he headed east on Railroad Street. He took if off again when he turned north on 2nd Avenue East. He could see the white, wooden church three blocks ahead with its tall steeple and church bell. A man stood outside on the front steps beside the open doors. The parking lot was full, but no one was going in. Webb put his hat back on again, thinking they were the last ones to arrive.

He pulled into one of the few parking places left, put the Chevy in neutral and turned off the motor. His heart pounded and his palms were sweaty.

The car wouldn't roll on the flat terrain, but Webb pulled on the hand break out of habit. What he wanted to do was back her up and head for the hills of Montana.

"Blanche," Webb cleared his throat. "I asked Julia to marry me last night…and she said 'yes.'"

THE ROAD TO LARETA

PART THREE
The Decision

26

Dorothy
Dunn Center, North Dakota 1939

Laurel, Dorothy's oldest brother, greeted Webb at the top of the steps, but he didn't smile. "Saw your car comin' up the road, Webb, kickin' up dust. We knew you were gonna try to make it so we held the service up for you." The two men shook hands.

"Thanks, Laurel. It's been a while." Laurel looked at him without a response. Webb wished he hadn't mentioned anything about how long it had been and thought Laurel still resembled his mother, Laura—the same square face, high cheek bones, thin lips and long narrow nose. Wire rim glasses sat high on the bridge of his nose. His wavy hair was cut short and neat. Laurel looked like the business man that he was, manager of a local grain elevator.

He handed Webb a black arm band. He was wearing one, too. It was tradition to wear the band for six months after losing a family member. It said to the everyone who saw it, 'Be gentle; this man is grieving.' The women wore black.

Webb removed his hat, took the armband and put it on. "This is my sister, Blanche. She knew Dorothy and

LaReta real well. Spent a lot of time with them. Came along to keep me company."

Blanche understood this wasn't the time to talk about LaReta, but thoughts about Webb's last comment in the car still had her wondering. Would he become the man Dorothy wanted him to be after all—but with Julia? If that was true and he planned to tell the Boes, his timing was horrible.

She shook Laurel's hand and they entered the sanctuary. The small church was full. Everyone in Dunn Center and living on surrounding farms knew the Boe family. It had only been a year since they had left for Oregon and townsfolk welcomed them back and came to pay their respects.

With every eye on them, Laurel ushered Webb and Blanche down the center aisle to the front row. Webb's footfall on the wooden floor echoed through the church, announcing his arrival. No one was smiling. A gawker leaned toward her neighbor and in a hushed voice, asked if she knew who that was with Webb. One of the "Lutheran Ladies" who'd prepared the church basement for later, ventured a guess. "Might be one of his sisters—I would hope so. I've heard he has a couple and Webb looks like her, don't you think?"

Ed and Laura Boe, Myra and her husband, Randeen, Laurel's wife Ada, and Melva sat in front on the right. Five of the Boe's grandchildren, including LaReta, were being cared for at a relative's home. Dorothy's other brothers, Miland and Aaron, and her two sisters, Naomi and Vernetta, were absent. It was unfortunate, but they couldn't afford the trip from Oregon. It had been hardship enough for Dorothy's parents to make the journey. The family nodded in greeting when they saw Webb and Blanche. Mrs. Boe and the women went back to dabbing their eyes with handkerchiefs. The men tried hard not to show their emotions. An organist was playing *What a Friend We Have in Jesus.*

Laurel directed Webb and Blanche to the front pew on the left. In front of the alter steps, a few feet from them, was Dorothy's beautiful casket. From the looks of it, Webb thought more folks than just family members had contributed money for the funeral. He wasn't one of them.

Three sculpted silver handles adorned the side of the casket. Webb knew there were three more on the other side to help carry Dorothy to her final resting place outside of town.

The top half of the casket was open. He saw the softly tufted, white satin lining, and Dorothy. She was dressed in white, lying in peace. A bouquet of red roses adorned her breast. The casket was surrounded by multiple sprays of ferns with carnations and lilies, more gifts of flowers than Dorothy had ever been given when she was alive.

The reality of her death stabbed Webb in the heart. *If only…Maybe if I had…Why her? She was so young.* His tears started to flow when the reverand asked the congregation to rise and sing *How Great Thou Art.* Webb couldn't help but see Dorothy over the pages of his hymnal.

"Is there anyone who would like to share their memories of Dorothy?" the reverand asked after he'd given a brief sermon.

A number of parents talked about Dorothy's dedication as a teacher and how their children enjoyed learning from her.

Richard Bailey spoke on behalf of his family and in particular his older brother, Arlis, who couldn't afford the trip back to Dunn Center for the funeral. As sad as Richard was, he tried to lighten the mood by telling stories of Dorothy's first experience snow sledding with him and Arlis, cutting ice from the river for the ice house, and the first time Arlis showed her how to shoot a rifle. "She was sure proud of how well she did, the first time she shot. She was hittin' the targets even better than Arlis." The congregation laughed.

Richard fiddled with the paper he'd taken to the pulpit to help him remember what he wanted to say. "And she loved to dance. Her and Arlis went every Saturday they could, and then to shows on Sunday." Richard looked at Webb to see if there was any reaction, but Webb's eyes were focused on the polished floor boards in front of him. He knew how Dorothy liked to dance and was glad she'd found someone to make her happy. He knew in the last couple years, he hadn't brought her any joy.

"We sure liked Dorothy a lot. And we're real sorry she's gone. We're gonna miss her and little Reta too."

Mrs. Bailey dabbed at her tears, proud that Richard had been able to say his piece, and sad at the thought of not having Dorothy and LaReta in their home any more. She also wept for Arlis, knowing how much he cared for Dorothy. If Dorothy had been able to join Arlis in Oregon like they were planning, she might have become Mrs.

Bailey's daughter-in-law. At least that was the talk.

Dorothy's oldest sister, Myra, climbed the two steps to the pulpit. She spread a piece of paper in front of her and took a deep breath. A handkerchief was in one hand.

Myra knew Webb. She'd known him for years. She married his cousin, Randeen, the year before they introduced Webb and Dorothy to each other in the summer of 1934. The four of them went dancing together, drinking together. Her voice was a whisper at first. The congregation leaned forward to hear.

"Dorothy was a good parent and she loved LaReta so much." Myra started crying and stopped to wipe her tears before she continued. Her voice got stronger.

"When she lived in Dunn Center and had to stay at her school all week, she couldn't wait to be picked up on Friday by one of my sisters, so she could get home to her daughter. And little Reta felt the same way. She always rode along to get her mommy. Even though Naomi warned Dorothy about it, she spoiled LaReta on the weekends anyway." Myra smiled and the congregation chuckled.

"But because they moved around a lot, back and forth between here and Billings and then to Gladstone so Dorothy could teach another year, she did worry that LaReta didn't have a place to call her own. The Bailey family was the closest they came to that for quite a while.

"Dorothy was also very grateful that when she was riding back and forth on the Bailey's horse to her school in Emerson, she had Mrs. Bailey to take care of LaReta during the week. The family was a godsend." The Bailey's smiled at the kind words, even though they were a little embarrassed by the attention. They were sitting in the row behind Webb and Blanche.

Myra looked at Webb. His head was still down. She spoke softly again. "I know my sister wanted what's best for LaReta and she still does." She paused. Webb raised his head and returned her gaze. He knew she was speaking to him.

"Some of you haven't seen LaReta since last year when they moved to Gladstone. At three and a half, she's grown a lot, but of course, she doesn't understand what happened. But the family has agreed, we'll do everything we can to make sure LaReta knows she's loved and that she will be taken care of." She stepped down from the pulpit and leaned over the casket. She kissed Dorothy on the forehead and sat down with the rest of her family.

Webb couldn't bring himself to say anything. He was too distraught and at a loss for words.

At the end of the service, everyone rose once more and sang *Amazing Grace*.

Ed and Laura Boe stood and walked to one side of the casket. Myra, Laurel and Melva took their place on the other side. Webb and Blanche remained where they were, unsure of what to do.

The reverend told the congregation Dorothy would be interred in the cemetery following the service, after which there would be a wake at 4:30 pm in the church basement. He invited those who wished to pay their last respects to come forward. Row by row, with ushers starting at the back, folks either came forward or left the church. Those who came forward shook hands with the family, took one last look at Dorothy and gently touched the casket, remembering who she was to them: friend, neighbor, teacher, relative or the daughter of Ed and Laura Boe.

Webb shifted in his seat, but didn't get up. A few of the men Webb knew from working around Dunn Center five years before shook his hand and sympathized about the loss.

Webb and Blanche were the last two to pay their respects. Blanche had never met Dorothy's family before, but she introduced herself and told them how much she loved Dorothy and LaReta. Tears flowed.

Webb was the last to go through the line. He shook Laurel's hand again and thanked him for his help. He hung on to Myra's hand longer and gave Melva a kiss on the cheek. He was too choked-up to say much of anything. He stopped to look at Dorothy and with tears in his eyes, kissed her forehead.

Laura Boe was sobbing and Ed had his arm around her as Webb faced the two of them. "I'm so sorry. I'm so sorry," was all he could think to say. He meant it.

A truck which served as the town's hearse was moved to the front of the church. Webb stepped forward as one of the pallbearers. After the lid was closed and secured, Webb, Ed Boe, Laurel Boe, Randeen Hoovestol, and two family friends picked up the casket and moved it to the front steps of the church.

The sun had come out and although it was cold, they'd been spared from more snow. There was a gentle breeze. The conditions were right for a photograph.

It was tradition to have a photograph taken of the

deceased in the casket, as a lasting remembrance. The casket was laid at an angle on the front stairs and the top half opened once again. Women of the church brought all the flowers to the front steps and placed them on the lower half of the coffin and around its base. Dorothy looked as though she lay in a garden. The fluffy white bows on the sprays fluttered in the wind.

Webb remembered something once said at another funeral he'd attended.

Dead people receive more flowers than living ones because regret is stronger than gratitude.

He shivered at the thought, knowing how true that was in his relationship with Dorothy. He walked over and touched the flowers, all the while looking at Dorothy's still, pale face.

The town mortician served as photographer. He adjusted his box camera to take photos from several angles. This would be a final remembrance of a daughter, sister, wife and mother.

When he finished, the flowers were removed and the lid closed again. Pallbearers moved Dorothy onto the covered truck bed for the four and a half mile ride to the cemetery, southwest of Dunn Center. All the flowers were placed onto the truck alongside the casket. The fragrance of the lily's wafted over family and friends who stood behind the vehicle.

The graveside service was simple. Family, a few friends and the photographer attended. The site was on a lovely hillside overlooking a lake. There was a gentle breeze whispering across headstones.

I joked about residents of this cemetery enjoying the view, the first time Dorothy and I were alone. Five years later, she's one of them. How could I have known?

Once lowered into its sarcophagus, family members and Webb took turns tossing a shovel full of dirt on top of the casket. It was their final goodbye. Life would not be handing Dorothy "another kick in the pants" ever again.

"That was harder than I thought it would be." Blanche's voice was soft as they drove back to the church for the wake. "I haven't been to an open casket funeral before and to see Dorothy like that…"

"I know. Hit me, too. Made her passing real, but I still keep seeing her sad face." Webb gripped the steering wheel with both hands, looking straight ahead. "And I wasn't expecting what Myra said. Thought she was talkin' right to me. Sounds as though the family has made up their minds about who's going to raise LaReta."

Blanche looked at Webb. "Isn't that your decision, since you're LaReta's father?"

"As far as I know, it is, but I have to talk to the Boes to see what they're thinkin'. This gatherin' is not the best place to do that."

The wake was a solemn affair, not much laughter or reminiscing other than guests sharing praise for Dorothy with her parents and siblings.

When elders passed away, people celebrated a life well-lived. They talked about contributions the person made and laughed about quirks and character traits. It was another story when someone as young as Dorothy died. It shocked the community and left people shaking their heads in disbelief, particularly those closest to her.

Webb chatted with friends he knew and some he didn't know, introducing his sister and solving the mystery for some of the women in town as to Blanche's identity.

A friend invited Webb and Blanche to stay with his family as long as needed. Webb accepted. He was grateful, since funds were limited and trying to find overnight accommodations for himself and Blanche was something he hadn't planned.

Conversation with the Boe family was limited. The Boes were busy talking to other reception guests, thanking them for their kindness and sympathy.

Laurel approached Webb as the crowd thinned. He handed Webb an unopened letter. The addressee: Dorothy Boe in care of the Dickinson Hospital. The hospital address was crossed out. The forwarding address: Mr. L.E. Boe, Halliday. Return address: Webb Bateman, Ogallala, Nebraska.

"This came this morning, Webb. Thought maybe you'd want to know Dorothy didn't get your letter before she passed."

Webb's felt a stab of pain again. He looked down at the floor. "I wanted her to know I cared about the fact she was in the hospital. I wished her a speedy recovery. I'm sorry she didn't see it."

Laurel grabbed one of Webb's shoulders and gave it a squeeze. Laurel was the one who first came to Dorothy's bedside in February at the Bailey's after her fall from the horse. He was the family member who took her to the hospital and stayed with her the first night. He'd been to see her every couple days after that until Myra and Randeen came from Watford City and the Boes arrived from Oregon. He was there on Tuesday, March 7th, when Dorothy had another stroke before leaving the hospital, and that night, he stood by her bedside when she died. She had been in the hospital exactly two weeks.

Webb spoke to Laurel in low tones. He took a moment to glance at the rest of the family, chatting with Blanche. "I hope Dorothy explained why I haven't been back here this past year."

Laurel tipped his head to one side, not sure what Webb meant.

"Did she let you know we decided to separate last summer and that we'd be gettin' a divorce?"

Laurel paused. "She may have written or said somethin' to Ma or my wife or her sisters, but she didn't come right out and say as much to me. But then she was in Gladstone and we didn't see her except at Christmas."

Laurel shifted his weight from one foot to the other. "I'm not surprised though. She talked about Arlis a lot and what a good time they were havin'."

Webb changed the subject to what was important. "There hasn't been a good time to ask about LaReta, but I want to see her tomorrow. Do you know where she's stayin'?"

Laurel's posture straightened. "She's with my mother-in-law in Halliday, east of here, along with our kids and Myra and Randeen's." He paused. "You're welcome to come out. Mom and dad will be there too."

"Thanks, Laurel. Guess Blanche and I'll head off to

Martin Olson's for the night. They're puttin' us up 'til Sunday when we have to head back. It's been a long day and I could use some shuteye. Please tell your folks I need to talk to them tomorrow when I come to see LaReta. I'll call first, but I have something everyone needs to know."

Webb and Blanche said their goodbyes to the family and left the church. Laurel's uneasy gaze followed them out the door.

Back Row: Ada Boe (Laurel's wife), Laura Boe (mother), Laurel Boe, Vernetta Boe, Dorothy Boe Bateman, and Ed Boe (father)

Front Row: LaVonne Boe (Ada and Laurel's daughter) and LaReta Bateman

Boe Siblings not pictured: Myra, Naomi, Miland, Melva, and Aaron
1937

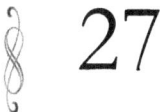

27

The Boes

Halliday, North Dakota 1939

Ed and Laura Boe were up early Saturday morning. Laurel told them the night before that Webb would be coming out from Dunn Center and would pick up Melva on the way.

They knew Webb wanted to see LaReta and had something to discuss with the family. The Boes had a sleepless night. Dorothy's death was enough of a shock and now they would have to deal with the father of their grandchild, a man they hadn't seen in a long time who may want to take LaReta away from them.

Ada, Laurel's wife, bulging with her third child, insisted on fixing breakfast for the elder Boes. It was hard to keep her mother-in-law out of the kitchen, but Ada understood the emotional toll Dorothy's death had on her in-laws and wanted them to rest as much as possible. The Boes would have a long trip back to Oregon in a couple days with thoughts of losing Dorothy as an unwelcome traveling companion.

"Where are the children, Ada?" Laura asked from the living room. Ed sat tight lipped and solemn on the couch beside her. From his vantage point he could see out the window and down the road toward Dunn Center.

"They're still at Mother's house next door, Laura." Ada wiped her hands on the apron draped over her protruding belly and came to the living room door. "I was over there earlier. I guess Roland and LaVonne had quite the time keeping LaReta company last night. Mother said she thought they would never get to sleep, but they were up again, bright and early this morning when Myra brought Donna and Kenton to join the party. It's not often the five cousins get together. Myra and mother have their hands full," Ada counted on her fingers, "with two five-year-olds, a four-year-old, three-year-old LaReta and two-year-old Kenton." Ada smiled. She was trying to lighten the mood.

"Myra's going to stay next door and help with the kids. Randeen's coming in from the trailer house to have breakfast with us. Did you get a chance to see the inside of the house on wheels they brought out from Dickinson yesterday before the funeral? It's really swell." Attempts to make her mother-in-law think of something other than Dorothy's funeral didn't seem to be working.

"No, we didn't see inside, dear. Maybe later today," Laura replied. She was glad the children were next door. Her mind was on the discussion they would be having with Webb. It would be an adult affair, not one for the ears of small children.

Ada went back to her work in the kitchen. She heard Laurel talking to Randeen on the back porch and could see cigarette smoke floating past the window. She insisted Laurel keep his smoking outside. Her pregnancy hadn't been easy and the smell of cigarettes made her sick. It also meant she limited visits to friends in the past months. All the men they knew and some of the women, too, smoked indoors no matter the time of year.

For the moment, Ed and Laura were alone in the living room with their thoughts.

"Just a year ago, we were trying to move the graves of the twins to the Dunn Center Cemetery. Didn't know we'd be putting another child there in less than a year." Laura said folding and unfolding the handkerchief in her lap.

At 52, Laura's build was slight and her dark hair starting to show signs of grey. As well it should. She had given birth to twelve children, including two sets of twins, in a one-room sod house on the homestead she and Ed settled in 1906, not far from Dunn Center. The first set of twin boys were born their first year of marriage and died the same year.

The homestead was barren of trees; there was no pine box for their burial. Instead, the twins were swaddled in blankets and buried together, not far from the house. A stone marker was etched and placed on the grave. Before leaving the homestead, Laura and Ed wanted to move the boys to a better place, to the Dunn Center Cemetery, where two other children of theirs had been buried. That wasn't to be. All they found were rusty safety pins used on the twins' diapers. "Dust to dust," Laura said at the time.

"We outlived five children. Not supposed to be that way," Ed, a man of few words, said solemnly. He looked even more severe than usual. Not one for change, his dark hair, greying at the temples, was still parted in the middle and raked back on the sides, the way he'd worn it from his youth. His face was chiseled with hard angles and ruddy from years of outdoor work on the farm. He looked tired. Life had worn him out. At 62, all he had toiled for was gone. He and Laura had abandoned their homestead the year before because of drought and the Depression. They'd moved to a relative's small farm in Oregon. Ed was hurt, angry and grieving.

"Ed, I don't know what I'll do, if Webb wants to take Reta. She's all we have left of Dorothy." Laura used the handkerchief to catch her tears.

"Have to see what he has to say, when he gets here." Ed continued his gaze out the front window toward the road. "Little Reta knows us. Doesn't know her dad."

"But he is her father. He does have the last say about who she lives with, doesn't he?" Laura asked, her brow furrowed with worry.

Ed didn't answer.

Laurel and Randeen walked through the back door into the kitchen. Randeen called out, "Mornin', folks." He walked into the living room while Laurel stayed to help Ada in the kitchen. "You should see the bunch at Mrs. Fockler's. They've been havin' a great time," Randeen was smiling, but his smile faded when he saw the solemn faces of the Boes. "So, Webb comin' out this mornin'?"

Randeen was an easy going guy, tall and muscled from growing up on a farm. He'd become a jack of all trades, earning money by painting grain elevators and building trailer houses. Randeen had known Webb from the time they were kids. They were cousins and he knew Webb had a good heart, but bad habits, so he understood the concern if Webb wanted to raise LaReta.

"Haven't heard from him yet, but figure he'll be here before noon," Ed responded.

Laurel called from the kitchen. "Breakfast is 'bout ready."

After breakfast, the men gathered in the living room, while Ada and Laura cleaned up the kitchen and started preparations for the noon meal. Laura refused to let Ada work alone. She washed dishes while Ada peeled potatoes.

"Before Reta went next door last night, she asked me where her mommy is," Laura confided to Ada, her tone worried. "Wants to know if she's still in the hospital. I don't know what to say, Ada. Dorothy wasn't a regular church goer, so I don't think LaReta understands about heaven. How do I explain to a three-year-old that her mommy died and she won't see her again?" Tears spilled down Laura's cheeks.

Ada stopped what she was doing and gave Laura a long hug. She imagined someone having to tell her own five-year-old son and four-year-old daughter they'd lost their mommy. With the difficulty she'd had in this pregnancy, Ada had her own fears and what-ifs to contend with, made worse by Dorothy's death. It was too much too think about. The two women clung to each other and wept.

Composing themselves, they wiped their tears and went back to the tasks at hand. Laura finished the dishes and excused herself to go next door. She wanted to check on LaReta.

"Tell Mother not to worry about fixing lunch for the kids. We have enough for everyone," Ada called after

Laura as she went out the door.

Randeen and Laurel sat on the couch in the front room and made small talk, hoping to keep Ed's mind off what Webb might have to say to the family. Ed sat in one of the overstuffed chairs. He chose the one with a view down the road.

"Whaddaya' think of that last Joe Louis fight in January, Ed?" Randeen leaned forward, both elbows on his thighs, hands clasped together under his chin. "Did you get a chance to listen on the radio in Oregon?"

"I heard about it. Guess he wins so much they're callin' the losers 'Bum of the Month.'" Ed showed signs of a smile.

Randeen was pleased he found something to talk about that was of interest to Ed. As long as Randeen had known his father-in-law, he still wasn't sure how to read him. "He cleaned the other Lewis' clock in that last fight in January. Knocked him out in the first round,"

Laurel added. "I read Joe is a pretty clean-living, okay kinda guy, but there are plenty of white folks who aren't happy about a Negro beatin' the hell out of white opponents. Not quite sure how I feel about it either. But then, we don't have many Negroes around here to get a feel for 'em."

Laurel, a couple years younger than Randeen, was sometimes quick to judge. The fact the two men didn't always see eye to eye had the brothers-in-law at odds more than once. Dorothy had written to her parents she wasn't sure all of them would be together for Christmas in 1938 because of differences, but the sisters-in-law nipped that in the bud. Myra and Ada made sure they were together, joined by Dorothy, LaReta and Melva. After all, they were the last members of the Boe family left in North Dakota. All the others had moved to Oregon.

Randeen smiled at Laurel's comment. "Let the best man win, I say. Gives negros something to be proud of. I hear every time Louis wins, thousands of his kind stay up all night to celebrate. They march out in the streets and cheer and yell and cry because he won. I don't recall hearing anyone else causing that kind of stir."

Laurel stood up, stretched, and leaned against the door frame leading to the kitchen. "You always were a bleedin' heart, Randeen." Laurel smiled, "But then again, with this Depression and people tryin' to survive, guess it helps to have somethin' else to think about, even if it does rile 'em up, one way or t'other. I know I could sure use somethin' else to think about. Not sure how much longer Ada and I can make a livin' around here. I've had a real good position runnin' the Occident Grain elevator, but with the drought and 'hoppers, there's not much being harvested any more. We may have to consider movin' out your way, Dad."

Ed leaned forward and looked hard at Laurel. "You hang on as long as you can, son. You put a lot of work into this house and it's your home. Movin' to some strange place away from everything you've worked for and know, it's…it's not easy. Somethin' dies." Ed sunk back in the chair and his chin dropped to his chest, eyes cast down.

Randeen sat back on the couch. "We're in the same boat, Laurel. Nobody's buying trailer houses. They can't afford 'em and the grain elevator painting business is dryin' up, too. So many farms have failed because of the poor soil, and like you said, what does grow gets eatin' by those damn 'hoppers."

Laurel crossed his arms in front of him. "I thought maybe you were on to somethin', Randeen. So many folks moving west to better opportunities, the idea of takin' their house with them on wheels made a lot of sense.

Twisting his wedding ring, Randeen said, "I did, too, Laurel, but for me to make a livin', folks have to pay for their trailer house. There's the problem. They may need a trailer house, but can't afford to pay for it. They're packin' everything they own into their vehicle and hopin' it will get them wherever they want to go. A lot of folks don't even know where they'll go."

He shrugged his shoulders. "So far, we're not as bad off as the folks in Oklahoma and Kansas that got run off their land by big banks they owed money to. I heard hundreds of thousands of those tenant farmers had to move from homesteads they'd worked for years. Tractors came and just plowed down their houses and left people standing there trying to figure out where to go. A lot of people goin' to California, but I'm hearin' they aren't welcome there. Too many comin' at once. When they do get there, they're treated like dirt. Can't get decent wages 'cuz so many need work. They thought they were goin' to a land of plenty and instead they're starvin'.

Randeen looked at Ed, realizing he may have added more pain to what Ed was already feeling about the loss of his farm and now, the loss of his daughter.

Ed didn't respond. He had turned his gaze out the

window toward the road to Dunn Center.

Webb held the Chevy's passenger door open for Melva as she got into the car. Blanche got in the back seat to give more time for Webb and Melva to catch up on family. He closed the door for Melva and walked around to get into the driver's side. They were getting a later start than Webb had planned. He'd slept in, unusual for him but much needed and the Olson's had insisted on preparing Blanche and Webb a big breakfast for which they were grateful.

"So how come you're livin' in Dunn Center, Melva? I thought maybe you would be out in Halliday with Laurel and Ada or in Watford City with Randeen and Myra."

Melva waited for Webb to start the motor. "My teaching position isn't far from here and I found a family to batch with, so it worked best for me to stay in town."

Melva folded her hands in her lap. She was a prim-looking young woman with the same fine features as her mother. All the girls shared their mother's poor eyesight, corrected by wire rim glasses. "You, know, we all have to do whatever's necessary to earn a living and I'm so grateful Dorothy helped me get my teaching certificate."

Nineteen-year-old Melva had been teaching in Dunn Center since the previous fall. Dorothy, with her earnings as a teacher, had helped pay for her six-week teacher training at the Normal School in Ellendale the year before. Dorothy had wanted to make sure Melva could support herself.

The Chevy headed east out of Dunn Center on Highway 200 through barren farmland. The terrain was flat and lifeless with the wind stirring up dust devils here and there. It was late morning and Webb had called ahead to let Laurel and Ada know they were on the way. It wouldn't take long to drive fifteen miles across an arid plain.

"Dorothy was a good woman, Melva, and you got that right about doin' whatever's necessary. I've had to keep movin' for a lot of years to find a job." Webb hesitated and then continued, "But I might settle back in Billings for a while. I can always get a truck drivin' job, if need be. Doesn't pay as much as construction, but allows me to be in one place for a time."

Melva wasn't sure she wanted the answer, but she asked anyway. "What's making you think about settling in one place, Webb?"

Webb glanced at Melva and found her staring at him in anticipation. "That's a discussion I need to have with the whole family. I don't mean to put you off, Melva. It's just that...frankly...I haven't put everything together I want to say. I know it's a tough time for everybody and I gotta keep that in mind when I talk about my plan."

Webb changed the subject. "Been goin' to any dances on Saturday nights, Melva? You interested in anybody?"

Melva grinned. She knew what Webb as doing, but until Dorothy's passing this week, she had been having some fun on weekends. "I've been to quite a few and I did meet someone I'm interested in, but he may be moving west, too, so I don't know where that will go. Seems like Dunn Center is shrinking in size with so many people leaving. I still have to finish teaching this year and that won't be till the end of April. With the folks in Oregon, I'm thinking I might as well head there too. Seems like

Myra and Laurel and their families will be going west pretty soon and if I stay, I won't have any family left here. We'd all be together again, if we move to Oregon." She paused, "Except for Dorothy, that is." Melva looked out the passenger window at the desolate landscape. "But maybe it's time for a fresh start."

Blanche leaned over the front seat and made small talk with Melva. The two had never met, but because of their ages, they had a lot in common. Blanche told Melva about her job and some of the dances she'd gone to in the past few months. They seemed to hit it off.

They turned left from Highway 200 onto Highway 8 toward Halliday. Within minutes, they were pulling into Laurel and Ada's driveway which wound around to the back of the house. The broad back porch was the entrance everyone used. If a stranger came to the front door, Laurel and Ada knew they were selling something.

Webb had never been in Laurel's home before. "Should we go 'round to the front, Melva? Might be more respectful that way?"

Melva laughed. "They'll think you're a pot and pan salesman, if you go that way. Besides, I saw Dad looking out the front window. They all know we're here."

Webb opened the car doors for Blanche and then Melva. He was nervous. They all walked up the back steps together. Webb took off his fedora and held open the porch door to the kitchen for the two young women to enter.

"Come on in. I'm just fixing food for lunch and the men are in the living room," Ada greeted them.

Randeen strode into the kitchen and shook Webb's hand. "Good to see you again, Webb. We didn't get much of a chance to talk yesterday. Ed and Laurel are in the living room. Laura and Myra are still next door with all the kids. Come on in." Webb felt a little more at ease with Randeen's greeting. They walked through the kitchen to the living room.

Blanche and Melva stayed in the kitchen with Ada. "How can I help, Ada?" Blanche asked, although she was anxious to see LaReta.

"I'm going to fry up some chicken so we'll have leftovers for a couple more meals, too. You could help cut up the bird and get it seasoned, if you will. Melva can show you where everything is. And we still have leftovers from the wake yesterday at the church. People brought so much food." Ada added, "Banquets are such a part of dying in North Dakota."

Webb had his hat in hand. He nodded at Laurel and Ed and shook their hands. Ed motioned him to sit in a second overstuffed chair opposite his.

"Didn't know if you would make it, Webb. Got a letter from Dorothy that you were working in Nebraska," Ed said.

"I was about finished with the job when I got your telegram, Ed. Real shock, but I know it was a shock for all of us. Still can't believe she's gone. So young. Such a shame. Musta been a hell of a trip for you and Laura, hearing about Dorothy in the hospital and then having to drive all the way back here from Oregon."

"Yup, it was."

Webb fiddled with his hat band. Conversation with Ed was going to be tough. "Mrs. Bailey told me there were even snow storms just a week ago that kept Randeen and Myra from getting' to Dunn Center sooner." Webb addressed his comment to Ed, but Randeen nodded in agreement. Ed didn't respond.

Webb decided he might as well broach the subject of his daughter. "Well, I'm anxious to see Reta today. I'm hoping she'll recognize me. It's been since last summer."

"She's next door. I reckon you can go over to see her if you want," Ed responded. His face was a blank. He showed no emotion, but sat straight with his hands on the arms of the chair.

"I'll walk over with you, Webb," Randeen volunteered. "I need to see how Myra's doin' and if she's planning to come back over here for lunch."

As the men headed out the door, Ada called after them, "Be sure to tell Mother we'll be bringing food over for her and all the kids. Maybe Melva and Blanche can spell Myra with the kids at lunch time." The men and the girls nodded in agreement. Blanche was eager for the opportunity to spend time with LaReta.

Walking across the stretch of trampled grass between the two houses, a stone's throw apart, they saw the kids playing in the back. Webb stopped to look at his daughter. She and LaVonne were playing tug-of-war with the arms of a doll. "Mine!" LaReta hollered, stomping her foot.

Randeen stopped beside Webb. "Guess it's kinda tough on her, 'cuz she's moved around so much and hasn't always had her own things. She wants to hang on to what she thinks is hers. At least that's what Myra says."

Webb's guilt rose to a new height. He knelt down on one knee and called, "Hey Reta!" LaReta stopped what she was doing and stared at the strange man calling her name.

"Come see your ol' Dad. Come here."

LaReta didn't move, but continued to stare.

"It's gonna take her a bit to get reacquainted, Webb. That's how kids are. Let's go on in and you can greet the women. Knowing my kids, Donna and Kenton, they'll come in 'cuz they'll be curious now and the rest will follow." Randeen waved at his children.

Webb and Randeen climbed the steps to Mrs. Fockler's back door and entered her kitchen. Myra and Mrs. Fockler sat at the kitchen table taking a break and having a cup of coffee. Laura stood at the kitchen window where she had observed Webb and LaReta.

"Morning, Webb. Need a cup of coffee?" Myra asked Webb as he entered the door. She got up and headed for the stove to pour him a cup.

"Can't turn one of those down, Myra. Morning, Laura. And you must be Mrs. Fockler, Ada's mother. Glad to meet you." Webb shook her hand and she invited the men to sit down. Laura moved to a chair and sat down. She hadn't returned his greeting.

Before Webb could take a drink, little heads popped through the back door, unsure whether they should come into a room where this strange man sat drinking coffee.

"Hi!" Webb grinned at the little tribe.

Led by the five-year-olds, Roland and Donna, they swarmed past and ran into the living room, all the while eyeing the adults at the table, Webb in particular.

"How long you staying, Webb?" Laura asked. The tone of her voice was not inviting.

"Got to leave tomorrow, Laura. Blanche has to get back to work. She's next door helping Ada and Melva in the kitchen. I guess they'll be bringing food over pretty soon. And I have to get back to Billings, too, and start lookin' for work again, so we won't be here long."

LaReta peeked around the door frame from the living room. Gathering more courage, she stepped partway into the kitchen. Her shoes and socks were gone, tossed into a corner as soon as she could get them off. Now, she stood on one foot, caressing the back of her leg with the instep of her other foot. Her arms were clasped behind her. She watched Webb with steady, small blue eyes, eyes the color of his. She looked up from under towhead bangs and gave Webb a pout instead of a smile.

"Want to sit on my lap, Reta?" Webb asked with a broad smile.

LaReta gazed at Webb, cocking her head to one side. For a moment, he thought he saw a flicker of recognition. "My mommy is in the 'ho'pital'. She's 'bery' sick and I'm goin' to see her." LaReta turned and ran to join the other kids. The air seemed to go out of the room.

Laura was the first to speak. "She doesn't know you, Webb. That's the problem. She knows us and we have to tell her about Dorothy." She was setting the stage for the conversation to come.

28

All of Your Own

Halliday, North Dakota 1939

Although Blanche and Melva chatted amiably as they took lunch next door to Mrs. Fockler's, Blanche's thoughts and emotions were mixed and elsewhere.

Blanche had bonded with LaReta from the time she first met her in the fall of 1935. The Bateman family had all relocated to Billings earlier and Webb, Dorothy and LaReta followed when Webb lost his construction job because of the Depression and lack of work in North Dakota.

The pain of her own loss still weighed on her daily. Blanche was only seventeen when she gave birth to her baby boy earlier in 1935. After the baby's birth, in Fargo at the home for unwed mothers, a cloud settled on her. An ache she didn't understand was ever present. The family didn't talk about her moodiness, fatigue and emotional outbursts—it wasn't discussed.

Blanche started helping Dorothy with LaReta, first out of boredom, but very soon it was because she couldn't wait to see the baby. Her spirits lifted and somehow, a void was filled. She found a reason to laugh and smile again. Hardly a day went by that Blanche didn't see LaReta. As she'd shared with Webb on the trip, she saw most of LaReta's firsts and they stuck with her. Those firsts were memories she could depend on to make herself smile.

Soon, Dorothy seemed like an older sister. The difference between Dorothy and Blanche's own sisters was she could talk to her about the birth of her baby boy and how she had afterward. Dorothy helped her understand those feelings, by listening. She didn't give medical advice or suggestions for what Blanche could have done differently; she simply let her talk about her feelings.

When Dorothy decided to move back to North Dakota and take LaReta with her, Blanche was in pain again. It wasn't the same, but it was still grief. She understood Dorothy needed her own family if Webb wasn't going to keep them together, but that knowledge didn't lessen her sense of loss, again.

Since then, Blanche had only spent a few weeks with LaReta, once in the fall of 1936 and again last summer, June of 1938. It was just enough time to resurrect feelings of love and longing for a child. Blanche hadn't learned how to protect her heart.

Now, here she was about to see LaReta again. She felt sorrow for a little girl who'd lost her mother and joy at the prospects of having LaReta in her life for what she hoped would be a very long time.

The screen door banged behind Blanche and Melva as they entered the kitchen carrying lunch Ada had prepared. Laura, Webb, Myra and Randeen were in the kitchen too, but soon headed back to Ada and Laurel's to eat and talk about LaReta.

"Hi, LaReta!" Blanche's voice was high and childlike. She had taken time to introduce herself to Mrs. Fockler and put down the food, but immediately turned her attention to the little blonde-headed pixie standing next to her in the kitchen.

LaReta's head tilted and she squinted her eyes. Her face was saying, *Do I know you?* Chubby pink cheeks adorned a sweet smile when her question-face became a more sure-of-herself-face and she asked, "Auntie Bwanche?"

Blanche bent down and scooped LaReta up. "Yes, it's me. I'm so happy you remembered me! I didn't know if you would. You are such a smart girl!"

"I know," was the reply. "I can count real high. Want to hear me?"

Blanche bounced LaReta on her hip. "Of course I do." The other four little ones who had been watching from the living room doorway chimed in at that point. Roland and Donna, both five, and four-year-old LaVonne, vied for who could count the highest. Two-year-old Kenton jumped up and down to get attention, mimicking sounds the others made. Blanche laughed and complimented all on their efforts.

LaReta put her hands on both sides of Blanche's face and turned it to make sure they were eye to eye. "Is my mommy in the 'ho'pital'? I want to see her. Can you take me?"

Blanche's heart cried. She tried in vain not to let her eyes show it.

Lunch time at Laurel and Ada's was filled with small

talk: Webb's job in Nebraska, Laurel's work at the grain elevator, Randeen's trailer house ventures, the long drive for the Boes back to Oregon, the impending birth of Ada's baby…everything but conversation about LaReta.

After lunch, Myra and Laura helped Ada clean up while the men went to the back porch for a smoke.

"Guess we need to have a conversation, Webb." Ed, looked at the pasture behind Laurel's place and took a puff from his pipe. He blew smoke in the direction of Mrs. Fockler's house.

"We do, Ed. Would be good if Laura, Myra and Ada could hear what I have to say, too. I know they have thoughts about what should happen with LaReta."

The men finished their cigarettes and flicked them into the grass. Ed, out of respect for Ada and her condition, tapped the bowl of his pipe against the porch railing to lose the ashes and remaining tobacco. They all returned to the living room. When the women came to join them, Laurel and Randeen got up from the couch to let the three women sit down. Ed and Webb sat in opposing overstuffed chairs.

Webb leaned forward, forearms on his thighs, hands clasped in front of him. He looked in earnest at Laura and cleared his throat. "Mrs. Boe, I know I haven't been the husband and father that Dorothy wanted. I went wherever I could find a job and when I could, I sent money. I could of done better with that, I know… It put Dorothy in the tough spot of havin' to go back to teachin' when she just wanted to have her and LaReta and me together as a family. But it didn't work out that way." There was a lengthy pause. No one responded.

"Because she passed the way she did, I'll have regrets the rest of my life." Webb rubbed his brow.

Silence.

Webb scanned the faces of Dorothy's family as they sat around the room. There was no forgiveness in their eyes. Webb twisted and straightened the black band on his arm. "Anyway, you may already know, when Dorothy and I were together in Billings last summer, we decided it would be best if we went our own ways. I had to keep movin' and Dorothy thought she would have a teachin' job again, here in North Dakota. She was gettin' comfortable takin' care of herself and LaReta. We did talk about gettin' a divorce, but it didn't seem we had to do it right away. We figured we'd work it out when we had to."

Webb cleared his throat. "She wrote to me later in the fall that she was havin' a good time with Arlis, goin' to dances and shows. I was happy for her. I wanted her to be happy. I didn't wish her any ill will, just because it didn't work out for us." Webb stopped and took a deep breath. He looked down at the floor. "I loved Dorothy the best I could. I know it wasn't good enough." He swiped a tear before it fell, sniffed and sat up straighter to gain control.

Laura spoke up. "Webb, we knew about your decision last summer. Dorothy wrote to us about it. What we want to know is, are you planning to raise LaReta?"

The question was out in the open and Webb knew he had to respond.

"Yes, mam...I am."

Laura gasped and twisted the handkerchief in her lap. Myra clasped an arm around her and Ada grabbed her hand. Laura straightened her back and Myra released her. Laura, normally quiet and calm, pushed her glasses up. With a steady but forceful voice, she began:

"How are you going to do that, Webb? You have to keep moving to get work. You can't expect your mother to raise LaReta when you're off for months at a time. What does a single man know about raising a little girl? How much time have you spent with her? She doesn't even know you." She laced her fingers together, her knuckles white."

"I saw out the window. LaReta didn't come running to greet you." Exasperated, Laura raised her hands in question. "How can you say you're going to raise her? I don't understand."

Her voice shook with emotion. "Doesn't matter how many children you lose, Webb, the pain worsens each time. It doesn't get better. One is too many. It hurts." Tears streamed down Laura's face. She took a stuttered breath. "There's pain, unbearable pain." She leaned forward, her face contorted. "Do you understand Webb? And now you want to take LaReta too?"

Everyone in the room reacted. Myra and Laurel had never seen their mother like this. Myra hugged her mother again. Laurel's face flushed with anger. Ada and Ed sat silent and rigid, glaring at Webb. Randeen tried to remain neutral. He leaned against the door frame, crossed his feet and looked at the floor.

Webb cleared his throat. "Mrs. Boe, I understand you or Myra or Laurel may want to raise her, but I have a responsibility to bring her up. I'm her dad." Webb said the words he'd been struggling with the entire trip. They were out and there was no taking them back. Once he'd made up his mind, he'd have to make his case.

"But how are you going to do that, Webb? Myra asked. "Mother and Dad have already decided they can take LaReta back to Oregon with them. They're living on a nice little farm that belongs to one of my uncles. She'll have one home and by the looks of it, all of us will be moving out there pretty soon too. LaReta will have her cousins to play with and other distractions to help her get over her mommy's passing. Why would you deny her that?"

"Myra, I have a plan. Dorothy wasn't the only one who got involved with someone last year. I met a woman. Her name is Julia. She has an eight-year-old son, is real hard workin' and we hit it off. We are talkin' about getting married and she's willing to take on raisin' a daughter too, so I wouldn't be alone. I know now it takes two parents to make a go of it with kids. As difficult as it is to say, I do believe that Dorothy and I would have gotten a divorce— her for Arlis and me for Julia—if she hadn't passed the way she did." Webb cleared his throat and continued, "Sounds like Arlis had gone off to Oregon to find work right before Dorothy landed in the hospital and that she was thinkin' she would head that way after school was out. I figured they would get together, too."

Laurel broadened his stance and crossed his arms. "Dorothy's been in the ground one day, Webb, and you're talkin' about gettin' married, right in front of her parents." He growled, "You got nerve."

Webb bristled, muscles tensed and his hands clenched

into fists. "Calm down, Laurel. I said this was difficult to say 'cuz of the timin'. I wish to God I wasn't havin' this conversation with you, but I am 'cuz I have to." It was Webb's turn to be forceful.

"Dorothy wrote me a letter from the hospital tellin' me what happened to her. In the letter, she even said how close I came to havin' a daughter all my own. She would have wanted me to raise LaReta." Webb patted his breast pocket. There was an envelope sticking out of it. "I have the letter right here in my pocket, if you want to see it." No one spoke.

"Strange as it sounds, I've even dreamed I saw Dorothy's face. In one of the dreams she has LaReta's hand and she's holdin' it out to me. That's a real sign that I have to figure out how to carry out her wishes."

"Webb, that was a dream," Ed spoke without moving from his rigid position in the chair. "Dorothy would want LaReta raised by family she knows, not one she doesn't. She's what we have left of Dorothy, so let her be."

Webb stood up. He knew he wasn't going to change their minds, but his own was made up. Once Webb decided on something, there was little anyone could do to change his direction. He'd been described as a 'bull in a china shop' on more than one occasion. He was used to moving dirt and bossing men. He'd honed skills that required carrying out decisions whether they were his own or someone else's. Once a decision was made, the result was what mattered, not how he got there. He had to move forward with the plan.

"I *am* her closest family, Ed. I haven't been the perfect

father— I know that, but I did send Dorothy money when I could. I bought her a new dress and some things for LaReta the last time we were together. I did care about what happened to Dorothy and LaReta. I drove all the way here to pay my respects. I know you want what's best for LaReta, but I've decided I'm what's best for her. I'm her father and I plan to raise her the way Dorothy wanted me to.

Blanche and I'll be headin' back to the Olson's for the night, but I'll be out in the mornin' to pick up LaReta. Blanche has spent a lot of time with her and they're next door gettin' reacquainted right now. She'll be a real comfort to LaReta on the way back to Billings. Once we're back there, I'll have time with her, too, before I go back to work and I'm planning to get local truckin' jobs so all this will work out. Have LaReta and her things ready when I come back in the mornin'. I'll be early."

He pushed past Laurel on his way out the back door. Randeen stepped aside as Laura crumpled into Myra's arms. Ada sobbed. Ed didn't move.

29

LaReta

Halliday, North Dakota 1939

The next morning, Webb and Blanche were eating breakfast with the Olson's, when the phone rang. Martin answered and with a worried expression on his face, shrugged and handed the phone to Webb, letting him know he didn't know who it was. Webb took the phone. "Hello."

"Webb, I can't believe you'd do such a thing! Where's LaReta? Did you come get her this morning?" a voice choking with tears, railed on the other end of the phone line.

"What the hell are you talking about? Is this Laura?"

"Yes." Laura continued to weep. "Did you pick her up already, before any of us could say goodbye?" The stress of the last few days and now LaReta's disappearance were too much. She couldn't bear any more loss.

"Laura, I wouldn't do a thing like that. Where is she? What happened?"

Laura's voice was more controlled. "All the kids, including LaReta, came back to Laurel's house to sleep last night. This morning when we got up, we couldn't find LaReta. The other kids say they don't know where she is, either. We've looked all through the house and next door, but haven't found her. We thought you'd come to get her somehow."

"Well, I didn't, but I'm comin' out right now. Are the men out lookin' for her? Thank goodness it's not too cold. We'll be there in half an hour." Webb handed the phone back to Martin. "We have to get out to Laurel's place. LaReta disappeared."

Webb grabbed his coat and hat and headed for the door. "Leave your stuff, Blanche. We can get it later. We have to find LaReta. If anything happens…" Webb was sick with worry.

The sun peeked over the eastern horizon. No one tilled the fields. The drought destroyed crops that might have been harvested the previous fall, and poor farming techniques had leached the earth. Nothing of substance grew. It was a desolate landscape, even for a three-and-a-half-year-old.

A small figure with tousled blonde hair, an open coat, one sock up, the other down, wearing her good Mary Jane shoes and clutching her doll's suitcase, kicked dirt along the road. LaReta knew where she was going, even if she didn't know how to get there. She could hear the morning birds chirping and the wind rustling in the grass alongside the road. A rabbit hopped across the road. LaReta laughed at the sight and ran to catch it. No luck.

LaReta's mind was made up. No one was answering questions, so she was going to find out for herself. She woke up with a plan, got dressed, found her doll suitcase, and put some of her own clothes in it. She slipped her coat off the hook in the hall. *I can be quiet as a mouse 'cuz I have to do this.*

LaReta was precocious. She'd grown up with adults and very few children her own age, except when she and her mom visited with Dorothy's siblings and their children. She'd learned to entertain herself with her dolls or whatever toys were at hand—and they were few. Play with her cousins usually ended in a tug-off-war over a toy she didn't have, but wanted very much.

Dorothy spoiled LaReta on weekends after she'd been away teaching school all week. In February, not long before her accident, Dorothy wrote to Webb from Gladstone where they were staying with the Baileys:

Dear Webb,

LaReta is getting so darn smart. She uses such words as 'favorite' and 'appreciate' and even 'application' and uses them right, too. We nearly die laughing at some of the things she says. I surely wish so often that you could see her now. I was just upstairs making the beds. She came in and said, "Mommy, shall I go over the floors with the dust mop?" She is really growing up.

LaReta was good at walking on her tip toes, too. She'd practiced tippy toe to sneak up on the sleeping cat at Mrs. Bailey's house. It delighted LaReta to see the cat jump into the air. She would howl with laughter, even when Mrs. Bailey scolded her for being mean. But this morning, she didn't make any loud noises, even closing the back door. Proud of her accomplishment, she hurried up the road before anyone woke up.

LaReta heard a car coming around the bend behind her. Afraid she'd be found, she slipped off the side of the road and lay down in the ditch. The grass was uncomfortable and wet with dew. It poked and prickled her. She didn't care if she got dirty or scratched, but was surprised by how wet her clothes were when she stood up. The car disappeared over a rise ahead of her.

Was that Uncle Laurel's car? she wondered. *Don't matter. I hid and he didn't catch me. I'm gonna go 'cross the field. They won't find me. I don't care if I'm wet. I gotta go.* The field LaReta chose to cross took her back toward Dunn Center.

Laurel's car was heading north from Halliday. Randeen, Myra and Ed stayed behind to scour the fields around nearby houses and talk to neighbors. Laurel and Ada's home was the closest one to Mrs. Fockler's. Other houses in the vicinity were farther apart and the family had a lot of ground to cover. It was decided Ada was too far along to be traipsing around fields, so while Laura gave the children breakfast, stopping now and then to wring her hands in worry, Ada made phone calls to neighbors.

"Webb, what happened at Laurel and Ada's yesterday? You didn't say much on the way back." Blanche was looking for answers again as they headed east toward Halliday. The old Chevy's high gear was being tested for speed. By the sounds of the motor, it objected.

"I didn't want to discuss the conversation I had with the family with Melva in the car. Thought it would lead to another dust up or somethin' and I didn't want to talk about it with the Olsons, either. Didn't mean to keep you in the dark. The timin' wasn't right to let you know what happened." Webb gripped the spoke steering wheel with both hands and leaned forward, willing the automobile to move faster. "I did tell the Boes we were pickin' up LaReta today and takin' her back to Billings."

"You did! I wasn't sure you'd made that decision, Webb. You didn't come right out and say it before." Blanche was thrilled.

The flat landscape rolled past. "I wasn't sure myself, Blanche, but the more I thought about it, I know it's what Dorothy wanted. She deserved a good husband and father for LaReta." Webb ran one hand through his hair. "I sure didn't make the grade as far as bein' a good husband is concerned, but I have a chance to do right by Reta. Now it's somethin' I have to do. And I do need your help 'cuz I'm still a stranger to her. It'll take a while for us to get to know each other. I don't think she remembers me at all."

"I think she remembers you a little, Webb. At lunch yesterday, she asked me if you were her 'Daddy Webb who went to Montana'. That's a start. She's shy right now."

Webb continued, "I also told the Boes you spent a lot of time with LaReta in Billings and were gettin' reacquainted with her next door. Sounds like maybe that was true."

"We did get to know each other again. She remembered me playing with her." There was a smile in Blanche's voice. "I had a grand time having a tea party with LaReta, LaVonne and Donna. Five-year-old Roland thought he was too old for tea parties and two-year-old Kenton kept grabbing the dishes and making the girls mad. But it was fun. I didn't realize how much I missed Reta 'til yesterday." Blanche paused. "We'll find her, Webb. I know we will."

Webb came around a bend in the dusty road. In the distance, they could see a small figure walking toward them. The figure ran toward the side of the road and disappeared over the bank.

"That's her, Webb! I told you we'd find her!"

"Thank the good Lord." Webb pulled to the side of the road and they both jumped out.

"LaReta!" Blanche called to her. "Reta, it's your Auntie Blanche. I've come to find you. Where are you?" Her voice was singsong and playful.

A small, smiling face popped up out of the ditch and the rest of her followed, disheveled and dirty, still carrying the doll suitcase. They hurried over to help her onto the road. Blanche knelt down and gave LaReta a hug.

"You scared us, Reta. Your grandma called and said you were missing."

"I'm not missin'. I'm right here," LaReta gave Blanche a surprised look, her head tilted and her little eyebrows arched. Webb stood by, afraid any gestures on his part might scare her off again.

"Where are you going?" Blanche asked.

LaReta looked at Blanche, still on her level, and then up at Webb, a giant of a man in her eyes, someone she thought she remembered, but wasn't sure of. LaReta burst into tears and looked back at Blanche. "I'm goin' to find my mommy. I'm 'bery' sad. Grandma won't tell me where she is, but I know she's still in that ho'pital where I saw her with the table." She drew quick gulping breaths. "I want my mommy." She threw her arms around Blanche's neck. "Why can't I see her?"

Tears welled in Blanche's eyes and Webb looked away so LaReta couldn't see his. For just a moment, words from a distant past—his mother's hotel in Almont, words from Elsa came back to him: *Webb, when you find somethin', make sure it's yours. 'Cuz if you don't, it's called stealin'.*

Webb scuffed the dirt with his boot, swiped a sleeve across his face and cleared his throat. He thought about Else's other advice. *You have to think before you do things that might hurt somebody.* Webb couldn't begin to count the times he'd ignored that advice, since first hearing it.

He turned toward Blanche and LaReta. "We better get in the car, ladies. We have to go find...some people."

At first, LaReta sat in the middle of the front seat between the two of them, not saying a word. She thought she was in trouble and what was worse, she hadn't found her mommy.

"Want to steer the car, Reta?" Webb asked. LaReta looked at her dad in surprise. The idea of driving a big car was too much to refuse.

"Can I?" Her face lit up. Webb hoisted LaReta onto his lap and he let her hold the steering wheel, quite a stretch for her short arms. He'd found a diversion from her original destination. They whooped, hollered and laughed each time she headed for the ditch and Webb grabbed the wheel to keep the old buggy on the road.

Even with the respite from concerns about LaReta's safety and the fun at hand, Webb's thoughts churned. He'd been touched to the core by his daughter's longing for her mother.

Dorothy and LaReta have been together all of LaReta's three and a half years. I've been in and out and now, I'm a stranger. Will LaReta accept Julia, another stranger, as a stepmother? Am I tryin' to steal her from her mother's family, the family she needs right now?

They pulled up and parked at the back of Laurel's house. Laurel drove in right behind them. Ada, Laura and the children poured out the back door to meet them. From the fields, Randeen, Myra and Ed had seen the car churning dust as it neared the house. They headed back to Laurel's, hopeful LaReta had been found.

Blanche got out of the car, holding LaReta's hand. There were questions on the faces of the Boe family, but they let Webb explain.

"We found her walking down the road toward Dunn Center. Said she was goin' to find her mommy." LaReta looked down at the ground. The family was gripped again by grief, loss and not knowing how to explain to this little girl that her mother was dead. They couldn't be upset with her.

Laura stepped forward. "Come on in, Reta. You haven't even had your breakfast. Maybe we can talk about mommy after you've had a bite to eat." They all followed Laura and LaReta into the house. Ada held the door open for Webb and Blanche to come in.

30

The Road

March 12, 1939

Webb had his hat in his hands. "Laura, while Reta's eatin' breakfast, can I talk to you and Ed alone?" His tone was soft. The three of them moved out to the back porch again and Ed lit his pipe.

Webb looked down, shifting from one foot to the other. "I made mistakes, Laura, first for not bein' a good husband to Dorothy, second for not bein' around for LaReta. Guess I was on the verge of makin' another big mistake—takin' her away from the woman she knows best."

"Webb, this has been…" Laura began.

Webb held up his hand. "I don't mean to cut you off, Laura, but let me say a little more, 'cuz this is hard enough to get off my chest. I was sure of bein' right to take LaReta back to Billings. I want to be a dad to her and I thought it was what Dorothy wanted. I knew I could count on Blanche and Ma and my other sisters to help, too. But hearin' LaReta want to find her mommy so bad, made me stop and think about what I'm doin'. Made me think about other times in my life when I did what I wanted without thought to how it would affect someone else." Webb

314

looked down. Images of Tobias, dead on the pool hall floor because Webb wanted his dad's approval; his mother, upset about her car because Webb wanted to have fun; Shorty shaking a stubby finger at him and telling Webb how he'd been screwed over because Webb wanted to be the center of attention—flashed across his mind's eye, like film clicking through an old time movie projector. "I realize, Laura, I can't replace Dorothy with me or my family, but I still think she wanted me to raise LaReta—maybe, not right now."

Laura looked at Webb with hope in her eyes. Ed gazed out toward the pasture, one hand in his pocket, the other on the bowl of his pipe. The sun shone and a golden hue washed the stretch of low rolling hills. The morning was still quiet, save for Mrs. Fockler's chickens clucking and scratching for worms.

"What did you have in mind, Webb?" Laura asked in a tentative voice. "You know we want to take LaReta back to Oregon with us. We have a small farm and it looks like the rest of the family will be moving out soon. We'll all be together in one area. We may be older, but we do know how to raise children."

Webb smiled at her. There was no arguing her experience raising children. "Don't get me wrong, Laura. I still want to have LaReta with me, but until Julia and I get married and I get a job, it's best if Reta goes with you."

"How long you figure we'll have her?" Ed asked.

"Three months maybe. I'll be able to see what truckin' opportunities there are around Billings. Day trips would be best for stayin' close to family and I've always been pretty good at findin' somethin' when there wasn't any work to find." Webb regretted what he thought sounded like bragging as soon as he said it. If what he said was true, he should have sent more money to Dorothy and LaReta. It wasn't that he didn't send any, he did, but not on a regular basis. He'd stuck his foot in it again.

"Anyway, I want to do better by Reta than I did by Dorothy." Webb looked at the two of them.

"We're prepared to raise her, Webb, as long as necessary. She needs a steady hand and a place to call her own. Poor kid has been bumped around so much, she doesn't know what a home is," Laura said.

I can relate to that. Webb thought. "Well, guess Blanche and I had better hit the road. We've got some ways to go, but sure not as far as you do. Are you leavin' in the mornin'?"

"Yes, we need to get back to take care of the farm. Belongs to my brother. He's been real good to us, giving us time to get our feet on the ground. We're hoping to find a place of our own before too long, but it'll be in the same area. You'll know where we are."

Laura turned square on to face Webb. "Thank you for changin' your mind, Webb. It would have broke our hearts to see LaReta go with you today. And I don't know how much these ol' hearts can take anymore." She looked over at Ed, who was as stoic and unspoken as ever. Webb held the door open and they walked back into the house.

"Reta, can I talk to you for a minute outside on the porch? Are you done eatin' breakfast?" Webb looked at his daughter sitting at the kitchen table. She was still dirty from her dives into the ditches. Her legs dangled restlessly from the chair she sat on.

So blonde and blue eyed, Webb thought. *She does look like the Bateman side of the family.*

"We gonna drive the car?" LaReta asked. Her whole face smiled at him, smudges and all.

"No, not right now. Your Aunt Blanche and I have to go back to Montana today. I just want to talk to you for a little bit before we go." Webb caught Blanche looking at him with dismay. She hadn't heard the conversation with the Boes on the back porch because she'd been busy talking to LaReta while she ate breakfast. Webb could only guess the questions she'd ask him when they headed out. Blanche had a stake in his decision, too, but it was his to make.

Webb and LaReta sat on the back porch step. "Are you my Daddy Webb?" LaReta asked.

"Yes, I am."

"Do you wiv in 'Ontana?"

"Yes, I do."

"Did I wiv there too?"

"You did. You and your mommy were there, not very long ago. You visited me last summer. Do you remember that?"

LaReta looked long and hard at Webb. "Maybe." she grinned, tilted her head to look at him and grabbed her knees to her chin.

"Reta, Blanche and I have to go back to Montana today 'cuz I have to go to work. But I'm planning for you to come live with me again real soon."

317

"Can mommy come, too?"

This was a conversation Webb wanted Laura to have with LaReta, not him. He wasn't prepared, but there was the question…He looked across the back yard, paused and then turned to LaReta.

"Your mommy won't be able to come with you, Reta. She got real sick. So sick that she…couldn't come home from the hospital."

LaReta looked at him wide-eyed. "She's in the ho'pital? I want to go see her."

"No, she's not there anymore."

"Where is she? I want to find her."

Webb rubbed his forehead, stretched his legs out, pulled his pants at the knees to shake them toward his shoes, then took a deep breath, cleared his throat and asked, "When you were at Mrs. Bailey's, did they have any animals, Reta?"

"Yup. Mommy rode Sweetheart to school every day. And they had a cow and pigs and some chickens. Some of the chickens got their heads chopped off for supper. Oh, and they had a kitty and a dog, too." LaReta was proud of being able to name all the animals at the Bailey's house. "I used to scare the kitty sometimes." LaReta wrinkled her nose and tilted her head at Webb again. "Mrs Bailey didn't like it when I did that, but it was funny." LaReta giggled and then got serious again.

"But where's mommy?" She was determined to get answers.

LaReta's story about chickens getting their heads cut off for supper dissuaded Webb from continuing his explanation about death using farm animals as an example.

Damn, I could do more harm than good with this talk. And it's one I never intended to have!

He wasn't sure if another tack would work or not, but decided to give it a try. From everything he'd been taught in Almont in the basement of the Lutheran Church, he believed it was true. At least for LaReta's sake and his own, he wanted it to be true.

"Reta. Your mommy got so sick she went to Heaven to be with Jesus. She's there now and someday, we'll all be able to be with her. She can't come live with us in Montana because she's in that beautiful place called 'Heaven' where no one is sick and everyone is happy. She misses you, but knows you'll be there with her one day, too."

LaReta looked at him with disbelief and then sadness. "Why didn't I get to go wif her to Heaben?" She started to cry.

Dear Lord, help me out here will you?

Webb wrapped his arms around his daughter. "Sometimes, Reta, that's just the way it is."

Webb sat back and held LaReta at arm's length. "Hey, want to drive the car again? I think we have time."

Sniffling, she bobbed her head up and down. Webb picked her up and galloped to the Chevy. That brought back giggles and smiles.

The car eased down the driveway and then picked up a little speed. "Wookit me! Wookit me!" LaReta bounced up and down in Webb's lap, her small hands stretched to the top of the big steering wheel. With one hand around LaReta's waist, Webb's other hand managed the steering wheel from the bottom as the old Chevy snaked it's way slowly down the road. His arms and heart were full.

One More for the Road

Blanche stared out the Chevy's front window. "Webb, you know I'm disappointed we aren't bringing Reta back with us. I would have taken care of her when I'm not working. And all of us would do anything for her—and you."

They headed south from Dunn Center to Dickinson. It was late afternoon by the time they got on the road. Saying goodbye to LaReta had been tough on both of them. They promised to see her soon.

Webb leaned on the driver's door and rested his right hand on top of the steering wheel. He looked at Blanche and returned his gaze to the road. "It was the right thing to do. I'm not in a position to make a home for her now. She needs one woman to fill in for Dorothy. You and Ma and Vivian, maybe Toots, takin' turns wouldn't be what's best for her. Laura was right and when Reta said she was goin' to find her mommy, that did it. Broke the stubborn streak I get when I make up my mind to do somethin'. I knew staying with Laura was the best thing for LaReta. I'm real sorry, 'cuz I know you wanted her in your life."

"I hope I'll see her when you get settled in Billings with a job and can bring her back from Oregon. How long do you think that will be?"

"I told them three months, but could take longer, Blanche. A lot has to fall in place to make it happen."

Blanche focused on the speedometer on the dashboard. The needle bounced around 45 miles per hour.

She didn't care about the speed, but needed a focal point. Blanche was still struggling with his decision. They were quiet until Dickinson was in the rear view.

Blanche sighed and grabbed the thermos Laura had filled for them. She poured herself a cup of coffee. "Want one?" she asked.

"Naw, not right now."

Blanche took a sip. "It's okay, Webb. I know LaReta can't take the place of my baby, any more than I could take Dorothy's place in LaReta's life. But I hoped I'd stop thinking about him with her around." Blanche took another drink and stared into the steaming black liquid.

Webb passed a slower moving vehicle ahead of them and when he moved back into the right lane, said. "I'm glad you're okay with this, Blanche."

She shook her head. "It wasn't my choice, Webb—it was yours. We all have to make our own choices."

Webb reached one hand under the front seat and pulled out a bottle. "Randeen gave me a goin' away present when we said goodbye." He unscrewed the cap with ease, tipped the bottle to his lips and swigged the whiskey in gulps.

Blanche looked over the top of her glasses at him, her eyebrows raised.

"Make it one for my baby…" He sang softly and took another drink. "And one more for the road."

EPILOGUE

Webb Bateman married Loretta Julia Skates Whitney on June 17, 1939, three months after Dorothy's funeral. (In the story, Loretta was called "Julia" to avoid confusion with LaReta). Webb and Loretta continued a nomadic lifestyle following construction and trucking opportunities for more than half their fifty years together. They lived in a trailer house more than once.

During World War II, they both worked in the shipyards in Portland, Oregon. Webb was a crane operator and Loretta, a welder. Webb was deferred from military service because of his color blindness.

Loretta's son, Raymond (Ray) Whitney, born on December 10, 1930, during her first marriage, lived with Webb and Loretta part of the time, but a tumultuous relationship developed between Webb and Ray. When he was old enough, Ray moved away and at age eighteen, joined the U.S. Army.

Bonnie Lee Bateman (the author) was born April 29, 1945, and because of her parents moves, attended thirteen grade schools, two junior highs, and one high school. Twelve years after Bonnie's birth, a son, James William Bateman, was born on July 26, 1957. Webb and Loretta's constant moves and the fact Ed and Laura Boe wanted

LaReta with them, kept LaReta in Oregon until she was fifteen years old. That's when she moved to Billings, Montana, to live with her dad and stepmother.

After years of moving between Montana, Oregon and Washington, Webb retired to be mayor of a small eastern Washington town, Benton City. He and Loretta later moved back to Billings, Montana, where Loretta passed away at age 77 on February 2, 1990. Webb followed seven years later on November 10, 1997, at the age of 86.

Whiskey was a companion his entire life, but he and Loretta were remembered by friends and family as kind, generous and loving people. They are buried in Sunset Memorial Gardens in Billings.

Evelyn (Toots) Ruth Bateman married Rolv (Ralph) Peterson on March 23, 1929. They had one daughter, Janet Maxine Peterson, born June 8, 1935, two months before LaReta's birth.

Ralph bought Jim Bateman's interest in the Town Talk Billiard Parlor, after which he owned other businesses in and around Billings. Because of their daughter, Janet, what began as a hobby evolved into a business in which they taught and marketed ceramic giftware for many years. They were also avid antique collectors.

Ralph died suddenly on June 9, 1978. Toots, as she was known her entire life, passed away June 10, 2001, at age 93. She outlived all her siblings. Ralph and Toots are also buried in Sunset Memorial Gardens in Billings.

Raymond(Ray) Wellington Bateman married and divorced Helen Norton in North Dakota prior to Webb and Dorothy's marriage. They had one son, Robert (Bobbie) Lee Bateman born September 9, 1928. Robert was raised by his maternal grandparents and barely knew Ray, who would stop by now and then with gifts.

Ray also had a daughter, Betty, who was born in 1935, the same year as LaReta. Betty never knew her father and was raised by her mother and a stepfather in California.

Years later, after her mother died, Betty found her half-brother Bobbie with the help of a daughter who was a librarian, and the advent of the Internet. They had lived not far from one another as children and when Bobbie and Betty finally connected by phone, his first words were, "Hi Betty. This is your brother, Bob." Someone in the family had told Bobbie when he was young that Betty was his sister. He never forgot.

With an aptitude for electronics and recording equipment, Ray ran a radio repair shop in Billings for many years. In his thirties, during World War II, he was employed by Western Electric in New York. (He's pictured with his second wife, Betty, in New York City. Her last name is unknown). He then moved to Inglewood, California where he worked for the National Broadcasting Company (NBC) in radio and later as a recording engineer in radio and television. He married again in Los Angeles in 1961, but was single when he was killed in a one-car accident in Northern California on December 6, 1964. He was 55 years old.

After **Walter (Walt) Harrison Bateman's** marriage to Juliet Jacobson ended in divorce in 1936, he moved to Billings, Montana, and in 1938, married Laura Haefer. During the war, they both worked for Kaiser Company on Swan Island in Portland, Oregon. Walt was a crane operator and Laura a certified welder. These were the same jobs that Webb and Loretta held at the same time in the same location.

Walt didn't finish high school and for most of his life earned a living as a truck driver. After the war, Walt and Laura returned to Great Falls, Montana where he went to work for George Taber, Walt's brother-in-law. He had married Blanche Bateman. Walt, Webb and George, and one other driver became trailblazers on the Alcan Highway, before it was paved. They hauled bombs, which they loaded in New Mexico, to Alaska for the United States Government ("Uncle Sam") because of North Korea's invasion of South Korea and mounting tension with Russia and China. The 8000-mile trip started in mid-October, took four weeks and was extremely dangerous. In his diary, Webb's last entry was, "Financially the trip was a success, but nothing exceptional when you consider all the hours we put in and the risk of losing your outfit and maybe more."

In 1961, Walt, with 1.6 million accident-free miles to his credit during the preceding nineteen years, was named Montana's top commercial driver. Laura preceded Walt in death. He later married Lucille Magnus in 1991 and passed away on May 11, 1995. He was 82 years old. He never had any children.

Vivian Lois Bateman married Harold H. Burnett in Portland, Oregon on July 24, 1939, just a month after Webb married Loretta. Vivian and Harold both worked in the shipyards, operated a couple of neighborhood businesses, and Vivian became a hostess at a restaurant in downtown Portland called

"Hillaire's." She also worked as the assistant manager of a beauty school.

In the early sixties, they returned to Great Falls, Montana, where they lived until Vivian passed away after a long and painful illness related to liver disease. Vivian died on May 19, 1967, at age 52. She and Harold did not have any children.

Blanche May Bateman married George W. Taber on March 1, 1941. They moved to Portland, Oregon, where George took up flying, and although he was too old for the military, he succeeded in becoming a civilian flight instructor for the Air Force in Florida. After the war and a temporary return to Portland, they moved back to Montana where they owned a flight service. They survived lean years by hunting coyotes for bounty from a Piper Cub aircraft. After selling the flight service, they moved to Great Falls, Montana where George operated Taber Truck Lines and employed his brothers-in-law, Webb and Walt. George was an entrepreneur, but he always attributed a great part of his success to Blanche, with her knowledge of business and a willingness to take chances and work hard. George later developed a logging business and is credited with inventing the Relay System that allowed delivery of logs to mills at night, a major efficiency improvement. He sold his business interests in 1968 to Crown Zellerbach.

Blanche and George retired to Mesa, Arizona where they became avid golfers. Blanche was always a reader and involved in many organizations. She died of pulmonary fibrosis on April 2, 1989 at the age of 71.

After her death, George established a major academic scholarship in her name in Wheatland County, Montana. Blanche and George never had any children. It's unknown whether Blanche ever tried to find the son to whom she gave birth at the age of seventeen.

James (Jim) Robert Bateman and Tomine Teodina (Dena) Ramsland Bateman followed their adult children to Portland during World War II. Webb, Walt, Blanche and Vivian were all there with their spouses. Family members continued to stick together over the years.

Back L to R: Webb, Blanche, Toots, and Walt
Front L to R: Vivian, Jim, Dena and Ray
1957

Following the war, Jim and Dena moved back to Great Falls, Montana, and finally to Billings. Dena died on February 25, 1963, at the age of 78. Jim stayed with Ray for a while in California, but the destructive drinking in which both men engaged caused Webb to drive to California and bring Jim back to Pasco, Washington where they were living. Jim eventually moved to Billings, Montana, under the watchful eye of his daughter, Toots.

Jim died July 18, 1970. Both Jim and Dena are buried at Sunset Memorial Gardens in Billings, Montana. They were married 56 years. The photo was taken in 1957 at the celebration of Jim and Dena's fiftieth wedding anniversary.

LaReta (Lore) Lois Bateman moved to Billings, Montana to live with Webb and Loretta the summer of 1951. She turned sixteen on August 8th of that year. Lore nicknamed herself to avoid confusion with her stepmother, Loretta. She didn't want to be called "Little Loretta." The name "Lore" was similar to her grandmother's name, Laura, and that's what she was called the rest of her life.

That summer Lore met John T. (Jack) Harrington, a handsome football player. He was an Irish Catholic from Butte, Montana, who was living with his father in Billings.

They married in November 1951. Lore was sixteen and Jack, eighteen. By the time Lore was 24 years old, she had five children, Danniel Timothy, Nicolette Louise, Michael John, Nannette Kathleen, and Kevin Patrick. She said all she ever wanted was to be a mother and have a family of her own.

Jack and Lore divorced after 22 years of marriage and in 1975, Lore married another Jack, Jack Curtis. During their dozen years of marriage and because Jack worked for Boeing, they were able to live in Turkey, Iraq  and Iran. They travelled extensively on vacations. This Jack, according to Lore, was the love of her life, even though he eventually left her for another woman.

Lore was devastated, but decided to move on and turned her home in Tukwila, Washington, into a boarding house that over the years welcomed men and women who came from countries around the world. Lore created long lasting friendships with many of them. Her most recent renters referred to her as "Mom."

Since two of her children, Nannette and Kevin, live on the "Big Island" in Hawaii, Lore acquired travel miles and used them for visits where she would find Nannette tending her 600 coffee trees, writing, editing and enjoying her animals.

Kevin and his wife, Rebecca, own their own plumbing business and Rebecca also works as a civil engineer. They have a daughter, Hailey. Kevin has two sons, Jack and Conner, from his first marriage to Adele Yamagata.

Lore was also an artist who worked with pastels and acrylics over the years. Her daughter, Nicolette, inherited her love of art and became an artist in her own right. She is a master weaver and an art teacher on Whidbey Island, Washington. She has two daughters, Laura (Ellie) and Dorie from a previous marriage. Her husband, Tim Hyatt, is a biologist and wood craftsman. They live in La Conner, Washington, home of many artists.

Dan is thinking about retirement, having worked for many years in information technology for various companies and the federal government. He's travelled extensively, but lives near his mother's home in Tukwila. For years, Sundays would find Dan reading the paper in her living room and discussing the week's events. Dan has one son, Lee, who resides in Alaska and is a speaker and published author.

Mike lives in Walla Walla, Washington, and commutes to his job as an environmental engineer with the Army Corps of Engineers in Richland, Washington. Mike has one son, Victor Jeremiah (VJ).

Most of her life, Lore suffered from a Bipolar Disorder which she managed well, but was diagnosed with breast cancer in 2011. Shortly after, she had a gall bladder attack, a heart attack, and suffered broken ribs due to an accident in the hospital. In spite of all that, she recovered and was cancer-free for five years. In 2016, she was diagnosed with bone cancer and, in spite of efforts to forestall the terminal disease, she passed away on June 14, 2016 at the age of 80.

In her own words, Lore said she lived a good life and her children, of whom she was very proud, were the ones who got her through tough times and made her life worthwhile. She loved them dearly and they love her. We all do.

Danniel, Nannette, Kevin, Nicolette, Michael
July 24, 2016

ACKNOWLEDGEMENTS

This was not a book I planned to write. In 2011, I was gearing up to write my own story about the road that led me to Australia, not the road to LaReta. As I researched the art of memoir, I got excited about sharing what I learned and began teaching a memoir writing class at the local senior center.

Teaching memoir writing classes paused the writing of my own story. At the same time, I toyed with the idea of writing a novel based on anecdotes that my father, Webb, had written in his youth, but I knew very little about his first wife, Dorothy.

In January 2015, my sister, Lore, then 79, told me of letters Dorothy had written to Webb in the 1930's. I couldn't wait to see them. Webb had kept the letters for over fifty years and finally, in the late 1990's, gave them to Lore's son. Dan was working on a genealogy project and Webb asked him to promise he wouldn't let Lore see them until Webb died. Dan kept the promise and the first time Lore read the letters from Dorothy to Webb was with me on a rainy day in early 2015.

Lore also kept other letters from her mother to relatives, but had only recently read them.

"I hadn't read the letters my mother wrote to relatives before because I always thought they would make me too sad, but after talking to you on the phone the other night, I sat down and read them. I'm glad I did. I found out how much my mother loved me."

Besides the anecdotes our father wrote and the letters Lore's mother wrote, this book would not have been possible without the other special people in my life and there are many.

It is with gratitude that I thank my husband, Scott, and our families for their unwavering love and support. I thank my dad—Webb Bateman—first for not being the scoundrel in my life that he had been in his youth and second, for keeping the letters all those years. Perhaps it's my mother, Loretta, who should be thanked. I remember her propensity for keeping anything she thought had sentimental value, including my horned-rim, rhinestone-studded glasses from junior high and the bite plate I wore after braces. They were neatly wrapped in tissue paper in a cedar chest I rummaged through, many years after ever needing them again.

My thanks also go to three of Lore's children: Dan for keeping his promise to Webb and Nicolette for inspiring the title of the book. Thank you Nannette, for a final edit of the novel. This was not an easy task given the quirky language and my tendency to tell, not show. You are a gem.

Throughout the writing, our cousin, Janet Peterson Esser, generously offered family history and photos in spite of far too many requests. A family reunion book on which she worked was invaluable: *Ramsland-Larson: A Family History 1852-2006*. Her Uncle Sigurd (Sig) Peterson's book, *Gone Are The Days: Facts and Hearsay,* about Sims and Almont, North Dakota, provided a wealth of information. My half-brother and Lore's step-brother, Raymond Francis Whitney, gave permission to use his father's name, Francis

Hackett Whitney, in the chapter describing the abuse he and our mother suffered at his hand.

The firm and fair guidance I received from my writers' group, the Wordsmiths, helped shape the novel from what could have been a recitation of family facts into a manuscript I'm hopeful my family and Lore's family will cherish and that others will enjoy. The Wordsmiths are Renette D. Harvey, Phebe Ward Tademy, Judy Bridges, Sabrina Teller Metzger, and Sydney Troi.

Those who were first to read the entire novel before publication and a final edit suggested structural and language changes that were invaluable. Many thanks again to Phebe Ward Tademy, Janet Peterson Esser, Sue E. Shoblom and Joan Tornow. Joan is the author of *Writing Memoir Together: A Roundtable Approach*. This was the teaching resource I used in my memoir writing classes.

Most important of all to this story was my sister LaReta (Lore) Lois Bateman Harrington Curtis, the one who lost her mother at age three and a half. It's been said that to lose your family long before you've had time to create your own causes a very specific kind of loneliness. Lore experienced a void all her life from the loss of her mother, but she filled it with love for her five children, seven grandchildren and a sincere interest in the wellbeing of all whose lives she touched.

Lore and I talked on the phone weekly. We shared family news and occasionally, she would drive the 25 miles from Tukwila to Puyallup to visit me. Most of the time, I would find myself sitting in one of her living room recliners sipping coffee, chatting about friends and family and enjoying the view of her deck with its massive tree, adorned with birdhouses.

We not only discussed the mundane, we shared the kind of information only close female friends dare to share. I miss my sister. She wasn't just my sister; she was my friend.